C000291850

Two

Previous books by Trevor Negus

The Coal Killer

The Exodus Murders

A Different Kind of Evil

(4)

FOR LORAINE

Two Wrongs

Trevor Negus (signature)

Trevor Negus

© Trevor Negus, 2018

Published by Bathwood Manor Publishing

All rights reserved. No part of this book may be reproduced, adapted, stored in a retrieval system or transmitted by any means, electronic, mechanical, photocopying, or otherwise without the prior written permission of the author.

The rights of Trevor Negus to be identified as the author of this work have been asserted in accordance with the Copyright, Designs and Patents Act 1988.

A CIP catalogue record for this book is available from the British Library.

ISBN 978-0-9955737-9-6

Book layout by Clare Brayshaw

Prepared and printed by:

York Publishing Services Ltd
64 Hallfield Road
Layerthorpe
York YO31 7ZQ

Tel: 01904 431213

Website: www.yps-publishing.co.uk

PROLOGUE

September 1983
Hyson Green, Nottingham

It was almost two o'clock in the morning and the streets were deserted.

The only vehicles on the road were taxis ferrying late night revellers away from Nottingham city centre.

Pc Tom Naylor stepped back into the darkness of a shop doorway to observe the street, he was very cold and very bored. This was his second set of night shifts; his tutor constable had taken great pains on his first set to explain the different approach needed when working a foot beat on night patrol as opposed to the same beat during the day.

Tom Naylor had listened carefully to his instruction.

He understood that it was vitally important on nights for him to see but not be seen. If he could observe people up to no good before they saw him, he would be able to do something about their criminal intent.

Tom just wished he could see somebody, anybody.

For the last hour of his lonely foot patrol he hadn't seen a soul.

The only living thing to cross his path had been a large tom cat out on the prowl.

This was the fourth night shift he had patrolled alone. So far, he'd seen none of the excitement he had envisaged when he considered joining the police force.

Tom had been a member of the Parachute Regiment and had served his country during the conflict to liberate the Falklands after the islands had been invaded by Argentina.

At the conclusion of the Falklands War, like many soldiers, Tom had become overwhelmed by a sense of anti-climax. Being a peacetime soldier was not what he wanted to do for the rest of his life, so he had made the difficult decision to leave the armed forces.

Being a young man of twenty-three, he still felt the need for excitement and he wanted to serve the community. It had seemed like a natural career choice to become a Police Constable. Having made his decision, Tom returned to the area of his birth and joined the Nottinghamshire Constabulary.

Within a month of being accepted, he had embarked on a ten-week training course at Dishforth Police Training College at the RAF base in North Yorkshire. When he first drove through the gates of the military establishment Tom briefly thought that he'd stepped back in time, but he quickly settled into the barrack style accommodation of the RAF base. He became popular among the other recruits who readily picked his brains about uniform preparation, and how to achieve the gleaming shine on bulled boots.

Having completed his training, Tom had been posted to the Hyson Green district of Nottingham. This inner-city area was full of the problems associated with that environment. Drugs were plentiful, prostitution was rife and violent crime and unemployment were both way above the national average.

The Hyson Green area had three police stations, Tom had initially been posted to Hamilton House Police Station.

This station covered the areas of Carrington, Sherwood and Mapperley Park.

When he first arrived at Hamilton House Police Station he was shown around the old building by his shift sergeant and allocated a tutor constable whose job it was to show him the ropes. The tutor had the important role of demonstrating how policing was done practically as opposed to the theoretical training acquired at Dishforth.

Fortunately for Tom, his tutor, Andy Gibbs had taken his role very seriously and imparted a great deal of knowledge and experience. The two men had gone their separate ways after one month.

Finally, Tom would be allowed to walk the beat alone.

His sergeant had allocated a foot beat in the Sherwood area for Tom to patrol. It was considered to be quieter than some parts of the police area covered by the Hyson Green Division and was ideal to introduce the new recruit to the public.

This was now Tom's second month walking the beat and he was slowly beginning to realise something that all experienced coppers know only too well. Police work is ninety per cent mundane, repetitive, boring work interlaced with a ten per cent mixture of heart stopping fear, excitement and adrenalin rushes.

The only problem for Tom was that he hadn't witnessed any of the excitement of that ten per cent, yet.

He soon discovered that he enjoyed working the night shift much more than the numerous day shifts his duty rota required him to work. He was still very much a fledgling police officer and at the moment he found the hardest thing to get used to, was the expectation on him to talk with complete strangers.

He found the whole process of interacting with the general public quite daunting.

Night shifts were different.

It was a lonely patrol.

He enjoyed the physicality of checking property on his beat, finding every alley, cut through and passage way on the area.

The only members of the public he engaged with on nights were the few individuals out and about on the streets in the small hours. Tom found he had no problem engaging with these people, trying to establish if they were involved in criminality.

This was his fourth shift of seven.

So far, he'd attended several domestic disputes between violent, drunken husbands and their abused, downtrodden wives. There had also been numerous reports of fighting and disorder in the pubs on his beat.

Frustratingly, these disturbances had always finished by the time he'd arrived on foot, leaving him feeling useless and redundant. He couldn't help but notice the suspicious looks fired in his direction from some of his more experienced colleagues in the Panda cars that had responded to the disorder quicker than he could.

Tom knew instinctively what they were thinking.

Had he deliberately taken his time to avoid confrontation? He hadn't yet had the opportunity to prove himself in front of his colleagues in a dangerous, violent situation.

He completed checking the last row of shops on Mansfield Road and made his way back along Hucknall Road to Hamilton House for a much-needed bite to eat and a hot drink. As he trudged back into the station he felt cold and demoralised. He began to wonder if he'd made the right career choice.

Taking his helmet and greatcoat off he realised that he needed to give his new career a period of time. After all, in the grand scheme of things, he'd only been here five minutes.

Having retrieved the lunch box from his locker, Tom made himself a hot drink.

He unbuttoned his tunic, sat down, took a sip of his coffee and reached for one of his ham and tomato sandwiches.

As soon as he took the first bite from his sandwich, his personal radio crackled into life, 'Control to Pc Naylor.'

Tom swallowed the mouthful of sandwich and picked up the radio from the table, 'Go ahead control.'

'Sorry Tom, you're going to have to leave your refs. I need you to see Sgt Jefferies in the front office immediately. The burglar alarm at Mayweather's Factory on Gladstone Street has just activated. Sgt Jefferies will convey you down there to check it out, over.'

'On my way, over.'

Tom felt like cheering out loud, at last a little bit of action. All thoughts of his ham and tomato on white and mug of coffee were quickly forgotten as he grabbed his gear and raced downstairs to find a waiting Sgt Jefferies.

Running out the door of the station, they raced to the nearest Panda car and jumped in. The Sgt revved the engine and then drove off at speed towards Gladstone Street.

On the way to the factory, Sgt Jefferies said in his growling, gravelly voice, 'There's a dog handler already on the scene searching the grounds of the factory. I'll drop you off on Bentinck Street; I want you to keep watch on the back wall of the factory, just in case the dog flushes anybody out and they climb over. You okay with that Tom?'

Tom nodded, quickly buttoning his greatcoat.

As he climbed out on Bentick Street and watched the sergeant race off in the Panda car to get to the front of the factory, once again Tom quickly felt deflated.

Here he was again: the new boy. Safely stuck out the way at the back of the factory while everyone else was inside catching the burglars.

He looked dejectedly at the back of the car as it sped off into the darkness along Bentinck Street.

Bentinck Street had the long, high factory wall on one side of the street and a row of terraced houses on the other. Tom put his hands in the pockets of his greatcoat and leaned against the wall of one of the houses, staring at the weather worn, grime stained brick wall of the factory. The burglar alarm was still ringing loudly and Tom began to imagine what he would do if a gang of desperate burglars suddenly started to clamber over the high wall.

Abruptly the alarm stopped ringing.

The silence was now deafening.

It was absolutely still; the only sound Tom could hear was the distant rumble of a coal train way off in the distance.

Suddenly, two houses along to his left, he heard the distinct noise of a sash window being raised.

Instinctively, Tom stepped back into the dark alleyway that ran between two of the terraced houses. He peered intently through the small gap between the wall of the house and the drainpipe.

He saw a man's head appear through the now open downstairs window.

Looking closer, he could see that the man was a young West Indian youth, wearing a black benny hat over dreadlocks.

The youth began looking in both directions along the dimly lit street, his head moving back and forth in jerky movements. Having checked that the coast was clear the head momentarily disappeared back inside the property, only to be instantly replaced by an arm holding a laden, cream coloured pillow case.

The full pillow case was laid carefully down onto the pavement.

Tom watched on intrigued as the young black lad then climbed backwards out of the open window.

As soon as the youth picked up the pillow case, Tom stepped forward out of the dark alley way and grabbed him by the upper arm.

The youth was shocked at Tom's sudden appearance; his eyes widened when he realised it was a policeman that had grabbed him. Trying to compose himself the youth managed to stutter, 'It's my stuff mister. This is my girlfriend's house. I'm just getting my gear coz I'm leaving her.'

Gripping his arm tighter, Tom replied, 'Sorry son, that's a load of crap. I don't believe a word of it.'

Without loosening his grip on the youth's arm, Tom looked inside the pillow case. It contained a collection of LP records, bits of jewellery and a transistor radio.

Tom put the pillow case back down on the pavement, looked at the youth and said, 'I'm arresting you for burglary.'

'No man, that's bogus, this is my stuff.'

Ignoring the protestations of innocence, Tom grabbed his radio and said, 'Control, I've detained one male on Bentinck Street on suspicion of burglary, could you arrange for transport please. Over.'

Tom placed the youngster in handcuffs and waited for the transport to arrive.

The youth was visibly shaking and said nothing.

Tom said, 'What's your name?'

'It's Billy, Billy Swan. Can't you let me go mate? I'm only fourteen. I've never done anything like this before.'

Tom could see that the youth was now panicking and he gripped his arm a little tighter, fearing the panic might make him attempt to struggle out of his grip and make a bolt for freedom.

After five long minutes, that to Tom seemed like an hour, Sgt Jefferies returned to Bentinck Street in the Panda car. As he got out of the car he said, 'Bloody hell Tom! Where'd this one come from?'

'He climbed out through the sash window of that house, carrying all this stuff in a pillow case.'

The old sergeant smiled.

'Well done Naylor, looks like you've bagged your first burglar.'

Tom looked at Swan who now had tears streaming down his face, 'He's so young sarge. He says he's only fourteen, still just a daft kid.'

The sergeant laughed out loud, 'Billy Swan here isn't fourteen, he's almost eighteen and even if he's never been arrested for burglary before tonight he already has a record for thieving that's as long as your arm. Look at it this way Tom, you and young Swan here are both virgins. This is your first burglary arrest, and it's also his first arrest for burglary. I would bet my pension that it won't be the last for either of you!'

Chuckling to himself, Sergeant Jefferies walked around to the driver's door as Tom placed a now quiet and surly looking Billy Swan into the back of the police car.

CHAPTER 1

7.30am 4th January 1987
Nottingham City Centre

The detective surveyed the scene before her with a resigned air, then let out an audible sigh that betrayed both weariness and sadness. Although still only thirty-four years old, Det Sgt Julie Piper had witnessed the scene that now confronted her more times than she cared to recall.

A career detective, Julie Piper had been a member of the CID for over ten years and a Detective Sergeant for five. Her dark blue business suit was crumpled and creased, her plain black shoes unpolished. She pushed the fringe of her short blonde hair off her face and examined the scene in front of her with an experienced and professional eye.

On the bedroom floor was the naked body of a beautiful young woman with long raven hair. She was curled up in the foetal position, her hands together in front of her stomach. The tell-tale signs of cocaine abuse were apparent on her top lip and at the base of her nose. Her full lips were pulled back over her teeth in a frozen grimace and her dull, dark brown eyes were wide open.

The room was full of the overpowering stench of vomit and excrement. The unfortunate young woman had been violently sick and her bowels had opened prior to her obviously painful and lingering death.

As she surveyed the pitiful sight, Julie wondered if the girl had been aware she was dying or whether death had mercifully overtaken her as she slipped into unconsciousness.

The bedroom the dead girl lay in was beautifully decorated, it had the look of opulence associated with extreme wealth. Everything inside the room was the height of stylish luxury and had been purchased with no expense spared. It was in keeping with the rest of the city centre apartment.

The tower block that housed the apartment was situated in the most desirable and exclusive area of the city, and any property in the block was amongst the most expensive properties available in the city.

Julie Piper was standing in the penthouse suite that took up the entire top floor of the prestigious ten storey high Bathwood Court. The views from the apartment were stunning. Julie looked out of the vast window that took up one entire wall of the bedroom at the cityscape beneath her.

The city gradually unfurled out across the Trent valley.

In the distance the Trent river was a ribbon of dark blue that glistened in the weak morning sun. Beyond the river she could see the countryside, a patchwork of different coloured fields and dark woodland that stretched from the edge of the city to the horizon.

As far as Julie was concerned, the only downmarket thing about the penthouse apartment was its owner.

Tony Banks was an overweight, forty something, balding scum bag who had accumulated his wealth through the illegal sale of drugs.

His associates were all suspected of being involved in large scale drug supply within the city.

Banks was an intelligent individual who maintained that

2

area of uncertainty that prevented the police from provi ᴖ any involvement in the sordid trade.

He also had a reputation in the city of being a man who regularly preyed upon young and somewhat naïve women, using his obvious wealth and connections to impress.

What Julie Piper couldn't understand was the fact that the women Banks seemed to attract were always stunningly beautiful and usually highly intelligent.

She found it difficult to comprehend what it was about Banks that attracted these types of women. Surely, they could see through his sickeningly false charade of decency and see him for what he actually was.

Banks was bad news.

What wasn't difficult for Julie to comprehend was the cause of this young woman's death. To her experienced eye, the dead woman was displaying all the hallmarks of a drugs overdose.

As the Detective Sergeant given the task of investigating this untimely death, she now had to try and establish if that overdose was a tragic accident, a case of misadventure or something more sinister.

The outcome of the post mortem examination scheduled for later that day would assist her enquiries greatly.

Upon her arrival at the apartment earlier that morning and after a cursory look at the scene that confronted her, she had immediately arrested Tony 'Shithead' Banks on suspicion of supplying the controlled drugs that had no doubt eventually killed the young woman.

Banks had been led away, loudly protesting his innocence to anybody who could be bothered to listen and claiming he was unaware the dead girl was a junkie.

en arrogant and indignant in equal measure,
v shocked he'd been when he woke up that
nd found the silly bitch collapsed on the floor at
.... his enormous bed.

Somehow Julie had resisted the overwhelming urge to punch the odious man in the mouth. Instead, she'd instructed a couple of the younger detectives on her team to remove Banks from the flat and take him to Central Police Station for questioning.

Now, looking around the bedroom, Julie saw a crumpled heap of women's designer clothes dumped on a chair next to the fitted wardrobe. The dead girl had obviously dropped them there as she had got undressed the night before.

Julie inwardly shuddered at the thought of the beautiful young woman lying naked in bed next to the bloated, middle aged Banks.

Scenes of Crime officers had attended earlier to photograph and examine the scene but had long since left. Julie was now alone in the bedroom with her thoughts while she waited for the undertakers to arrive and remove the body.

While she waited she started to examine the clothing on the chair.

Still wearing blue latex gloves to prevent scene contamination, Julie picked up a pair of size 8, Victoria Principle denim jeans from the top of the pile.

She began to empty the contents of the jeans pockets, spreading the found articles on the bedroom floor. There wasn't much, but what there was would prove very useful in her quest to identify the woman.

From the back pocket of the jeans Julie recovered a small black leather wallet that contained a Nottingham University Student Union card.

4

This card bore a photograph showing the face of a very beautiful and very happy, smiling young woman with huge brown eyes, perfect white teeth and long jet-black hair.

The face on the Identity Card belonged to the woman lying cold and dead on the bedroom floor; the smile had now changed to the rictus grimace of death.

The card identified the deceased as Francesca DeLuca, an Italian Medical Exchange Student, studying medicine at the nearby Nottingham University.

Placing the wallet and contents into an evidence bag, Julie muttered, 'Welcome to England, sweetheart.'

The pointed remark was said in a sorrowful, almost apologetic way in response to the sad fate that had befallen the young woman in England.

Her thoughts were interrupted by a loud banging on the apartment door. The uniform constable maintaining the scene log signed in two burly undertakers from the on-call list.

Julie called out, 'Body's in here gents.'

The undertakers walked into the bedroom carrying a black PVC body bag and a fold up trolley on wheels.

Julie stepped back away from the young woman and said, 'Good morning gents, I need you to take her to the mortuary at Nottingham City Hospital. Thanks.'

As the undertakers began the grim task of placing Francesca DeLuca into the black plastic body bag, Julie's thoughts turned to the young woman's family.

Very soon, somewhere in Italy, somebody would be given the news that their precious daughter had been callously ripped from their lives forever. Julie found it impossible to imagine the feelings of devastation and sadness this news would bring to that family. It was always the families left behind that upset the experienced detective. For the deceased it was too late for emotion.

Julie was only too aware that whatever the truth behind the woman's death, it would inevitably be marked down as a tragic accident. She knew that without evidence to prove their culpability, the people actually responsible for her death, the pushers and the suppliers of the evil poison that had killed her, would never be brought to book.

In her head Julie could already hear the Coroner at the inquest making the same tired platitudes about the evil of the drugs trade and the dangers of recreational drug abuse.

As she followed the undertakers carrying the black bag that contained the body of Francesca DeLuca out of the penthouse apartment, Julie muttered under her breath, 'What a shit world this is.'

CHAPTER 2

3.00am 21ˢᵗ June 1987
Rolleston Village, Nottinghamshire

Danny Lee was shivering violently; he was unsure if it was the bitterly cold night air or his nerves causing him to tremble.

'For fucks sake Danny, what's wrong with you tonight?'

The gruff, aggressive voice belonged to Jimmy Smith.

'Nothing Jimmy, I'm alright honest. I'm just bleeding freezing!'

Now Jimmy's twin brother Nathan joined in and began picking on the youngster, 'Freezing my arse! It's the middle of summer, you're shitting yourself, aren't you?'

Both the brothers now chuckled at the boy's expense.

Danny didn't say a word, trying to ignore the ridicule of the two older men. He liked the Smith brothers, but he was also very scared and threatened by them. All he ever wanted to do was impress them. He believed that by coming on jobs like this he would eventually earn their begrudging respect; he desperately wanted to be accepted by them.

Danny Lee was only fifteen, he lived with his mother and three younger brothers in a cramped, scruffy caravan on the Tanley Road gypsy camp at Newark. He'd always been small for his age and was still short and very skinny. There was never any money coming in at home and Danny always felt scruffy in his patched-up jeans, old sweatshirts and hand me down fleece jacket. The boots he wore had never seen polish and holes were beginning to appear in the soles. His lank, dark hair was down to his shoulders and with his babyface features he could quite easily have been mistaken for a young girl.

His father had pissed off four years ago just after the birth of Danny's youngest brother.

His mother didn't really give a shit where Danny was at any given time, she was just glad of the extra space in the caravan.

As a direct result of his slight stature and the fact that he had no father or older brother to stick up for him, Danny was constantly bullied by the other kids of his age on the Tansley Road site.

That bullying had stopped overnight when Jimmy Smith stepped in and prevented Danny from getting another beating. Danny had latched onto the twin brothers and had hung around with them ever since, becoming further and further embroiled in the criminality the brothers were involved in.

Jimmy and Nathan Smith were five years older than Danny. They too lived with their elderly mother on the Tansley Road site, their father had died two years before from alcohol related liver disease. The twins had provided all the income for the family since they were both fourteen, when their father first became seriously ill. That income came from petty crime and thieving.

As the brothers got older and grew from sullen teenagers into strong, angry young men, other travellers on the Newark site stayed out of their way. With justifiable cause, they believed the brothers were extremely dangerous individuals who could only ever be a bad influence on their own youngsters.

Both the twins considered themselves to be the top men on the gypsy site and strutted around with an air of arrogance, they feared nobody and had no respect for the elders on the site who had tried unsuccessfully to curb their violent ways.

They already had long criminal histories with the police and both were extremely violent. It was when they were together that they were particularly dangerous, they were renowned for inciting each other into committing acts of grossly unnecessary violence.

Tonight, the three young gypsies had been watching the large house for over an hour. Having travelled from Newark to the village of Rolleston in an old, rusting flatbed lorry, they had patiently waited for darkness to fall.

The house they were watching was a large Elizabethan manor house, set well back from the remote country lane where they had left the flatbed lorry. The picture postcard property was surrounded by beautifully tended gardens and perfectly manicured lawns.

It had been the beautiful gardens of the house that were responsible for them being there. The grounds were part of a scheme that allowed visitors into private gardens during the summer months.

This had given Jimmy Smith the opportunity to walk around the property unchallenged towards the back end of the summer of last year. During that visit, which cost him the paltry sum of one pound towards some local charity, the young gypsy had discovered that the house was owned by a wealthy retired businessman who now lived alone in the large house. He'd committed the location of the house to memory and had made his mind up to pay the home owner a visit in the not too distant future.

Jimmy Smith was never one to let such a golden opportunity pass him by.

Now, as he waited with his two accomplices in the darkness, the only light showing on the ground floor of the house was suddenly switched off, plunging the entire house in darkness.

Almost immediately that light was replaced by another being switched on, this time in one of the upstairs rooms.

Jimmy muttered under his breath, 'Won't be long now boys, looks like the old bastard's finally going to bed.'

'Not before time', moaned Nathan.

'Are you sure this is the right house Jimmy?' asked a still very nervous Danny.

Jimmy shot the scared youngster a dangerous look.

'Of course it's the right fucking house you dope! Look Danny, if you're going to bottle it piss off back to the truck, I haven't got the time to wet nurse you!'

'I'm fine Jimmy, sorry.'

The upstairs light in the house was switched off and once again the house was in total darkness.

The only sound was the distant barking of a dog on one of the neighbouring farms. There were no such obstacles at this property, Jimmy had made sure that there was no guard dog at the house.

Sitting in the darkness Jimmy immediately began to issue orders to the other two.

'Right that's it, come on you two. Nathan, scout round and find the alarm box. Danny, have you got the can of foam I gave you?'

'It's right here Jimmy.'

Within a couple of minutes Nathan had located the

alarm box. Both of the brothers hoisted Danny onto their shoulders so he could reach the bright yellow box.

Jimmy hissed, 'You know what to do Danny.'

Danny took the lid off the canister of foam and filled the cavity of the bell box. Within seconds the building foam had set rock hard, rendering the burglar alarm useless.

The brothers lifted Danny back down to the floor and Jimmy whispered, 'Have you got the doings Nat?'

Nathan grinned and passed Jimmy a small jar of jam and a sheet of brown paper from his jacket pockets.

Jimmy smeared the sticky jam onto a transom window at the rear of the house. The window he'd selected to gain entry was well away from where they had seen the last light go out.

Once the window had been smeared with jam, Jimmy applied the brown paper to the sticky substance, then using a piece of stone from a nearby rockery, Jimmy reached up and smashed the pane of glass. The noise from the breaking window was nothing more than a dull thud, the fragments of glass had stuck to the jam and as Jimmy pulled away the sheet of thick paper the glass came away with it.

Jimmy turned to Danny and whispered, 'In you go then young 'un, sharpish!'

Danny quickly put on the pair of old black leather gloves that the brothers had given him earlier and began to pull the last remaining bits of glass away from the window frame.

With a leg up from Nathan, Danny climbed through the transom window and into the property.

As soon as he was inside he opened the larger window, directly below the transom so the brothers could also climb in.

As he climbed in Nathan winked at the young gypsy, 'Well done Danny boy, now for the fun part!'

Danny knew only too well what Nathan meant by his comment and right at that moment he wouldn't have traded places with the old man for all his money.

Danny followed the brothers through the dark rooms and then up the polished wooden stairs of the mansion, as they tried to locate the room where they had seen the light go out.

At the top of the stairs Jimmy stopped, turned to face the other two and whispered an order, 'Right, get the masks on boys, let's scare the shit out of this old bastard!'

All three men quickly pulled on black woollen ski masks.

Jimmy then slowly opened the heavy, oak panelled door to the room where the last light had been extinguished.

The room was dominated by a large four poster bed.

Danny could see that the old man was alone in the bed and that he was already in a deep sleep.

The three men could easily have left him sleeping and ransacked the entire house without disturbing him at all.

Unfortunately for the old man, that was never going to be an option for the sadistic Smith brothers.

Jimmy and Nathan stood either side of the bed watching the old man sleep, listening to him snore and both men began to giggle.

Danny knew what was coming and began to get really scared, he whispered under his breath, 'Jimmy can't we just rob the place and fuck off? Do we have to mess him up?'

It was Nathan who answered in a low menacing growl, 'Yes Danny, we do have to mess this fucker up. It serves him right, the rich old bastard. He wouldn't piss on the likes of us if we were on fire, fuck him!'

With that Nathan ripped the heavy quilt back, pulling it

off the sleeping figure before pulling the old man out of the bed and throwing him roughly to the floor.

Jimmy stepped round to that side of the bed and both brothers began laying into the old man with boots and fists.

After two minutes of a sustained, violent beating the old man lay bloody and bruised on the bedroom floor. He'd curled up into a ball and was groaning in pain.

Jimmy leaned down and put his mouth close to the old man's ear, 'Where's the money old man? You'd better tell me sharpish or you'll get another kicking.'

The old man's voice was barely a whisper as he tried to speak.

The words were mumbled as they escaped from his bloody and bruised mouth, 'Everything's in the wall safe behind a painting in the dining room downstairs. Please don't hurt me anymore. I'll give you everything, anything you want. I'm begging you, please just leave me alone.'

Without saying a word, Nathan grabbed the old man by both of his wrists and began to drag him face down along the polished wooden floor. When he reached the top of the wooden stairs Nathan didn't stop. He continued to drag the old man down the stairs, almost running as he did so.

Danny could hear the bones in the old man's legs breaking as they smashed off the hard-wooden stairs.

The youngster was shocked at the level of violence being used.

He knew the brothers were bad, but this was pure evil. He was only too aware that if he said anything or tried to stop it, both the brothers would turn on him and give him a beating too.

He looked away and dry retched as he heard the old man scream in pain.

'Where's the safe?' shouted Nathan above the pitiful wailing.

The old man raised a frail arm and pointed to another oak panelled door that led into the dining room.

Once again, he was dragged unceremoniously into the room

Nathan snarled, 'Where?'

A bony finger pointed to a landscape painting on the wooden panelled wall of the dining room.

Nathan removed the painting and saw the grey safe. He turned, lifted the old man off the floor, propped him up in front of the safe and snarled, 'Open the fucking thing then.'

The battered old man was confused and barely conscious, his body racked with pain he mumbled, 'I'm trying to remember the numbers.'

Nathan punched the man on the side of the head knocking him back down to the floor and screamed, 'Try harder you bastard!'

Danny gasped and grabbed Nathans sleeve, 'For fucks sake, you're going to kill him at this rate!'

Nathan rounded on Danny, 'Shut it you little twat, or you'll be next!'

Jimmy now grabbed Nathan's arm, 'The kid's right, he's had enough. If he passes out we'll never get into the fucking safe.'

Jimmy now bent down to the pathetic heap lying on the floor and whispered in the old man's ear, 'Last chance mister, give me the numbers for the combination to that safe or we'll fucking do you once and for all.'

'Twenty-six, thirteen, ten and five.'

'That's better', said a smiling Jimmy.

He stepped over to the safe and carefully dialled the numbers of the combination. With a slight hissing noise, the heavy metal door swung slowly open. Jimmy and Nathan reached inside and started to pull out bundles of bank notes. Through their ignorance, the twins totally ignored the extremely valuable jewellery, bonds and banker's orders that were worth far more than the cash.

Grinning from ear to ear Jimmy said, 'Right you two, as the shepherd once said, let's get the flock out of here!'

Wearing a grim expression Nathan turned to Jimmy, 'This will only take a minute bruv.'

'It had better not take any longer, I'm not waiting for you. Don't be long, see you back at the truck.'

As Danny followed Jimmy back through the dark house he could hear the sounds of punches and boots going in as the old man received yet another savage beating from Nathan.

Danny whispered to Jimmy, 'Your brother's a fucking psycho! He won't be satisfied until he's killed the poor bastard!'

Jimmy grabbed Danny by the front of his fleece jacket and pulled him in close, 'And if he hears you talking like that Danny boy it will be you next. Just button your lip for Christ's sake son.'

Five minutes later and the three men were all sitting in the flatbed lorry parked on the quiet, deserted lane.

As rain started to fall outside Jimmy sat in the driver's seat and quickly counted the cash.

He smiled triumphantly and said, 'Good stuff. There's about four and a half grand here. That's a grand for you Danny boy, me and Nathan will split the rest.'

Nathan growled, 'Why can't we give the little twat five hundred? That way we'll have a couple of grand each.'

'Because I say so Nat, that's why!'

As they drove away from the manor house, all three men began to think about how much amphetamine they could buy with the cash from the burglary.

For Jimmy Smith in particular it had been imperative that they got something out of tonight's job. He already owed the gang at Phet Row well over a thousand pounds for drugs that had been laid on when he'd been skint.

Suddenly, he shouted 'Fucking stuff!', and slammed his hand against the steering wheel, causing a startled Danny to glance in his direction.

Jimmy hated the fact that he was dependant on the drug, but he knew that first thing tomorrow morning he would be driving over to Phet Row, or as it was otherwise known, Hammond Street on the Renton council estate in Worksop.

As they drove away, not one of the three young gypsies spared a thought for the badly injured old man who was now desperately crawling along the floor of the large hallway, trying to reach the telephone to summon help. He feared that both his legs were broken and he could feel that his jaw had been displaced. He was struggling to see as the bruised flesh around his eyes rapidly began to swell.

At least I'm alive, he thought to himself as he willed himself along the floor. He'd been convinced that he was about be murdered by the thugs that had broken into his home.

After twenty pain racked minutes, he finally reached the telephone table. Using the last reserves of his failing strength, the badly injured old man grabbed the wire and pulled the telephone from the table. He dialled three nines and lay next to the handpiece on the floor.

The phone was answered immediately and he heard a clear voice say, 'Hello emergency, which service do you require?'

The old man croaked into the receiver, 'Help me please', before passing out completely.

CHAPTER 3

7.00am 21ˢᵗ June 1987
Linby, Nottinghamshire

Tom Naylor had been running steadily for three quarters of an hour. He was in that rhythm all serious runners know well, where the sound of his training shoes hitting the wet tarmac dictated the pace of his easy breathing.

The rain that had been falling heavily had now stopped and Tom pulled the hood of his sweat shirt back, allowing cool air to envelop the sweat on his head. Refreshed and energised by the sudden feeling of cold, Tom took a deeper breath and lengthened his stride.

Another fifteen minutes at this faster pace and he would be home.

The smell of freshly ploughed fields either side of the lane was even more evident after the heavy rain. The sun had now broken through the rapidly diminishing clouds and the warmth from the first rays caused wisps of steam to begin rising from the earth as the heat quickly warmed the sodden ground.

At just under six feet tall and weighing twelve and a half stone, Tom had never been a big man, but he was very fit and carried no surplus fat. He kept his dark brown hair short, down to a grade two crew cut, out of a preference honed by his military background.

Whenever he could, he would always go for a run on Sunday morning, through the country lanes that surrounded his cottage. There was nothing better to clear your mind of the previous week's trial and tribulations.

Probably, the major perk of being a member of Nottinghamshire Constabulary's Special Operations Unit was having virtually every Sunday off work.

The majority of men deployed on the four sections of the Unit would be involved in policing football matches or public order duties in the city centre on Saturdays.

The four sections would take a rest day on Sundays. A call out rota was maintained should a situation develop that required an armed response or other emergency mobilisation.

Tom was running on automatic now, head still, arms pumping as his pace got faster and faster, forcing the blood through his veins. His lungs were burning by the time he rounded the last bend in the lane and his small cottage on the outskirts of Linby came into view.

He smiled, slowed to a walk, opened the gate and fished his door keys from the zip pocket of his navy-blue tracksuit bottoms.

He walked inside, locked the door of the cottage behind him and made his way upstairs where he got straight out of his wet running gear and into a steaming hot shower.

Fifteen minutes later and wearing a freshly laundered, black crew neck sweater and a pair of light blue Lee jeans, the order of the day was breakfast.

Tom lived alone at the two-bedroom cottage, having purchased the property almost six months ago. He'd taken the decision to get on the property ladder after living in digs in the Woodthorpe area of Nottingham for the last couple of years.

He'd moved into the cottage one month before transferring from Hyson Green to the Special Operations Unit.

Tom had been pleasantly surprised when his application to join the Unit had been accepted. He was deployed to C Section and had now been on the specialist department for five months.

As he thought about what he wanted to do with the rest of his day off, he quickly rustled up fresh brewed coffee and a fried egg sandwich. Otherwise known as a 'Banjo', the fried egg sandwich was a throwback to his life in the military.

Tom had joined the army straight from school as a junior soldier in 1975, much to the disappointment of his father, who felt he could have put good school exam results to a better purpose. Despite his father's misgivings Tom knew he had made the right decision; he revelled in the discipline the army provided, that and the hard, physical training. Even back then he soaked fitness work up like a sponge.

Once in the army he also discovered that he possessed a natural gift for marksmanship and as soon as he joined the regular army on his eighteenth birthday, he was quickly fast tracked for sniper training.

At least this part of his chosen career pleased his father, who himself had once been the small-bore rifle champion of Southern England, during his time doing National Service at Bicester camp near Oxford in the fifties.

When Tom had broken the news of his sniper training, his father had laughed and said, "It's all in the genes son, all in the genes".

Tom loved the army so much that in 1978 he applied for and passed selection for the Parachute Regiment, fully intending to make the military his career for life.

Had it not been for some despot General from Argentina deciding to invade the Falkland Islands in 1982, he would probably have still been a member of the armed forces now.

Before they travelled to the South Atlantic, hardly any of the lads in the Regiment knew where the Falkland Islands, or as the Argentinians would have it, the Malvinas, were.

By June of 1982, the war that he'd trained so hard for was over and he and the rest of the servicemen that had fought to liberate the islands returned home victorious.

During that conflict Tom had fought and killed the enemy. The victory had been achieved with a high price; the cost of losing too many good friends.

Having returned home to a hero's welcome, something Tom didn't relish at all, he'd found it extremely difficult to revert back to being a peace time soldier. Everything he did felt pointless and he was surrounded by a huge feeling of apathy.

After what he'd been through and what he'd witnessed in combat, being a peace time soldier was just too much of an anti-climax.

In an effort to try and pep his interest in the military up again, he applied for selection onto the Special Air Service. His attempt at the rigorous selection process ended in failure after he badly sprained an ankle on one of the many forced marches in the Brecon Beacons.

As a result of the injury he was unable to continue on selection and was returned to the Parachute Regiment.

Within six weeks of being RTU'd Tom bought himself out of the army, leaving behind the career he'd always thought would be his for life.

Five months after leaving the army, Tom was wearing a different uniform and pounding the beat as a police officer in inner city Nottingham. He worked at Hyson Green for four years before transferring to the Special Operations Unit, the armed response team of the Nottinghamshire Constabulary. His military background and his specialist skills as a sniper had no doubt helped him to be successful in his application, so young in service.

Having wolfed down the fried egg sandwich Tom was still sipping his hot mug of coffee when the telephone on the table next to his armchair began to ring. He picked up the phone immediately and said briskly, 'Hello, Tom Naylor.'

A flat, monotone voice on the line said, 'This is Inspector Henson in the Force Control Room. Pc Naylor, are you sober?'

Tom grinned and replied, 'Yes sir I'm sober, I didn't go out last night.'

The truth was, he hadn't been out for two weeks, ever since he was unceremoniously dumped by the woman he'd been seeing for the last three months. He'd been seriously disappointed at the rejection as he had very strong feelings for the woman and had actually thought she might be the one he could eventually settle down with.

He was aware the woman was trapped in an abusive marriage that she was desperate to get out of. He'd dropped plenty of hints to her that she should seriously consider leaving her brute of a husband and move in with him. The day before he was going to ask her that very question she had called him on the telephone and unceremoniously dumped him.

Inspector Henson's relentless, boring voice snapped him out of his reverie, 'Pc Naylor, you need to get yourself in to

Headquarters as soon as possible. There's a job developing and you're required now. The rest of C Section and D Section have been called out and are already on their way.'

'Okay, I'll be there in twenty minutes sir.'

Monotone voice replied, 'Logging this call at 0835, do not be any later than 0900.'

The line went dead.

The Control Room Inspector had been his usual happy, chatty self.

Tom grabbed his car keys from the sideboard, locked the front door of the cottage and jumped in his car. He didn't bother changing, anything he needed would already be in the lockers at Headquarters.

He drove his Volkswagen Golf carefully through the quiet country lanes knowing he would arrive at Headquarters well before nine o'clock.

As he cruised through the lanes he resolved to try and contact the supposed love of his life again that evening, he needed to try and establish exactly what had gone wrong.

He felt compelled to try. He thought what they had was something special and he didn't want to let Jaycee walk out of his life so easily.

CHAPTER 4

8.50am 21st June 1987
Force Headquarters, Nottinghamshire

As Tom drove his car into the car park at Police Headquarters he started to speculate on what this call out could be for. It must be something pretty big to warrant two full sections, exactly half their strength.

The Special Operations Unit was made up of four sections. Each of the sections A, B, C and D were staffed by a sergeant and ten men. There were two Inspectors, each Inspector was responsible for supervising two of the sections.

In overall command was a Chief Inspector.

It was a very small, tight knit group of officers who were expected to deal with some of the most dangerous aspects of police work including providing a firearms response for incidents in Nottinghamshire.

No firearms had been mentioned by the Control Room Inspector this morning so that ruled out drawing weapons from the armoury for an armed response.

That meant the call out could be for anything. The possibilities ranged from an abducted child, a murder enquiry that required their search capability or door to door enquiries that needed completing, or even an aeroplane crash. Such was the diverse nature of the roles the Unit was expected to carry out.

Tom parked his car and stopped speculating, one thing was for sure he would be finding out soon enough.

He got out of the car and walked towards the buildings that housed the Special Operations Unit, a cluster of prefabricated buildings known by the men who worked there as simply 'The Huts'. These shadowy buildings were the only premises in the entire Force that were not accessible using the general issue police key.

Access to these buildings was strictly by invitation only, whatever your rank.

Tom could see other team members arriving, one of whom was his best friend and sniper team partner Matt Jarvis.

Matt walked over to Tom grinning and said, 'What's happening Tom? This has seriously put paid to my plans for the day. Mrs Jarvis is not a happy lady.'

'No idea mate, Happy Henson said fuck all on the phone, as usual.'

Matt Jarvis had arrived on C Section two months before Tom at a time when the section had no sniper capability. Virtually as soon as Tom had arrived, he and Matt were selected to undergo the rifleman training course at the Firearms Training School in order to fill that void and become the section's snipers.

Even though they had now specialised and were a sniper team they were still very much the new boys on C Section.

Walking into the huts, both men made their way to the main briefing area, a large room that would comfortably accommodate sixty men.

The windows of the room were all fitted with one-way glass to protect from prying eyes; it was totally soundproofed and had a large white board that completely covered one of the end walls.

There was a large map of the county of Nottinghamshire and maps depicting each of the county's larger conurbation areas along the length of one of the side walls.

Most importantly of all there was a large hot water urn that was permanently switched on. This vital piece of equipment would provide the hot water for the endless cups of tea or coffee that were an integral part of any planning session or major briefing.

Tom and Matt stopped to look at the written instruction on the white board at the end of the room.

ALL STAFF, FULL BODY ARMOUR AND NATO
HELMETS. KIT BAGS CONTAINING LIGHT WEIGHT
CLOTHING, ASP BATONS AND PLASTICUFFS.
BRIEFING WILL COMMENCE AT 0900

Tom glanced at his watch; it was now eight fifty. The assembled staff had ten minutes to get both kit and transport ready. The huts suddenly became a hive of frenzied activity as the instruction was carried out by the men.

There was no mention of drawing any weapons from the armoury so that definitely ruled out any kind of firearms job.

As the large clock in the briefing room moved onto nine o'clock, twenty-two men were kitted up ready to go. All the bags had been stowed onto the vans and the men sat quietly in full body armour with their navy-blue NATO riot helmets between their feet.

Before he transferred onto the Unit, Tom had heard rumours that briefings for jobs were legendary. Those final few minutes before the actual briefings began were always very light hearted with a lot of banter flying in all directions. Tom knew from his army days, it was just a mechanism for the release of tension. If you are too tense it's possible to actually miss vital parts of a briefing.

This was the reason why, although not actually encouraged by the command team, it was never prevented either.

All the men knew that once the briefing actually started the banter would stop and they would revert to being the consummate professionals they were.

Strangely, on this occasion the banter was very muted.

Tom looked around at the assembled officers: every one of them had a grim expression set on their face.

Sgt Mick Davies and Sgt Graham Turner, the sergeants in charge of D and C Section respectively, were in a huddle at the front of the briefing room with Inspector Gary Reeves, the Inspector responsible for the two sections.

All three men were engaged in animated conversation.

Tom and Matt sat next to each other on the second row of seats near the front of the room and Tom now strained his ears to try and hear what his supervisors were discussing.

The general hubbub of whispered conversations from the rest of the men as they chatted about the impending job, drowned out the supervisor's conversation and made it impossible for him to hear.

Inspector Reeves suddenly shouted, 'Stand up!'

The men in the briefing room immediately stood as a mark of respect to the man now entering the room.

Chief Inspector Jim Chambers walked to the front of the room and looked at the assembled men. He looked like a man who had been awake all night, his eyes were red and bloodshot and it was obvious from the dark shadow that he hadn't yet shaved.

'Sit down, gents', he said calmly.

He started speaking, his delivery concise and factual, 'Last night at approximately ten thirty, two officers from Mansfield Division were called to an extremely violent domestic dispute at a house in Cuckney, a small village located to the north of Mansfield. The house they attended was 55a Porter Close on the edge of the village.'

Suddenly, Tom's blood ran cold and every nerve jangled in his body. He sat bolt upright staring at the Chief Inspector.

Tom knew this address well and the people, or rather the woman, who lived there very, very well.

This was Jaycee's house.

The woman who had so unceremoniously broken off their relationship two weeks ago.

Tom was very much a single man but he knew full well that Jaycee was a married woman. She was married to a violent and abusive husband who regularly beat her.

Beneath the heavy body armour, Tom felt himself beginning to sweat as disturbing thoughts raced through his head.

Had he in some way been responsible for whatever had occurred at that address? Had it happened just because he had broken his own cardinal rule and got involved with a beautiful married woman?

Make no mistake, Jaycee Stasuik was indeed a very sexy, very beautiful woman, even though at forty-one she was quite a bit older than he was.

Tom had been attracted to her from the very first time she had smiled at him while he was having a quiet drink on his own in The Gate public house at Warsop. They had started talking in the pub and after spending a very pleasant couple of hours in her company, he had found himself not only invited back to her house in Cuckney but making love to a woman he had literally just met.

From that night, Tom had found himself immersed in a torrid passionate affair. She had told him on many occasions about the abuse she constantly suffered at the hands of her husband who worked away on oil rigs in the North Sea and that her kids had all left home.

Jim Chambers continued with the briefing, 'This violent domestic occurred between the woman of the house, Jaycee Stasuik and her nineteen-year-old son Kyle Stasuik.'

Fuck! Tom was now panicking big style inside.

He was in a state of shock.

Had the Chief Inspector really said Kyle Stasuik? He knew that Jaycee had a son but he thought he was away at University in Bristol.

Jim Chambers continued, 'For whatever reason, it would appear that the initial argument was between Kyle and his sixteen-year-old girlfriend Emma Simpson. This argument had become heated and quickly progressed to violence. Kyle used a kitchen knife to slash Emma once across the top of her left arm. It seems that Mrs Stasuik had then tried to intervene and was stabbed once in the chest by her son Kyle using the same kitchen knife.'

Fuck! This was rapidly turning into Tom's worst nightmare.

Was Jaycee dead?

The colour drained from Tom's face and a concerned Matt Jarvis sitting next to him whispered, 'Are you alright mate? You look like death. Were you out on the piss last night?'

Tom hissed back, 'No, I'm fine. I'm just cooking in all this gear.'

The Chief Inspector continued, 'When the two section officers from Mansfield arrived at the property, they found Mrs Stasuik on the floor of the lounge bleeding heavily from a single puncture wound. They also found Kyle Stasuik and Emma Simpson upstairs. They could see the young girl had also been injured and attempted to help her. Kyle threatened both officers with the knife before dragging the girl into the master bedroom where he promptly barricaded himself in blocking the bedroom door.'

A voice inside Tom's head was screaming, what about Jaycee?

As if in answer to that loud imaginary voice Jim Chambers said, 'One of the responding officers took the decision to leave his colleague at the house to contain the situation and then drove Mrs Stasuik to the Casualty Department at Mansfield Hospital in his patrol car with the blues and twos on. This decision undoubtedly saved her life and after undergoing emergency surgery last night, she's now in a stable condition and off the critical list. Her injuries are no longer thought to be life threatening.'

Thank God, thought Tom, at least she's going to survive.

Tom let out an almost audible sigh as relief flooded over him.

Matt whispered, 'Are you sure you're okay mate?'

'I'm fine', Tom said tersely under his breath.

'Okay, okay.'

The briefing continued as Jim Chambers provided more

detail, 'The house on Porter Close has been contained overnight and we've had a hostage negotiator there since early this morning trying to communicate with Kyle. The negotiator has confirmed that Emma Simpson isn't seriously injured but he's getting concerned that Kyle's becoming increasingly more agitated and unstable. There's now a genuine fear that Kyle could do Emma further harm or worse. From the information we're getting, it seems that Kyle's now totally undressed himself and has forced Emma to strip, both are now totally naked. Kyle's thrown all the clothes they were wearing out of the bedroom window. The negotiator has confirmed that Kyle is still in possession of a large black handled kitchen knife which he's constantly holding at the young girl's throat. Every now and then he drags her to the bedroom window to shout and scream abuse at the negotiator. As the situation's gradually becoming more volatile and could get even worse very quickly, the Chief Constable's taken the decision that we need to get in there as soon as possible and get Emma out of that house before she comes to any further harm.'

Jim Chambers wearily turned to Gary Reeves and said, 'Gary, could you take it from here please?'

Inspector Reeves stood up and said, 'We've got good intelligence for the surrounding area and it shouldn't be a problem for a section to approach the house from the rear without Kyle seeing them from the front bedroom window. The big problem we've got is this: the house itself is a very large detached property which the Stasuik's constructed as a self-build project four years ago and we've got absolutely no idea of the interior layout of the building. We've de-briefed the two uniform officers who attended last night and although what they've remembered has been useful, there are still any number of rooms inside the house that we have no clue about. As the name would suggest, Porter Close is a cul de sac and that will obviously assist us to contain the situation. The target premises are located at the very end of the cul de sac.'

Gary Reeves paused and then continued, 'The husband of the injured woman, Glen Stasuik, is already on his way down from Aberdeen. He was airlifted from the rig he's been working on by helicopter this morning. He's due to arrive here later this afternoon. As the current situation is so volatile, I don't think there's anyway we can delay this raid to await his arrival.'

The Inspector glanced towards Jim Chambers who shook his head slowly, confirming that the raid would not be put off to wait for Glen Stasuik.

Gary went on, 'It would appear that Kyle is quite a complex character. He's a top student at Bristol University studying computer science. Some of his lecturers are already speaking of him as being the next Bill Gates, he's that highly regarded. However, three years ago when he was only sixteen, he badly assaulted one of his father's closest friends outside the family home on Porter Close. The police were involved initially as a baseball bat had been used to inflict some quite serious injuries. Kyle was arrested and interviewed, but he refused to make any comment when questioned. After speaking with Glen Stasuik, the family friend declined to press any charges of assault. Consideration was given by the CPS about the merits of pressing home an offensive weapon charge but without the assault going through and because of Kyle's previous good character, the CPS decided, in their wisdom, that there was little prospect of achieving a conviction at court.'

After a further pause he continued, 'So, we've got this extremely intelligent young man who for no apparent reason suddenly flares up and commits the most horrific acts of violence. We've asked his father for his observations about this behaviour pattern, but he's refused to say anything about his son or these attacks until he gets here.'

Tom was listening intently. He thought to himself, it was obviously a case of like father like son. Kyle had probably grown up witnessing countless acts of violence by his father towards his mother and now feels that this is a normal way to behave.

Gary Reeves looked at the men and said decisively, 'Right. I want D Section rolling to Porter Close immediately. I want this whole area sealed off completely. I know that uniform officers are already there doing a containment job, but I want this place locking down tight. The last thing we need now is for the press to get wind of what's happening and start causing interference.'

He turned to Sgt Davies and said, 'Mick, can I leave that for you to organise?'

'No problem boss', was the quick reply and with that D Section were on their feet and moving out of the room. Within two minutes they were in their vans and heading out of the car park.

Tom looked around the room at his colleagues, they were all grinning like Cheshire cats. With D Section detailed for containment that meant only one thing; it would be C Section doing the raid and ending the siege.

All units of this type have a fierce rivalry. Although very capable of working as one cohesive unit, each individual section considered themselves to be the best among the best.

In reality the training is such that each section is equal and all are well capable of doing any task delegated to them.

With D Section gone Gary Reeves turned to Sgt Graham Turner, 'Graham, you've got just over an hour to sort a plan of entry out. I want C Section at the rendezvous point in Cuckney no later than ten thirty and in position ready to commence the raid on the property at eleven o'clock. Okay?'

'No problem boss.'

Immediately the team got into a tight huddle and got to work trying to establish a workable plan of action.

Tom quickly took Matt to one side away from the group, his stomach was churning and his mouth felt bone dry. He looked directly at Matt and said quietly, 'I've got a big problem mate. You remember that woman I told you about a few months back, the one from The Gate pub at Warsop?'

'Yeah, I remember. Drop dead gorgeous but married, right?'

'Yes, that one.'

Matt looked at him quizzically before his face began to break into a grin, 'Please, don't tell me you've been caught at it by her old man.'

'No mate, it's much worse than that. The woman I've been seeing is Jaycee Stasiuk.'

The grin on Matts face vanished instantly and he whispered, 'Shit!'

He then moved closer to Tom's ear and whispered conspiratorially, 'You've got to keep your head down mate. If Chambers finds out about this you'll be history. Your feet won't touch the ground, they'll throw you off the Unit.'

'That's the problem though, I can't keep quiet about it. I know that house from top to bottom, every room. I've been inside there enough times.'

'Yeah right, especially the fucking bedroom you idiot!'

Matt took a deep breath before continuing, 'You're right mate, you've got to say something. Your knowledge of the house layout could mean the difference between Emma Simpson getting seriously injured by that nutter, or us getting her out of there safe and well.'

Tom already knew what he had to do, but it was good to hear Matt confirm his own thought process.

Matt said, 'Good luck mate', before turning to re-join the group planning the raid.

Tom could see Chief Inspector Chambers standing alone near the door of the briefing room. He took a deep breath and walked across the room towards him.

Tom said quietly, 'Sir, I need to talk to you urgently.'

'Christ almighty Naylor! I'm sure you've got things you need to attend to right now. I know I have.'

Tom stared directly into his senior officer's eyes and said, 'Now sir, it's important.'

CHAPTER 5

8.50am 21st June 1987
Renton Estate, Worksop, Nottinghamshire

Jakub Kowalczyk was a very proud man.

He had first arrived in England in June 1940 just after his twenty fifth birthday. That was forty-seven years ago. Jakub had made the long and dangerous journey across occupied Europe to England to continue the fight against the German army that had conquered his beloved Poland.

When the Third Reich had smashed their way through Poland in September 1939, the Nazi SS stormtroopers had slaughtered his entire family simply because they followed the Jewish faith.

Jakub had somehow managed to escape the death and destruction, constantly hiding from the German soldiers. Eventually he had reached Ostend in Belgium and managed to smuggle himself aboard a fishing trawler heading for Hull.

As soon as he reached England, Jakub made his way south to London. Having no papers or identification he went to the nearest police station in the beleaguered city and handed himself in to the authorities. He told them his story and that he wanted desperately to continue the fight against the evil Nazi regime.

Things moved quickly for Jakub as soon as he told the authorities that he had been trained as a pilot in the Polish air force. The Nazi's advance through Poland had been so swift that he had been unable to get to his base to fight the invaders.

In August that year he was integrated into the Royal Air Force and was posted to RAF Northolt where he became part of the famous 303 Squadron that was made up of young Polish fighter pilots. He was quickly trained to fly the Hurricane fighter plane. The fast, manoeuvrable aircraft was a far cry from the old, dated biplanes he'd previously flown and he quickly fell in love with the graceful but deadly aeroplane.

Throughout the Battle of Britain, Jakub had fought courageously against the Luftwaffe. Constantly being vastly outnumbered by the Dorniers, Junckers and Messerschmitt fighter planes of the German air force.

During the conflict Jakub shot down many enemy aircraft and contributed massively to the final victory. He was decorated for personal bravery on three separate occasions.

Throughout the summer and autumn of 1940, he was based at RAF Northolt just outside London.

At the end of September, just as the Battle of Britain was coming to a conclusion, he had suffered a minor injury when a bullet from a Messerschmitt 109 had struck the fuselage of his Hurricane. Fortunately, the bullet hadn't struck anything vital on either the plane or Jakub. It had grazed the top of his right arm however and he was forced to spend the next three days grounded until the mobility returned to his arm.

Jakub found it impossible to sit around at the base while his friends took off again and again to take the fight to the enemy. Feeling the need to get away from London for a few days, Jakub got a lift into London; from there he caught the first train from St Pancras that was heading north. When he first arrived in England he had enjoyed the countryside as he made his way south down to the capital. He decided he would take a trip back to the north to clear his head and relax after the stress of the daily conflict in the air.

By pure chance, the train he caught took him to the beautiful midlands city of Nottingham.

As Jakub strolled leisurely along the tree lined embankment that runs alongside the sparkling blue river Trent, the young fighter pilot first met and fell instantly in love with his beloved Glenda.

Glenda was just seventeen years old, but Jakub was instantly struck by her long red hair, sparkling green eyes and beautiful smile. Glenda had been equally smitten by the tall, slim fighter ace with the mop of flaxen coloured hair and the bright blue eyes.

As they walked hand in hand alongside the beautiful river, Glenda had invited Jakub to travel with her to her home town of Worksop to meet her family and have a meal with them. Jakub had readily accepted her kind invitation.

Glenda's father was a coal miner at the Renton Colliery in Worksop; he had been excused military duty as the country desperately needed coal to fire the war effort. He had thoroughly approved of the courageous young Polish fighter pilot his daughter had brought to his house.

Just three weeks later, in October, the old miner had been delighted when Jakub had returned to Nottinghamshire to ask his permission to marry his daughter. He readily gave his blessing and the young couple were married the following weekend just as victory in the Battle of Britain was being declared.

It seemed as though everything moved at a lightning pace in those dark days; romance and marriage were no exceptions.

The war years were a difficult time when he had been sent overseas to continue the fight against the Germans after D Day and the invasion of Europe.

At the end of the Second World War and with the Allies victorious, Jakub had been unable to remain in the Royal Air Force.

He returned to England from the base in France and had taken the decision never to travel back to his native Poland that was now in the hands of the Russians. He was one of a few in his squadron that were able to remain in the country they had fought so hard to protect from the Nazis.

It was only because he had married his English sweetheart that he hadn't been forced to either repatriate to Poland or to seek a new life in another country.

Having been allowed to remain in the country, he decided instead to settle in Nottinghamshire with his war bride and try to earn a living in the coal mine alongside Glenda's father.

It had been very difficult in the beginning; for the first few years after the war Jakub and Glenda had occupied a single room in the house owned by her father. The house was small and conditions were cramped, but early in 1949 Jakub and Glenda had moved into a brand-new council house on Hammond Street.

The house was on a new estate in Worksop called the Renton Estate, it was absolutely beautiful. The vast majority of the people living there were mining families who took great pride in their new homes. The gardens at the front and back of the houses were meticulously cared for. As the majority of the homeowners were miners they were not rich, but they were not short of money either.

Jakub worked hard down the mine to provide for his wife. He grew vegetables and tended his garden while Glenda looked after the home and cooked beautiful meals.

This was a golden time for Jakub, life was sweet.

Glenda became pregnant soon after they had moved into their new home and when his daughter Anna was born he thought his life could never get any better.

The fates had other ideas and tragedy came quickly to the young family. His infant daughter contracted viral meningitis and died in his arms when she was just two years old.

His loving wife never really recovered from the devastating loss of their beautiful daughter and although they tried to have more children, Glenda never fell pregnant again and the couple remained childless.

Shortly after he retired from the mine, his wife was diagnosed with cancer and after a very brief battle with the illness she lost her fight and left Jakub on his own.

He'd lived alone ever since, his only company being his faithful mongrel dog, Molly.

Jakub was now disgusted by the condition of the once beautiful Renton Estate and in particular the state of Hammond Street. Everywhere was so scruffy and dirty, nobody cared about the condition of their houses or gardens anymore.

Jakub was now in his seventies and he was the only resident who bothered to cut the grass in his garden.

The streets on the estate were strewn with litter or worse, burning cars that had been stolen were regularly dumped. The Fire Brigade would turn up and put out the fire but the burned-out wrecks were left on the streets for weeks.

Some days Hammond Street reminded him of his home town in Poland after the Nazis had stormed through burning and destroying everything in their path.

Nobody bothered to talk to their neighbours anymore and there was a tangible feeling of fear on the estate. Jakub, who had fought so bravely during the war and who had feared no man, was now too terrified to venture out of his house after dark.

His own health had deteriorated after the death of his wife. He had put weight on, had a heart condition and suffered badly with rheumatoid arthritis.

One of the few pleasures he had left was taking Molly for long, slow, meandering walks. Most days they would set off at first light and make their way along Hammond Street. At the end of the street, where it turned the corner, there was a large gap in the row of houses. Once through this gap they were immediately onto the old pit tip that covered over ten acres of land. This part of the tip hadn't been used by the mine since the late seventies; Renton Colliery itself had closed shortly after the 1984 miners' strike.

This area of the old spoil tip had very quickly become overgrown and was now a beautiful place to walk. It rose quite steeply away from the gap in the houses but once he had taken his time and reached the top it was always worth the effort; he and Molly would spend hours on the old tip enjoying the wildlife, listening to the birdsong and admiring the views and fresher air.

Ironically, what had once been the ugliest part of the estate had now become the most beautiful.

Jakub saw it as his own personal refuge away from the grime and decadence of the estate and the scum that now lived there.

The 'scum' as he called them, were getting more brazen and aggressive every day. He had watched on disappointed, as they gradually became more and more emboldened in the way they openly flouted the law. He watched them every day selling drugs and God knows what else to the loud-mouthed yobs who arrived in droves, horrible loud music blaring from their flashy cars.

At first the dealers had operated out of the shadows, only venturing out onto the street when a car actually pulled up. Now it was a different story, they sat out in deck chairs, lounging on the corner of the street drinking beer and smoking.

The sale of drugs was now done openly.

Jakub had to pass these drug dealing louts every morning when he and Molly went for their walk up onto the pit tip. He always eyed them warily and with disdain. The big fat one who was obviously in charge always stared hard at him as he walked by. Jakub had nicknamed this man Hermann as he reminded him of Hermann Goering, the fat, bloated leader of the German Luftwaffe.

Jakub felt that Hermann stared at him in that way trying to goad him into saying something. He always averted his eyes from this man and just kept slowly walking.

He did feel intimidated by Hermann but he was not prepared to allow him and his yobs to ruin the last remnant of pleasure he had left in his life.

All these thoughts were racing through Jakub's mind this morning as once again he made his way along Hammond Street towards the corner, intending to go onto the pit tip with Molly.

As he walked, he felt inside his coat pocket for the little bottle of pills that he always carried. His doctor had told him to always make sure that wherever he went he kept the little lifesavers with him.

Jakub had suffered with severe angina for the last four years; it was now second nature to him to pop one of the little black pills under his tongue whenever he felt the familiar tightness begin to cramp his chest.

To his dismay, Jakub saw that even though it was still early, once again all the dealers were out there, about seven of them in total. He'd hoped he would be early enough to miss them. They were all sat in deck chairs drinking cans of lager even though it had only just passed nine o' clock in the morning.

Hermann was also sitting there and as usual began staring at Jakub, but this time the fat man spoke in a voice laden with menace, 'And where the fuck do you think you're going old man?'

Jakub was stunned; it was the first time Hermann had ever spoken to him. Stunned or not, he responded defiantly, 'I'm going to walk my dog. What business is it of yours where I go?'

Hermann now raised his fat frame out of the deck chair and said mockingly, 'Oh, walking the dog is it?'

He then started to waddle slowly towards Jakub saying, 'It's like this old man, I'm pissed off with you walking through my corner every day without a word, so this is what's going to happen. From now on you're going to walk that flea-bitten rat somewhere else or I'll rip its fucking legs off one by one, got it!'

Jakub felt an anger rising inside him.

He had not felt a rage like this since he was forced to flee Poland.

Suddenly, he forgot he was a seventy-two-year-old man with a heart condition; once again he was Jakub Kowalczyk, Battle of Britain fighter ace.

He took a step towards Hermann and shouted, 'Who do you think you are big shot? Some kind of Al Capone gangster? I'm not scared of you tough guy. I fought the Nazis and I'm sure as hell not scared of you, you fat bastard!'

Jakub knew instantly he'd gone too far by the expression on Hermann's face. The fat man took another pace forward and punched Jakub straight in the mouth, knocking the old man to the floor.

He stood over Jakub and growled menacingly, 'Obviously I didn't make myself clear old man. If I see you anywhere near the corner of this street again, I'll kill your fucking rat first and then you. Do you understand that?'

Shakily, Jakub got to his feet and looked at Hermann, he could already taste the blood in his mouth. He said quietly through gritted teeth, 'I know what you're doing here you fat piece of shit, you're selling the drugs here. I'll call the police tomorrow and tell them everything. You can't tell me where I can and can't go!'

Hermann drew back his hambone fist and feigned to punch Jakub again, involuntarily the old man ducked and cowered away.

The other drug dealers watching began to laugh.

Jakub felt ashamed and began to walk slowly away. With Molly still walking alongside him he carefully retraced his steps back to the sanctuary of his own home.

Hermann shouted after him, 'On second thoughts, don't worry about where you're going to walk the dog old man. After tonight, it's a problem you won't have to worry about!'

Jakub ignored the comment, he kept his head down and carried on walking.

As he walked away from the drug dealers along the litter strewn street, he desperately began feeling for the little bottle of pills in his coat pocket. He could already sense a familiar feeling of tightness starting to draw in around his chest.

CHAPTER 6

9.15am 21st June 1987
Force Headquarters, Nottinghamshire

Chief Inspector Jim Chambers studied Tom Naylor's face carefully and then said quietly, 'Okay Naylor, get in my office and close the door behind you.'

Filled with trepidation Tom followed his boss across the corridor, into his spacious office and as instructed closed the door behind him.

The Chief Inspector had propped himself against the edge of his desk, facing Tom with his arms folded across his chest and a concerned look on his face. Tom stood directly in front of him and waited courteously for the senior officer to speak.

Jim Chambers took a deep breath and said, 'Alright Tom, what's so urgent that in the middle of this shitstorm you need to speak with me?'

Tom came straight out with it, 'Sir, I know Jaycee Stasuik. I met her on a night out in a pub some months ago and ever since then we've been in a relationship.'

For a second, Tom thought Jim Chambers was going to explode, his face went bright red and he stared at him with a withering look that sent shivers through him.

Just as suddenly, his face changed and Tom saw the colour drain from his features. When he finally did speak, it was obvious that the senior officer was desperately trying to suppress his inner rage.

He looked at Tom through hooded eyes and hissed quietly, 'A relationship? You mean you've been fucking her, am I right? Were you aware she was married?'

Tom replied too quickly, 'Yes. I knew she was married, but her husband's a bully who physically beats her and subjects her to the worst kind of mental cruelty. She's already tried to leave him several times in the past.'

Jim Chambers was old school and having none of it, 'Christ man! Spare me the pitiful, whining, self-justification. The bottom line is you should know better. If, God forbid, this operation goes wrong today and then the press get hold of this little gem they'll quite rightly crucify you and not only that, they'll crucify the Special Operations Unit and the Force as a whole. Right at this moment I can't see any sort of future for you on this department, maybe even this job. I can't believe you've been so fucking stupid!'

Tom had never seen his boss this angry.

Chambers growled, 'I do have one question Naylor; why the fuck are you telling me all this now? Don't you think my day's been bad enough already?'

Tom hesitated for a second then said, 'Sir, I know what I've done is stupid, but what me and Jaycee had is now over. It ended two weeks ago.'

'Well fucking Hallelujah!' Jim shouted, a sarcastic edge to his voice.

With nothing to lose now, Tom pressed on quickly, 'Look sir, in answer to your question why am I telling you all this now? The answer's simple, rightly or wrongly, I've spent a lot of time inside that house recently and I know it like the back of my hand.'

'Wrongly Naylor, definitely wrongly, but go on.'

'What I'm saying is this, we don't need architects plans. I know the layout of the house both inside and out and I think I know a way to get us into that master bedroom without Kyle Stasuik knowing we're even in the house.'

Tom was talking fast now, he realised this might be his last shot at having any hope of staying on the Unit.

He had his Chief Inspectors full attention now and continued, 'There's an en-suite off the master bedroom that has a twin access door into a neighbouring bedroom. In effect the en-suite is shared by the two bedrooms. Jaycee always kept that door into the other bedroom closed, but not locked. I think there's a good chance that Kyle doesn't know it's unlocked and in his current agitated state of mind he probably hasn't barricaded it.'

Tom had finished talking; he could see that Joe was thinking deeply about what he'd just heard.

He stroked the stubble on his chin and said more to himself than Tom, 'That's an awful lot of supposition and probably, maybe's, Naylor.'

He levered himself away from his desk, still glowering at Tom. He walked across to his office door, opened it and bellowed, 'Sgt Turner. Get your arse in here now!'

Almost immediately Sgt Turner appeared in the doorway. Jim Chambers gestured for him to come in and said quietly, 'Close the door Graham. Right, Pc Naylor, tell your sergeant everything you've just told me and I mean everything, dickhead.'

Tom quickly repeated the whole sorry tale and saw the look on Graham Turner's face turn from incredulity to disgust, then to something akin to relief and finally almost joy as he realised that what he was hearing, probably offered them the best possible way to resolve the siege and get Emma Simpson out of the house relatively unscathed.

When Tom had finished speaking, Jim Chambers fixed him with a steely look and said, 'I hope for your sake and for Emma Simpson's sake that you can come up with a viable rescue plan. Whatever happens today, what you've told me will still have to be dealt with once this job is over. Be under no illusion, I'll be seriously considering whether or not you've any future on this Unit, Pc Naylor. Both of you get out and get cracking.'

'Yes sir', said Tom quietly.

As Tom started to follow Sgt Turner out of the office, Jim Chambers said finally, 'Tom, I know it wasn't easy for you to come in here and spill your guts like that. I also know that the reason you did it was because you care about getting that young girl out of the house safely. Right at this moment, that's all you've got going for you. Now go and achieve it, get her out of there.'

Tom said nothing and just nodded.

As he closed the door behind him he was confronted by Graham Turner who just looked at him and said quietly, 'Tom, you dickhead!'

That was all that was said, then it was straight back into the briefing room where Tom started to impart his ill-gotten knowledge to the rest of the team, missing out entirely how he'd acquired such valuable intelligence.

CHAPTER 7

9.00am 21st June 1987
Rolleston Village, Nottinghamshire

For a supposed summer morning, it was bitterly cold, the wind whipping across the courtyard felt like it was being blown directly down from the north pole. The sky overhead was full of dark clouds scudding quickly through.

Dc Sue Jenkins zipped her Barbour jacket up to the top as she walked towards the impressive oak doors of the Elizabethan manor house. Trying to get some circulation going, she strode purposefully across the gravel courtyard.

Just as she reached the front door it was opened from the inside and Sue was confronted by a figure dressed from head to toe in a white forensic suit. She recognised the ghostly apparition and said, 'Good morning Greg. Jesus, what's wrong with this bloody weather, it's so bloody cold. What have we got?'

Greg Martin, the senior Scenes of Crime officer pulled back the hood of his forensic suit, revealing a completely bald head. He shook his head slowly and said, 'It's that wind, if that dropped it wouldn't be bad at all. What have I got? Sorry Sue, not much at all I'm afraid. I think there were two, possibly three offenders, all wearing woollen gloves of some description. Follow me.'

Greg walked around the outside of the beautiful building followed by Sue. Eventually, at the very rear of the property he stopped.

He pointed to a smashed transom window and said, 'This is the point of entry. They initially smashed the small transom window into the kitchen using the jam and brown paper method; you can still see the remnants of it on the floor over there', he indicated a piece of thick brown paper covered in jam and glass fragments that had been discarded about a yard from the window.

'Any chance of getting anything off that, Greg?'

'No, it's too wet from the rain earlier. It would have been difficult with the jam anyway.'

Greg pointed at the open window below the transom, 'This is how they got in. I think initially one of them has climbed in through the small transom and then opened this larger window for the others.'

Sue nodded, 'What about the burglar alarm?'

'The box is at the front of the building, it's been filled with builder's foam. It's useless.'

'So, the MO's exactly the same as the other three burglaries.'

'My thoughts exactly detective.'

They walked back around to the front doors and into the large hallway. Sue followed Greg up the wooden stairs and into the master bedroom, pleased to be out of the biting cold wind at last.

Greg said, 'The homeowner was asleep in here when the offenders first attacked him. He was then dragged down the stairs to the dining room where the safe was located. The safe has been opened using the combination so I'm assuming they must have beat the numbers out of the poor bastard. How's the old chap doing Sue? Do you think he'll recover?'

'He'll live Greg, his injuries were horrendous but he'll survive. Will he ever recover? That's a totally different question, who knows? It's a wonder we're not starting a murder enquiry. All of these burglaries have been carried out using so much extreme, and totally unnecessary, violence. It's obvious that whoever's doing them just enjoys dishing it out.'

'Come back downstairs Sue and I'll show you the safe, then I'd better crack on. I've still got to photograph everything yet.'

As they walked back down the hard-wooden stairs, Sue had an image in her mind of the old man being bodily dragged down them, the bones in his frail legs cracking on the hard, unforgiving edges of the wooden treads.

In the dining room she saw the open safe and carefully looked inside, 'It's exactly the same as the others, Greg. Have you seen what's been left behind?'

'I know, all that jewellery must be worth a small fortune. It definitely looks like the same crew alright. I'll leave you to it Sue, I want to go over the entire scene again and have another look just to make sure I haven't missed anything. These bastards need catching, and quickly before they do kill someone.'

'Thanks Greg, I appreciate that. I don't think for one minute you'll have missed anything though.'

Having seen everything she needed to. Sue walked out of the manor house and back to her car. She was deep in thought and very worried. This series of burglary offences was something new for the Newark area. What she couldn't understand was the apparent need the offenders had to inflict such gratuitous violence. The other question that worried her greatly and that she needed an answer for was, why the offenders had an apparent need to carry out offences so frequently?

Her thought process kept bringing her back to the same theory; these offences had to be related to drugs.

After the first two burglaries, Sue had started to put the word out to a few of her old informants in an effort to obtain some sort of breakthrough. She knew only too well that addicts would quite happily sell out their own grandmothers for the next fix.

As she drove away from the manor house, intending to revisit the hospital at Newark to check on the progress of the latest victim, she became even more convinced that she would find the answers she needed lurking somewhere in the dirty world of drug abuse.

All she needed was that first snippet of information, that first link, however tenuous. It needed to come quickly though, she feared the next burglary would result in someone being killed. The level of violence being used was gradually increasing, the offenders had a real taste for it now.

CHAPTER 8

10.10am 21st June 1987
Cuckney Village, Nottinghamshire

The two unmarked white Transit vans carrying the men and equipment of C Section arrived at the final rendezvous point at the entrance to Porter Close at Cuckney.

The vans were parked side by side, approximately fifty yards from the target premises and completely out of the line of sight of Kyle Stasuik.

Sgt Turner looked at his watch; it was now fast approaching ten fifteen, three quarters of an hour to go.

As always, he started his final briefing with the same sentence, 'Right gents, this is the news. This will fundamentally be a four-man operation.'

Quietly and confidently he continued, 'Only four of us will actually make entry to the property as the room to manoeuvre in the bedroom may be restricted and I don't want us tripping over each other. The other factor for this decision is that the more people we put into the property, the more chance there is of us being compromised and if that happened the consequences for the young female hostage could be dire. Any questions so far?'

The men remained silent so Graham continued, 'Okay, so the four making entry will be Tom as Raid One, Matt Raid Two, myself as Support One and Steve Support Two.'

The numbered system was used to easily identify the individual roles on the forthcoming operation. This had already been fully discussed at the planning stage at headquarters, but now it was formal.

Raid One is responsible for leading the team through the house and is directly responsible for the arrest of the offender. He is backed up in that task by Raid Two. Support One and Support Two are just that, they are there to support the Raid Team in anything else that needs doing during the operation. It would also be the role of Support Two to administer any emergency First Aid to the hostage should anything go wrong.

Graham Turner continued the briefing, 'We'll approach the target premises along the bridle path that runs along the rear of the houses on the left-hand side of Porter Close. Kyle Stasuik has no view of our approach if we stick to the path. The entire section will advance to the rear of the target premises. The four-man raid party will then make the final approach into the rear garden and make entry into the house via the back door. The rest of the section will remain in position outside the property until the four of us have secured the premises.'

He directed his next comments to the men who would be remaining at the rear of the property, 'You'll only enter the house after a direct command from either myself or Tom. I don't need to tell you that this will be a silent approach. I will seriously damage any one of you who coughs, farts or sneezes while you're outside the property. Silence must be absolute from the moment we get on that bridle path. Has everybody got that?'

Nobody said anything.

The men just nodded that they had fully understood the graphic message. The tension among the men was mounting steadily as the time for action drew ever closer.

Graham now turned his focus on Tom, Matt and Steve, 'When we reach the target premises, there's a low wall that we can easily get over to gain access into the rear garden. It's only a small garden and again it isn't overlooked by the master bedroom of the house. The rear door is a UPVC frame so we'll need to take the hydraulic door opener. Steve, I want the HDO to be your responsibility. I know it's been checked before we left HQ, check it again please. It will be down to you to pop the door.'

Steve nodded grimly.

The Hydraulic Door Opener or HDO was a brilliant piece of kit, designed specifically to access UPVC doors. It functioned by exerting a very gradual increase of pressure onto the door locks until the door eased open with a barely audible pop. It was virtually silent and therefore perfect for this type of operation where stealth was key.

Graham continued, 'It's imperative that once we're inside the house we remain silent. Communication will be by way of throat mikes and covert ear pieces. Once inside, we'll use sign language wherever possible other than that it will be the two clicks for yes and one click for no system. I don't want to hear anything else, understood?'

Tom had seen Graham serious before, but never as intense as this.

The burly sergeant now looked squarely at Tom, Matt and Steve and said, 'I don't want this nutter knowing we're inside until we're all over him like a rash in that master bedroom. Tom, I want you to guide us into and through the house. Matt, you'll be directly behind Tom, followed by me and lastly Steve.'

He looked directly at Steve and said, 'I want you to carry the HDO as we move through the house in case we encounter any other locked doors but make no noise with it for fucks sake!'

'No problem Sarge.'

The HDO, although very good, was also very heavy with quite a few moving metallic parts. Steve Grey was a big strong individual and Tom knew he was more than capable of cradling it through the house and not allowing any rattle from those moving parts.

The final briefing was now coming to an end.

Finally, the sergeant began to outline the individual responsibilities expected from the raid team after they had made entry into the master bedroom.

The tension in the air was now palpable.

In a voice devoid of any emotion, Graham spoke to Tom and Matt, 'Once we get into that master bedroom I want you two straight in for Kyle. I want him controlled instantly. I'll be straight in behind to assist you, should you require it.'

He then looked at Steve Grey, 'Steve, once we've achieved control of Kyle, I want you to get hold of the female and get her out of there. As soon as Kyle's secured I'll break radio silence and get the Paramedic's inside the house. Any first aid necessary will be down to you Steve. Have you got everything you need in the first aid kit on your belt?'

'I've got everything I'll need for an emergency wound kit, which should be enough till the Paramedics can get in.'

Graham ended the briefing by saying, 'That's it guys. Any questions about what I've said so far or is there anything else concerning you?'

Steve Grey voiced what the rest of the team were thinking, 'Have we had any confirmation on the licensing check to see if there are any firearms listed yet?'

'There's nothing listed for this address for either firearms or shotgun licenses, but you know as well as I do that's only ever a guideline. There could be unregistered weapons in the house. Personally, I think if Kyle had access to any guns he would've been showing them off to the hostage negotiator by now. Is there anything else?'

The team stood in stony silence.

Graham again looked at his watch. It was fast approaching ten thirty, the raid was due to commence at eleven o'clock.

'Right, you've got twenty minutes to sort your gear out, I want us on that bridle path at ten fifty and outside the back door of the house at eleven, ready to go. Get sorted.'

As the rest of the men started to organise their kit, Graham took Tom, Matt and Steve to one side and said, 'Gents, this job will stand or fall on how quietly we can move through the house. At the moment we've got this bloody heavy body armour on. Would you consider wearing just the lightweight stab proof vest and changing down to Polo shirts, lightweight trousers and trainers? We know Stasuik is armed with a knife so I can't order you to do it but I think it would be safer in the long run. We'll have far more problems if we're compromised and the consequences for the girl could be fatal.'

Nobody said a word, but all three men immediately started to get the full armour off ready to change into the lightweight kit.

The three men accepted what their sergeant had said was correct and that there would be much more of a risk to the girl and to themselves if they were discovered early.

It only took a few minutes to change and then they joined the rest of C Section in position on the bridle path.

As he took his place at the front of the line of men, Tom quietly reflected how it now seemed a lifetime ago since he was in his own peaceful world, running through the early morning rain along the country lanes near his home.

CHAPTER 9

10.45am 21st June 1987
Newark Hospital, Nottinghamshire

Holding out her warrant card Dc Sue Jenkins said, 'Good morning. I'm Dc Jenkins, Newark CID. I've come to check how Mr Reginald Mulvaney is doing? I'm the officer dealing with the burglary at his home.'

Sue was addressing the young nurse sitting behind a desk located outside the Intensive Care Unit at Newark Hospital.

The nurse stood up and said politely, 'Wait here detective, I'll go and find out for you.'

'Okay, thanks.'

The nurse disappeared into the ICU, as the door opened Sue got a glimpse inside and she could see Mr Mulvaney in the bed opposite the door. She could see the wires and intubation tubes attached to the badly injured old man. She was shocked to also see the concerned expression on the face of the young nurse as she walked back to the door. The nurse closed the door softly behind her.

With real concern in her voice Sue enquired, 'Is everything okay?'

'I've just spoken to Janine, the Staff Nurse in charge of Mr Mulvaney's care. She says he's been placed in an induced coma as the pain he was experiencing from his multiple fractures was a bit too much for a man of his years to take. He'll stand a much better chance of making a full recovery from the induced coma. There's a new concern though, the consultant neurologist is calling in later this morning to re-assess him as he's concerned about some swelling on his brain that the first CT scan revealed. I'm afraid Mr Mulvaney's still critically ill, detective.'

'Thank you. Would it be possible for someone to keep me informed if there's any change or if his condition deteriorates at all?'

Sue handed the nurse a card with all her details.

'Yes, of course we will. He could be like this for days, it all depends how his body reacts to the enormous trauma he's suffered. Do you know if he's got any immediate family?'

'As far as I can ascertain at the moment, there's no immediate family, but I'm still looking.'

'I think you should detective, just in case he takes a turn for the worse and doesn't pull through.'

Sue nodded grimly and said, 'Let's just hope he pulls through, shall we?'

She turned and walked away from the desk.

How could these animals do this to such a defenceless old man?

Her blood was boiling as she walked out of the hospital and back to her car.

Just as she unlocked the car door she heard her name being called on her personal radio, 'Control to Dc Jenkins.'

She fished the radio out of her coat pocket and replied, 'Dc Jenkins, go ahead control.'

'Sue, we've taken an anonymous telephone call from someone who says he may have information you're interested in. He refused to give any details but said he'd meet you on Waverley Street at quarter past eleven this morning. Over.'

'Thanks control, I'm on my way back to the nick now, would you get hold of Pete Thomas for me and tell him I need to see him in the office as a matter of urgency when I get back in please. Over.'

'Will do, control out.'

As she started the car Sue allowed a fleeting smile to cross her face. Somebody who wants to see me on Waverley Street? That can only be one person. Maybe things were about to take a turn for the better. There was only one informant who liked to meet on Waverley Street.

CHAPTER 10

10.55am 21st June 1987
Cuckney Village, Nottinghamshire

With only five minutes to go until the raid started, the men of C Section set off in Indian file along the bridle path. The air was perfectly still, the wind that had been blowing hard and so bitingly cold earlier had now dropped completely. The men walked in stony silence, the only noise to be heard was the sound of birdsong from the tall hawthorn hedge that ran along one side of the path.

The sun had finally broken through the thin clouds and the day was starting to warm up. Soft sunlight filtered through the hedgerow, casting shadows on the black clad men as they made their way stealthily along the bridle path towards the rear of the target premises.

As they set off, Graham Turner spoke softly into his throat mike, 'C Section moving towards target premises now. Over.'

Then came two barely audible clicks in Tom's covert ear piece as the control room acknowledged receipt of the radio message.

At the same time as C Section began their covert approach towards the rear of the property, the hostage negotiator began desperately trying to engage Kyle Stasuik in further dialogue in the hope it would help to divert his attention from the events unfolding behind the house.

After four minutes C Section had reached the low wall that formed the boundary of the target premises. Very slowly and without making a sound each of the men climbed over the wall and made their way across the sloping lawn at the rear of the building.

There was a small step up from the lawn onto a wooden deck area. The men stayed in single file but now positioned themselves tightly against the rear wall of the house.

Tom and Matt were crouched directly below the kitchen window to the left of the back door.

Steve Grey made his way forward and got to work on the UPVC door with the HDO.

As the hydraulic pressure increased on the door locks, a tense minute passed, then there was a soft popping sound and the back door eased slowly open.

Before Tom made entry into the house, Graham whispered into his throat mike, 'Commencing entry into target premises now, observe full radio silence until my next message. Over.'

Again, Tom heard the quiet double click in his ear piece.

The back door opened inwards, so using the back of his hand Tom very slowly pushed it open taking great care not to dislodge anything that may have been propped against the other side of the door. He moved stealthily into the kitchen and remained in the crouch position. Once inside he stopped and listened for any movement coming from upstairs.

The house was still and silent.

The only sound was the beat of his own heart thumping steadily inside his chest. He half opened his mouth, as an aid to hearing, and listened intently.

Still no noise anywhere.

Tom now took stock of his surroundings and looked around the spacious kitchen. The obvious signs that there had been a violent struggle in the room were everywhere. Upturned breakfast bar stools, smashed cups and plates on the floor, spilled food on the worktops.

Suddenly, he was confronted with the memory of the first time he'd been in that kitchen with Jaycee Stasuik.

After spending the night together at a local pub, they'd gone back to her house. Jaycee had gone into the kitchen to make coffee and Tom had followed her in.

They hadn't been able to take their eyes off each other and it hadn't been long before they began kissing passionately for the first time. That electric kiss had been followed by a mad scramble through the large house to the master bedroom, discarding items of clothing as they went.

Jesus! Tom chided himself.

He needed to snap out of it and concentrate on why he was there now.

Tom turned back to face the back door and was about to signal the other three members of the raid party to enter the property when he froze.

He had heard a noise.

There was definitely the sound of movement coming from the other side of the door that he knew led from the kitchen into the dining room. He signalled for the other three men to hold their positions and he began to crawl silently across the tiled floor towards the door.

As he reached the door he heard the noise again, it was like a very soft scratching coming from the other side of the closed door.

Tom signalled for Matt to join him.

As Matt made his way into the kitchen and across the tiled floor, he gave Tom a quizzical look. As soon as Matt reached the door, Tom signalled for him to listen.

The scratching noise was still there and if anything, it was getting a little louder.

Tom gripped the door knob and slowly turned it.

Matt, his asp baton now in hand, tensed his muscles ready to engage whatever threat lay the other side of the door.

Tom opened the door about a foot and instantly an orange flash shot straight past him and Matt nearly bumping into them in the process.

Matt mouthed silently, 'Fucking cat!'

Tom had completely forgotten about the ginger tom that was Jaycee's pet. He was just grateful that the cat hadn't screeched as it fled passed him bolting for the outdoors. He looked at the open back door and saw Graham with a concerned look on his face. Tom signalled for him and Steve to now enter the house. All four men remained crouched in the kitchen waiting for Raid One to progress deeper into the house.

Now that the door to the dining room was open, Tom could hear muffled, angry voices coming from upstairs. It was the hostage negotiator trying to engage Kyle in meaningful dialogue.

It wasn't working.

Kyle was responding by ranting streams of abuse at the negotiator.

The raid team now made their way into the dining room and across to the door that led into the large opulent lounge. In this room, there were further signs of a violent struggle. A couple of the expensive Italian limed oak dining chairs had been tipped over and pieces of a broken vase were all over the floor.

Tom thought to himself, what the fuck happened here? It looked like all hell had broken loose.

Having reached the closed door that led into the lounge, Tom paused before slowly opening it a couple of inches. Once again, he paused and listened intently trying to make out what was being said upstairs.

The only noises he could hear were the same as before, the calm muffled voice of the negotiator punctuated by the much louder and clearer, angry abusive ranting coming from Kyle Stasuik.

Tom opened the door a little wider and crept through. He paused before signalling the other three to also make their way forward. There was plenty of time and they only had one chance to get this right.

Suddenly, he felt a change of air pressure inside the house as an upstairs window was opened.

Instantly, everything became much noisier, the voice that had been muffled was now crystal clear. He could hear the negotiator's voice promising Kyle that if he just remained calm and showed a little more patience everything would be sorted out.

More worryingly, Tom could also hear Kyle's agitated and aggressive voice making threats that if he didn't get what he wanted then it would be all over for Emma. The only thing Tom couldn't quite catch were the demands Kyle was making. The only thing he heard clearly during the troubled teenagers rant was the word father.

Was all this trouble and violence down to Kyle's father? That arrogant, violent excuse of a man.

Why wouldn't Jaycee make the right decision for her and her family and get him out of their lives once and for all? Why couldn't she see the terrible influence his violent ways were having on their son?

While all the commotion was going on upstairs, Tom quickly called the raid team forward and they made their way through the lounge.

Tom passed a large pool of blood, where the cops had tended to the wounds suffered by Jaycee the previous night. The blood was next to a large, cream coloured sheepskin rug in front of the sandstone fireplace.

Once again Tom's mind wandered and for a second his thoughts turned to the many hours he and Jaycee had spent lying on that very rug, gently caressing each other in front of a huge roaring fire.

In that instant Tom made a promise to himself. When all this was over he was going to get her out of this sham of a marriage and away from this monster.

If it cost him his job, so be it.

He scolded himself again that he needed to concentrate, to move forward and get this job done.

He felt Matt's hand on his shoulder. Tom turned and Matt glanced at the blood and mouthed, 'Are you okay?'

Tom gave him a steely look and nodded.

Having made their way through the lounge, the team were now at the foot of the oak staircase.

Fortunately, the carpet on the stairs and landing was very thick. They still made painstakingly slow progress as they eased their way up the stairs onto the gallery landing. It took nearly fifteen minutes for all four of them to negotiate the stairs. Each man carefully checked each step they took to avoid treading on a creaking step or floor board that would instantly betray their presence.

They regrouped on the gallery landing and Tom indicated the door to the master bedroom which lay two yards along the hallway. From within that room all four of them could now clearly hear the hysterical rants from Kyle. His voice was sounding increasingly agitated and aggressive.

Ignoring the door into the master bedroom, Tom guided the team to the door that led into the bedroom that shared the en suite with the master bedroom.

Having reached the door, he slowly turned the large brass handle. Every nerve ending in his body was now tingling with anticipation and his heart was beating fast as adrenalin coursed through him.

He eased the door open just far enough for him to see across the bedroom, past the large double bed that lay between him and the door to the en suite.

The door to the en suite was closed.

He signalled for the rest of the team to follow him into the bedroom and they all made their way across the thick carpet, until once again they were stacked outside the door that led into the en suite.

Now that he was this close, in between the ranting and the shouts from Kyle, Tom could hear another distinct sound coming from the master bedroom. It was the sound of muffled sobbing coming from the terrified young girl. Every so often this sobbing was broken by a more strident shriek of fear or pain.

What the hell was going on in there?

Every instinct in Tom's body was screaming at him to rush through the door and get Emma Simpson out of there before it was too late.

CHAPTER 11

11.15am 21st June 1987
Newark, Nottinghamshire

'Pete, if you must insist on smoking that rolled up camel shit, at least wind the window down a bit, for fucks sake!'

Dc Sue Jenkins' comment was aimed at her colleague, Dc Pete Thomas.

They were sitting in an unmarked car on Waverley Street, Newark, waiting patiently to meet an informant.

Pete wearily wound down the car window half way and flipped the last of the roll up out of the window, 'Sorry Sue, I forgot you don't smoke. What time's this arsehole supposed to be here?'

Sue didn't reply to the question, she just shrugged her shoulders.

After putting the word out that she needed information about a recent spate of burglaries, the control room had earlier received a very vague telephone call from somebody claiming to have just such information. Sue was hoping that the call had been made by an old informant that she hadn't heard from in over a year and a half.

She hoped the man making the call was Pip McGuire.

McGuire was one of a very rare breed indeed, an informant from the gypsy community. Sue had always found him to be a very reliable source, the information he provided was normally pretty solid.

She glanced at her watch again, it was now almost twenty-five minutes past eleven.

If it was McGuire, he was already late.

The fact that the phone call stipulated Waverley Street convinced Sue it was the old gypsy she would be meeting.

The location was the perfect place for a meeting with an informant.

Waverley Street ran alongside the back of the main sewage farm in Newark and was well away from any prying eyes. Nobody ever came to Waverley Street. The air here was thick with the smell of human waste being processed.

Another five minutes passed and just as Sue was about to give up she saw a shuffling, shambolic figure turn the corner and slowly make his way along the street towards the car.

As the man drew alongside the vehicle, Sue wound the window down, 'Hello Pip, long time no see.'

'Good morning detective, still the best-looking woman at the nick then.'

'I like to think so Pip.'

Sue smiled and reaching over the seat she undid the back door and gestured for McGuire to get in the back of the car.

Her colleague tutted disdainfully at the thought of the stinking, urine stained, scruffy individual getting in the car. McGuire made the stench outside the car seem positively fragrant.

Sue shot Pete a withering look that non-verbally told him to shut the fuck up.

Pete got the message. He wound down the driver's door window, lit another cigarette, took a deep drag and disinterestedly blew the smoke out the window.

Sue turned her attention to McGuire, 'Okay Pip, why all the mystery? What have you got for me?'

'I have to be careful detective, you know that. It's good info this, gonna be worth a lot of money.'

'Come on Pip, you know how this works, just tell me what you know and let me be the judge as to what it's worth, okay?'

'By God, you're still as tough as ever detective.'

'Just tell me what you know. I'm always fair, you know that.'

'Okay detective, this is what I've got. A little bird tells me you're interested in some bad fellas doing big country houses, and that these fellas you're after like to cause a bit of mayhem at the same time. Would that be right?'

Sue sighed and said firmly, 'Pip, you're definitely on the right track, but if you don't tell me what you know in the next ten seconds I'll be forced to ask Dc Thomas here to throw you into the sewage. Are you getting my drift?'

She smiled sweetly at Pip who responded by raising both his hands in a gesture of appeasement, 'Okay, okay. I keep hearing the same name. There's two bad brothers called Smith who live on the gypsy camp at Tanley Road. The word is these brothers are very handy with their fists and they don't give a fuck who they hurt.'

Once again Pete Thomas tutted and then mumbled under his breath, 'Smith eh, give me strength.'

Sue swiftly gave her partner a sly dig in the ribs to shut him up, turned back to McGuire and said, 'That's all very well and good Pip, but as you know only too well half the gypsies that live at Tanley Road are called Smith.'

'Yes miss, I'll grant you that fact, as it's very true right enough. There are one or two Smiths on that site and I do know that, but the word is these brothers are twins.

They're already looking for their next job and there's every likelihood it's going to be another big house out in the sticks somewhere, so I'm told.'

'It's getting more interesting Pip, is there anything else you've heard?'

'I think I'll be able to find out the vehicle they're going to use for the next job and I'll be able to let you know what it is nearer the time.'

'Not bad Pip, not bad. I think I could rush to a tenner for that little gem.'

'Aw come on miss, don't be tight now. I can also tell you why they're having to go out so often as well.'

'Don't keep me in suspense then Pip.'

'Okay, listen in detective. These brothers have both got a raging drug habit. Apparently, the poison of their choice is amphetamine and they've got in with some really heavy dealers over in Worksop. One of the twins in particular owes a small fortune to this gang. As violent as the brothers are, they're both shit scared of this bunch.'

'That's great Pip, anything else?'

'There's only one other thing I've got for you today. I keep hearing about a place referred to as Phet Row. Have you heard of that?'

Sue shook her head, 'Can't say I have. Right, here's twenty quid. It would have been thirty but I've got to give Dc Happy here a tenner to fumigate his car now you've been sitting in it.'

She grinned and McGuire smiled a toothless grin back, 'Detective Jenkins, sometimes you say some really hurtful things.'

Sue handed over the twenty pounds and said, 'Here you go Pip, buy some food will you?'

He quickly stuffed the cash in his coat pocket and nodded.

As he got out of the car she said, 'Pip, take care now and thanks. There'll be another payday if you can find out when the next job is and what vehicle they're using.'

'No problem detective. I'll call you for another meet as soon as I hear about the vehicle. You take care as well miss.'

Just before he turned to walk away he winked at Sue and said loudly, 'I'm sorry about the car Mr Thomas, I hope you get it cleaned up okay!'

He walked away cackling.

CHAPTER 12

11.20am 21st June 1987
Cuckney Village, Nottinghamshire

As he waited outside the door to the en suite, Tom knew he had to stay calm.

Very slowly he eased the door open fraction by fraction, just enough for him to see through the small gap and be able to see the door opposite that led into the master bedroom.

He saw that door was already slightly ajar. That explained why they could hear so much of the conversation from inside the bedroom. The fact this door was open would make their entry into the en suite extremely hazardous, but at least it meant they had unrestricted access into the master bedroom.

There were no barricades to hinder their progress.

Tom could now clearly hear every word of the conversation between the hostage negotiator and Kyle Stasuik. The negotiator was doing a fantastic job of keeping Kyle pre-occupied. By his patient, measured response he appeared to have also calmed the troubled teenager down a little.

The guy must have the patience of a saint, thought Tom.

He could hear Kyle talking rationally now, which was good news as it meant he was concentrating fully on what the negotiator was saying.

Tom knew if they could get across the en suite without Kyle discovering them, the raid team stood a very realistic chance of getting the girl out without her sustaining any further injuries.

Silently the four-man team quickly crossed the travertine tile floor of the en suite. Steve Grey had abandoned the HDO on the floor of the guest bedroom once he realised it was no longer needed.

The team gathered themselves at the door of the master bedroom in the order they had planned at the briefing.

Tom squinted through the small gap between the door and the door frame and the sight that confronted him froze his blood.

Kyle was now standing by the main picture window with his back towards him, he was holding a large black handled kitchen knife in his right hand and a handful of Emma's long hair in his other hand. He had brutally pulled the young girls head back exposing her throat to the blade of the knife.

Both Kyle and Emma were completely naked and Tom could see the dried blood on her left arm. The large wound previously inflicted by the knife stretched between her shoulder and her bicep and was three inches long.

Kyle was starting to get agitated again. He began gesticulating wildly with the knife at the open window.

Suddenly, his whole demeanour changed again and he screamed at the negotiator, 'I'll kill this bitch! All women are liars and they deserve to die!'

There was no time for any further delay. Tom quickly checked that the team were good to go and gestured a silent countdown with his fingers.

Three, two, one. Go!

He quietly pushed open the door then silently and swiftly crossed the carpeted floor. He never crossed his legs and maintained a rock steady platform to avoid any chance of stumbling.

He moved smoothly, fluid like.

Totally focussed on Kyle, he was now unaware of anyone else in the room.

Tom reached the couple just as Kyle became aware of his presence in the room. The troubled teenager's eyes widened, not out of fear but out of anger. He drew his right arm up and back and thrust the deadly blade down towards Emma's neck. At the same time, he pulled the girl's hair hard, once again exposing her vulnerable throat.

Instinctively, Tom snaked his arm around Emma's neck as if putting her in a headlock. He immediately felt a burning sensation down the length of his right forearm as the blade of the knife sliced open the flesh on the back of his forearm.

As the blade was withdrawn, Tom saw a flash of steel as Matt smashed his Asp baton across Kyle's right wrist. Tom heard the crack as the heavy blow snapped the bone in Kyle's wrist, followed swiftly by the clatter of the knife as it fell from his numb hand onto the window sill.

The final noise was a very loud howl of pain from Kyle as he staggered back away from the window, finally releasing his grip on Emma's long hair.

Tom pulled Emma back and away from Kyle then pushed her bodily towards Steve Grey.

He turned back towards Kyle just in time to see Graham Turner land a very heavy kick into the naked crotch of the teenager, effectively ending any further resistance.

Matt moved swiftly in and handcuffed Kyle, ignoring his howls of protest about the injured wrist. Tom looked quickly round and saw that Steve had grabbed the quilt from the bed and had wrapped it around Emma to cover her modesty.

As soon as Kyle was secured, Graham was instantly on the radio, 'Premises secured, offender arrested. Send in the paramedics immediately, Emma has no further injuries but I've an officer with a knife wound to the arm and the offender has a suspected broken arm.'

Tom looked down at Kyle Stasuik who was now lying curled up on the floor, sobbing. He wondered what it was that had so comprehensively sent the young man over the edge that he would have stabbed his own girlfriend in the throat.

None of it made any sense.

Tom glanced at his right arm and saw a gaping slash that went along the top of his forearm from his elbow to his wrist. The cut was deeper near the elbow and the skin had pared back over the muscle tissue below, as is the case with most slash wounds.

Tom could feel an intense burning in the area of the wound as the nerve endings responded to the trauma.

The paring back of the skin made the wound look ten times worse than it actually was. Blood was beginning to slowly seep from the wound and was dripping off his fingers onto the thick white carpet on the bedroom floor.

Seeping slowly was a good sign, thought Tom, it meant no major blood vessels had been severed. Slowly he wiggled his fingers and winced as the pain bit deeper. He could move them all easily which was more good news. No tendon damage, he reassured himself.

Feeling a little light headed as the pain grew more and more intense, Tom sat down on the edge of the bed. Plenty of stitches he thought, but no major dramas.

Just as he sat down two female paramedics came into the

room carrying heavy trauma bags. The bags were huge and looked as though they carried enough equipment to have dealt adequately with an aeroplane crash.

The older of the two Paramedics, a dark haired stocky woman, went directly across to Emma and checked the wound on her upper arm and began treating her for shock. The wound appeared to be quite shallow but would still probably require quite a few stitches.

The second Paramedic approached Tom and said, 'Tom? Tom Naylor, is that you?'

Tom looked up and met the gaze of the young Paramedic observing him. She was roughly the same age as him, very slim, with blonde hair tied back in a ponytail; she had the brightest blue eyes and a very attractive smile playing on her full lips.

'It's me, Bev Wilson, from school', she prompted after seeing Tom's blank look.

The penny finally dropped for Tom, 'Christ Bev, I haven't seen you since the day I left school. How are you?'

She smiled, 'Better than you right now by the looks of things. That arm's going to need some serious sewing. Let's get you downstairs and off to the hospital sharpish.'

It came as no surprise to Tom that the injury to Kyle's arm was the last to be looked at by the paramedics.

Tom stood up off the bed, probably a little too quickly, and suddenly felt dizzy and light headed; he felt his legs buckle slightly.

Bev grabbed his uninjured arm and said, 'Whoa! Take it easy, Tom. Let me organise a chair to get you back downstairs.'

'No way', said Tom. 'Just give me a minute and I'll be okay to walk down the stairs.'

After a couple of minutes Tom's head cleared and he walked, with Bev supporting him, down the stairs to the waiting ambulance, which he shared with a shocked, ashen faced Emma Simpson.

As Tom waited inside the ambulance Chief Inspector Jim Chambers appeared by the back doors, 'Great job Tom, well done. Get that arm seen to and we'll discuss that other matter when you get back to work.'

He winked at Tom and said, 'But don't go typing out any resignation letters just yet. Okay?'

Tom remained stony faced as the ambulance doors closed.

As the ambulance pulled away from Porter Close, Tom wondered if Jim Chambers would still think that way once he discovered his plans to leave the Force and start a new life with Jaycee.

CHAPTER 13

12.30pm 21st June 1987
Renton Estate, Worksop, Nottinghamshire

The pains in Jakub Kowalczyk's chest had finally subsided.

His mouth was still bruised and tender to the touch. He dabbed the tea towel into the bowl of warm salty water and carefully washed the dried blood from his lips and chin.

He was more concerned about his dog.

Molly had been shivering and fretful ever since he'd been attacked on the street. He finished cleaning himself up, tipped the bowlful of bloody water down the sink and walked into his living room.

Molly was lying on the rug in front of the hearth, a sorrowful and forlorn expression on her face. As soon as she saw Jakub walk in her tail started to wag and she got up and walked towards him.

As he sat down in his favourite armchair Jakub made a big fuss of his little companion, he stroked the dog and said softly 'It's alright Molly, we're not going to let that bastard Hermann get the better of us, are we girl?'

When the assault had first happened, he'd been extremely shaken. Even after he'd taken his heart pills the pains in his chest had taken a long time to subside. It was the worst attack he'd suffered in a long long time.

Even now he felt light headed and strange, but at least the pain had stopped.

He sat quietly stroking his dog's ears thinking about what he should do next. Doing nothing was not an option, he was determined not to let the bullies get away with what they had done to him and more importantly what they were doing to his neighbourhood.

His mind was made up, instead of taking his usual stroll onto the pit tip, tomorrow's walk with Molly would be to the police station.

He smiled at his old dog, 'What do you think Molly? Do you think the police will be interested when we tell them what fatso Hermann is up to?'

The little dog yapped and continued to wag her tail.

CHAPTER 14

1.15pm 21ˢᵗ June 1987
Mansfield Hospital, Mansfield, Nottinghamshire

Tom Naylor hated hospitals with a passion.

The smell of disinfectant, the general feeling of sadness and depression that permeated the very walls always got to him.

The doctor attending to him finished the last of the twenty-three stitches in his forearm and said, 'That's all done Pc Naylor, just keep the area clean and dry and we should be able to have those stitches out in a week to ten days' time, depending on how well you heal.'

'Thanks doctor. Am I okay to get going now?'

'Yes, we're all finished. When the pain starts to kick in after the local anaesthetic has worn off, just take Paracetamol as you need them. Have you had a tetanus injection?'

'Yes Doc, the nurse gave me that before you came in to deal with the cut.'

'In that case, you're good to go.'

Tom felt like a pin cushion. As well as the tetanus and several local anaesthetic injections, he'd also been given intravenous anti biotics.

He detested injections and needles almost as much as he hated hospitals.

He walked back into the waiting area and saw Matt reading a magazine.

When Matt saw him, he stood up and said, 'All done mate? I've been hanging on to drive you back to headquarters for the debrief. How's the arm?'

'It's bloody sore but could've been a lot worse. Luckily for me the blade missed anything important. Thanks for having my back in there mate.'

'No problem mate, you got everything?'

Tom nodded then paused and said, 'Look, can you give me ten minutes? I want to check on someone on the wards while I'm here.'

Matt shrugged, 'Sure, I'll come with you.'

They walked down the long corridors until they came to Nightingale Ward. Tom had managed to find out earlier that this was where Jaycee Stasuik was being treated.

He paused outside the door to the ward and said, 'Won't be a minute pal.'

'No problem, I'll wait out here in the corridor.'

Tom opened the double doors and walked onto the ward, where he saw a Staff Nurse standing by a trolley. He walked over and said quietly, 'Hello. I'm looking for Jaycee Stasuik. I understand she's being treated on this ward. Can you tell me which bed she's in?'

'Are you a relative?'

'No, I'm a very good friend of hers. I just wanted to see how she's doing.'

'It should be relatives only, but as you're a policeman, I don't suppose it will do any harm. She's supposed to be resting so don't stay too long. Mrs Stasuik is in a private room just along the corridor. Go back outside the ward, it's the second door on the left.'

'Thank you', said Tom and he hurried back out into the corridor where he passed a puzzled looking Matt.

Tom found the correct door, knocked once and then stepped inside the room.

The lighting in the room was subdued but he could see Jaycee sitting up in bed, wearing a plain white hospital gown. She was attached by various tubes and pipes to a cluster of medical machines and equipment, the lights of which were blinking brightly in the half light.

Jaycee was wide awake.

As soon as she saw Tom walk in she hissed, 'What the fuck do you want?'

Tom was shocked and taken aback by her harsh tone. He said quietly, 'I just wanted to make sure you're okay.'

'She's fine', said a soft-spoken voice behind him.

He spun round quickly and for the first time saw a slightly built, bespectacled man sitting at the back of the room, immediately behind the door Tom had come in by.

The man put down the book he'd been reading and said matter of factly, 'Who wants to know?'

Tom said, 'I'm one of the officers who rescued Emma Simpson from Jaycee's house today.'

'No doubt you're also one of the officers who arrested my son Kyle and broke his arm in the process.'

It was more of a statement than a question.

The softly spoken man continued, 'What's your name officer?'

'Pc Naylor.'

'Ah, I see. Pc Tom Naylor. Now it all becomes clear. You see, my lovely wife has already told me so much about you officer.'

'I beg your pardon?'

Jaycee butted in and said, 'Tom, why are you even here? I told you it's finished between us a fortnight ago. It was never

85

going anywhere, you were just a bit of fun. Why can't you take the hint? Go on, just piss off!'

Jaycee's husband stood up and said to Tom, 'I think you and I need to step outside and have a little chat officer.'

The softly spoken man then opened the door and stepped outside into the corridor.

Tom said to Jaycee, 'Are you sure you're okay?'

'Just piss off Tom and for Christ's sake get the message! It was fun while it lasted, but I can't be doing with all this serious shit.'

A crestfallen Tom walked out of the room where Jaycee's husband was waiting for him. He was still reeling from her vicious outburst. He couldn't believe how stupid he'd been.

Glen Stasuik stood directly in front of Tom and said, 'Do you want to know what really happened in my house last night? Why my beautiful son Kyle lost his mind?'

Tom knew he was going to be told anyway, so he said nothing.

Stasuik said, 'Kyle found my lovely wife, your lover, being screwed by yet another man in our bed. Again.'

The words hit Tom like a hammer blow, how could he have been so blind?

Stasuik paused for effect, smiled and said, 'Come on officer, did you really think that you were the love of her life? Did she tell you that I was a wife beating monster? That I constantly made her life hell? That I subjected her to the worst kind of mental torture on a daily basis? Yes, of course she did. That's what she always says.'

Tom looked down at the floor, remaining silent. Stunned by the stinging words.

'I can tell by your silence that I'm bang on the money officer. I don't suppose you're aware that Jaycee and I have been married for twenty-one years. During that time, the longest my wife has been faithful to me is six months, apart from the time when she was carrying our children, that is. Well, I say our children, I know that Kyle's definitely my son, but I don't think I'm the biological father of our twin girls, even though I've raised them as if they were my own. The problem for me, Pc Naylor, is a very simple one, I still love my wife. I always have, but it seems my love just isn't enough for her.'

Greg Stasuik was now in full flow.

Tom raised his head and stared at the short, ineffectual man, transfixed as Stasuik continued to eloquently chastise him, 'You see Tom, every time my wife does this with another man, it hurts me exactly like the first time, the pain is the same. Kyle knows this and has begged my wife to stop her adulterous dalliances for my sake. That time, a few years ago now, when Kyle assaulted our so-called family friend it was because he'd caught them fucking in our marital bed. That's the only reason the bloke didn't press charges, because his wife would have found out about his sordid extra marital affair. It was the same last night, Kyle found Jaycee screwing this other bloke and threatened him with the knife, ordering him to leave the house. She attempted to take the knife from Kyle and got stabbed during the struggle. The only reason he wanted to harm his own girlfriend afterwards was because he's now totally broken down. The preliminary diagnosis by the psychiatrist who's seen him a few hours ago is that he now sees every woman as being the same as his mother. I don't know how long it'll take him to come back from this, if he ever does.'

Tom could now see the tears welling up in the man's eyes, magnified by the thick glasses he wore.

He looked directly up at Tom and prodded him in the chest, 'I think you should leave now, Pc Tom Naylor. I just wanted you to know what an insignificant piece of shit you are and that you mean absolutely fuck all to me and my family. Just go.'

Tom said nothing. He turned and walked away along the corridor to where Matt was waiting.

As Tom reached him, Matt fell in step and the two men began walking along the corridor to the hospital entrance.

Tom said, 'Did you hear all that?'

'Yes mate, you okay?'

'Apart from feeling lower than a rattlesnake's belly, yes I'm okay. How could I have been such an idiot? Come on let's get out of here, I can't stand the smell of the bloody place.'

They reached the entrance to the hospital and walked out into the car park, passing the ambulance bay.

Standing by the open doors of one of the parked ambulances, Tom saw Bev Wilson. The blonde Paramedic was busy sponging blood from the sleeve of her green uniform.

As he walked by Tom said, 'I hope that's not my mess?'

'It most certainly is. How dare you bleed all over me?' she replied with just the hint of a playful smile on her lips.

She continued, 'I reckon you owe me at least one drink, to cover my dry-cleaning bill.'

'Bev, I'd like nothing more than to buy you a drink and catch up, but I reckon you're going to have to give me at least a couple of weeks so this arm can heal.'

She reached into her top pocket and grabbed a pen and a slip of paper. She quickly scribbled down her phone number and handed it to Tom, 'Make sure you call me when you're feeling better.'

Tom took the piece of paper and smiled before walking across the car park where Matt was standing a couple of yards away grinning.

'What are you grinning at mate?' Tom said with a smile.

Matt looked straight past Tom and in a loud voice aimed at Bev, he shouted, 'Excuse me love, just one thing, you're not married, are you?'

Bev smiled and shouted back, 'No. Footloose and fancy free, me.'

'Thank Christ for that', muttered Matt as he waved at Bev.

Tom shouted to Bev, 'I'll call you next week.'

'Make sure you do Naylor, just remember it might be me removing those stitches', she replied laughing.

As they walked across the car park to the waiting van Matt said, 'In all seriousness Tom, it seems to me that young Emma Simpson wasn't the only person who's had a narrow escape today.'

'My thoughts exactly mate. It's a lesson learned alright, how can I have been so bloody stupid?'

'Let's hope the Chief Inspector thinks you've learned your lesson as well Tom or I'll be looking for a new sniper team partner.'

'Oh, Christ. I'd forgotten about seeing Chambers. I'll just have to hope he sees that I was given duff information and that I've been an idiot.'

'I think he already knows you're an idiot mate! Come on let's get back to headquarters.'

CHAPTER 15

3.00am 22nd June 1987
Renton Estate, Worksop, Nottinghamshire

Jakub Kowalczyk was getting ready for bed.

Wearily, he undressed and put on fresh pyjamas, folding his clothes and placing them on the back of the chair in the bedroom. He had felt too unwell to go to bed earlier, he felt strange, there was a fluttering in his chest that he hadn't experienced before. He didn't like to admit it to himself but he had been afraid to go to bed in case he went to sleep and never woke up. He was overwhelmed by a feeling of dread, but eventually tiredness had taken control and he fell asleep in his armchair. When a noise outside the house had woken him with a start he decided it was time to go to bed.

He walked into the bathroom and rinsed his mouth with warm water to try and ease the pain of his swollen mouth and cut lips.

Jakub had decided he was going to make the fat bully pay.

First thing tomorrow morning he would walk to the police station in the town centre. He would tell the police everything he knew about the drug dealing scum living on his doorstep.

He used the toilet then walked into the bedroom, turned off the light and got into bed, pulling the sheets tightly round him.

Subconsciously, he reached out from under the bedclothes and felt for the small bottle of pills on his bedside table. He needed to know they were close, he was concerned that he wasn't feeling as he should. Having located the bottle, he gave it a little shake and listened to the rattle of the pills inside.

Feeling reassured he finally settled down in bed.

Just as he was dropping off to sleep he heard his dog whimpering downstairs. Without raising his head from the pillow Jakub shouted, 'Settle down Molly, there's a good girl.'

The whimpering noise from the dog abruptly stopped.

Lying awake in bed, Jakub thought even Molly knew something wasn't right, as once again he tried to drift off to sleep.

Suddenly, the door to his bedroom burst open.

The dim light from the street lamp directly outside his bedroom window cast enough light into the room to illuminate the figures of three men standing in the room at the foot of his bed.

Jakub sat bolt upright and shouted at the men, 'Get the fuck out of my house you bloody bastards!'

One of the intruders then switched on the bedroom light and the sight that confronted Jakub filled him with fear. The three figures standing in his bedroom were all wearing terrifying horror masks. To the old man it looked like the devil himself had come calling.

He was in a state of shock and could not move.

Strong arms began pulling him from his bed and one of the men growled, 'So old man, you're going to the police, are you? I don't think so.'

Having pulled him from his bed, the biggest of the men now dragged Jakub to his feet so his face was only inches away from the terrifying mask.

The menacing voice behind the mask said quietly, 'We've killed your pet rat downstairs and you're next, you stinking Polish grass!'

Jakub could smell stale fags and booze on the man's breath, he could also see that the man holding him was very fat and in that horrifying split second he knew exactly who his attackers were.

The ageing Polish fighter ace had never felt so scared in his life; he realised that he was powerless to do anything to stop the men.

Desperately, he tried to call out for help but the only sound that escaped his dried, battered and bruised lips was a pathetic wheezing sound.

Suddenly, he felt a familiar feeling as his chest tightened. It felt like a steel band was encircling his chest, slowly constricting until it was virtually impossible for him to breathe. He then felt searing pains streaking up and down his left arm. The pain then went flying from his armpit into his chest like bolts of lightning.

The agonising pains in his chest were new; he had never experienced pain like it and he began to panic even more. In desperation he attempted to reach out and grab the small brown pill bottle from the bedside table.

One of the intruders grabbed the bottle first and mockingly said, 'Is this what you want, old man? Looks like we're not the only ones round here who rely on drugs.'

All three of the intruders were laughing cruelly now, the man holding the pill bottle unscrewed the top and allowed the contents to spill out onto the bedroom floor.

Jakub could no longer withstand the intense pain, grabbing at the side of his chest his legs buckled and he almost passed out. The fat man holding him up allowed him to fall backwards back onto the bed.

Jakub lay on his back staring up at the ceiling, focussing on the bright light bulb above him. His head felt as if it was about to explode. The sound of his own heart beating faster and faster filled his head.

One of the intruders laughed and said mockingly, 'Looks like the old bastard's having a heart attack!'

Another snarled, 'Good it'll save us a fucking job.'

Jakub stared straight up as the light in the room began to fade, he knew he was slipping away. The pain that had been coursing through his chest was easing. It wasn't so intense now and suddenly he felt light headed and warm.

Was this what it felt like to die?

Jakub was ready to go; he could see his darling wife Glenda smiling at him, she was holding their beautiful baby daughter Anna in her arms.

He mumbled, 'I'm coming sweetheart.'

Finally, his pounding heart stopped and his now sightless eyes remained open looking up at the ceiling.

The youngest of the intruders stood open mouthed at the side of the bed before saying, 'Fuck me dad, the old bastards dead!'

The fat man took charge now, 'Okay you two, stop gawping and put him back into bed properly. It'll just look like he's had a heart attack, reached for his pills and then dropped the bottle before he could take one. Happens all the time.'

'I don't know dad, it seems wrong.'

The fat man exploded, 'Are you fucking mad, just scaring him like that makes it murder you soft twat! Do exactly what I'm telling you and don't say a word about this to anybody. If we all stick to the story, we'll be fine. I'll get your mother to call the cops in a couple of days and say she hasn't seen the old codger around for a bit and that she's worried something might be wrong. The cops round here are thick as fuck, they'll think it's a heart attack and that'll be that. Neither of you have taken your gloves off while we've been in here, have you?'

The other two shook their heads and held up their gloved hands as if to confirm the fact.

The younger one of the two never said a word about the five war medals stashed in his jacket pocket. He'd picked them up from the old man's sideboard downstairs and planned on selling them once the dust had settled. Should be a nice little earner.

The fat man looked down at the dead man lying under the bedclothes. He leaned forward and took the old man's arm out from under the sheets, he then dropped the dead man's hand onto the bedside table, placing the empty pill bottle in the outstretched fingers.

Stepping back, he inspected his work and said, 'That looks better.'

He then turned to the other two and said, 'Okay let's get out of here. You two make sure you pick up the dead dog. We need to get that fucking thing out of here and buried up on the pit tip. When we leave, make sure there's no sign of a break in. Everything will be fine, you've got to trust your dear old dad.'

The three men left the house carrying the dead dog in a black bin liner. They left Jakub Kowalczyk, Battle of Britain hero, dead in his bed, his gnarled bony hand still reaching out for the pills he'd been so callously denied.

CHAPTER 16

10.00am 24th June 1987
Renton Estate, Worksop, Nottinghamshire

As he parked his car outside the semi-detached house on Hammond Street, Dc Gary Watts could see the small crowd that had already gathered around the ambulance. The ambulance crew closed the rear doors, got into the cab and began to drive the vehicle slowly away.

Gary Watts had worked as a detective in Worksop for the last four years, he was approaching thirty-five and sweating on promotion. He was a fit, muscular man with crew cut, dark brown hair. He wore a white, short sleeve shirt with a dark blue tie, the top button of the shirt remained unfastened and the tie was knotted loosely. He'd left his suit jacket on the back of the chair in the office when he got the call to attend the suspicious death. He reached into the glove compartment of the car and removed a pair of latex gloves which he stuffed into his trouser pocket.

As he got out of the car he was approached by Pc Len Jackson, the local beat officer for the Renton estate.

Len Jackson said, 'Morning Gary, thanks for coming out so quickly. I've just released the ambulance and called out the deceased's own GP. The on-call undertakers are on standby. Looks like the old boy's been dead for a few days, but it's a weird one mate. Everything looks like he's had a heart attack. I've called you out for another opinion, there's something about this scene that just doesn't look right to me.'

Gary gave Len a puzzled look and said, 'In what way? What doesn't seem right?'

'That's the problem, I just can't put my finger on it. I know we need more than hunches to work with, but I've got a bad feeling there's been some sort of foul play here, that's all.'

'No problem, I'll go and take a look.'

As an experienced detective Gary knew better than to disregard what his uniformed colleague was telling him. Very often it was the uniformed officers working the same beat every day that had an insight into the events and happenings on an estate such as this one.

He would take that into account, but the detective also knew that if he was going to call this sudden death as being the result of foul play he would need some hard facts to work with.

Gary walked towards the house and said, 'Come back into the house with me Len, you can point out what it is that's making you so uneasy. I'm going to need a bit more than your bad feelings before I call out the Detective Inspector, Scenes of Crime, a Home Office pathologist and the rest of the circus mate.'

'I know that Gary and I'm sorry I can't be a bit more forthcoming with some hard facts for you.'

As the two officers walked along the street towards the house Gary said, 'Who called it in Len?'

'And that's just one of the things that doesn't sit right; the person who called it in is that glorious specimen of humanity over there.'

Len nodded towards a woman standing across the road staring at them. She was in her forties, short and very fat with lank dark brown hair that fell scruffily around her shoulders. She held a cigarette in one hand and a can of extra strength Kestrel lager in the other.

Gary said, 'That's Dawn Street isn't it? Wife of drug dealing, murdering low life Shane Street.'

Pc Jackson nodded, 'It most certainly is. What you might not be aware of yet, is that Shane is very much back on the scene and up to no good. I've tried my hardest to get near him and his cronies who all congregate on the corner over there, but they're aware as soon as I walk out the front door of the nick.'

Len Jackson pushed open the front door of Jakub Kowalczyk's house and Gary followed him inside.

Gary instinctively slipped on the pair of latex gloves and began looking for any signs of a forced entry. He checked every ground floor window and both the front and back doors. He found nothing, everything looked perfectly normal. He then concentrated on finding any signs that would indicate a struggle had taken place inside the property or that possessions had been moved around and looked out of place.

Again, he saw nothing that aroused any suspicion.

Gary walked upstairs and into the old man's bedroom.

Jakub Kowalczyk was still lying under the bedclothes exactly how Pc Jackson had found him earlier. One of the dead man's arms was hanging out from under the sheets as if reaching for the bedside cabinet.

Gary had attended countless sudden deaths throughout his service and he could see the tell-tale signs of heart attack all over the dead man's face. The swollen, blackened head, bulging eyes and the white froth that had dried around the man's lips.

As he moved around the bed Gary saw the pills scattered on the floor and the small bottle in the outstretched hand. He picked the bottle out of the deceased's hand. Reading the label, he saw the words Metoprolol Tartrate.

He held up the bottle and turned to Lenny, 'These are heart pills mate, they're used to treat angina.'

The Pc nodded grimly.

Gary pulled back the bed sheets and looked at the body closely. He unbuttoned the pyjama jacket and examined the chest and abdomen. He rolled the body over and examined the dead man's back. The only injury he could find was some minor bruising around the lips. It was difficult to tell the extent or the age of the injury because of the swelling of the head generally. The body looked to have lain undiscovered for two or three days and was already beginning to deteriorate.

Gary turned the deceased back onto his back and buttoned up the pyjamas before finally replacing the bed sheets.

Pc Jackson stood with his arms folded across his chest in the doorway to the bedroom, 'I know what you're thinking Gary, there's nothing that looks out of place is there?'

'If there is mate, I can't see it.'

There was a knock on the door downstairs and a woman's voice called out, 'Hello, it's Dr Armitage!'

Pc Jackson went downstairs and returned moments later with a middle-aged woman carrying a black bag.

She walked into the bedroom and saw Jakub Kowalczyk on the bed.

As she walked in to the bedroom Gary said, 'Morning doctor, I'm Dc Watts from the local CID. I've had a look at the man's chest and abdomen and can find no obvious marks of violence.'

Dr Armitage turned to him and said, 'Good morning detective, I'm Sara Armitage, Mr Kowalczyk's GP. I've been treating him for acute angina for years. I prescribed the pills that are now on the floor. They're a beta blocker that will stabilize his heart in the event of an angina attack. It looks like Jakub's heart finally gave out and he couldn't grab the pills in time.'

Gary asked, 'Will you be able to certify his death?'

'I'm afraid not officer, I checked the records before I came out here. I haven't seen Mr Kowalczyk for well over eight months. These pills were on a repeat prescription. Everything looks like it was a heart attack, but I'm afraid it will have to be for the pathologist to say so for certain. The Coroner will have to issue the death certificate. I do know that he has no surviving family that you could contact.'

'Okay doctor. Thanks very much for coming out.'

'No problem. It's such a shame, Jakub was such a lovely man.'

Pc Jackson escorted the doctor back downstairs and out of the house.

When he returned, Gary said, 'You might as well get the undertakers to attend now Len. I'm not going to call out the circus for this one. If the post mortem shows something different later, I'll admit I was wrong. I just can't see anything other than the old boy has suffered a massive heart attack during the night and couldn't get to his pills in time.'

'I understand what you're saying Gary, I totally agree

with you about not calling everybody and his dog out on what's here.'

'You heard what the doctor said Len, I think she's of the same opinion.'

The beat officer looked thoughtful and said, 'Mentioning everyone and his dog has just reminded me, come to think of it, I know for a fact that the old man had a dog called Molly, Christ knows I've seen him walking it often enough. The old boy adored that dog and it's nowhere to be seen. We both know that generally a dog will always stay near the body in cases like this. Obviously, it's your call detective and all I'll say is this; there's any number of things that can bring on a heart attack.'

'I hear you Len, let's see what the pathologist says at the post mortem this afternoon.'

Gary left Pc Jackson in the house and walked back out onto the street. Now that the ambulance had gone the crowd had thinned out.

As he made his way across the street back to his car he saw a bulky, overweight figure dressed in a dark purple shell suit. There was something familiar about the fat man standing on the corner of Hammond Street.

As Gary reached his car the fat man waddled towards him and said, 'Well, well, Detective Watts, long time no see. What brings you out to the Renton estate this fine morning?'

Hearing the high-pitched, whining voice Gary knew instantly who it was, 'Shane Street. I should be asking you the same question, what brings you back to this lovely area? You had enough of the bright lights of Nottingham?'

'It's all about the family for me Mr Watts. Me and Dawny are giving it another go for the sake of the lads, you know how it is. My boys need a father figure to look up to, don't they?'

'How old are the boys now Shane? You've got four, haven't you?'

'Do you know what, you should've been a copper with a memory like that. Yeah, four lads, eldest is nineteen youngest twelve. Me and Dawny were at it like rabbits back then.'

He laughed at his own joke before saying, 'I'm hoping they're all going to follow their old man into the family business.'

'And exactly what business would that be, Shane?'

Shane Street winked, allowed a sly smile to play across his features then turned to walk away. As he strolled slowly away he said, 'You know I can't tell you that detective. You have a good day now, hope you catch some criminals!'

Gary opened the car door and was about to get in when Shane Street shouted across the road, 'It's a terrible business detective. The old man and his dog dying like that!'

How did Shane Street know the dog was even missing let alone dead?

Feeling a rage growing inside him, Gary slammed the car door shut and strode across the road to confront Street. He grabbed him by the front of his shell suit top and pulled his face in close to his own. Quietly, but with real menace the detective hissed, 'What the fuck do you know about the death of this old man and his dog, Street?'

Shane Street smiled a malevolent smile and whispered, 'Exactly the same as you copper, fuck all. Now unless you're going to nick me get your fucking hands off me.'

Gary knew he didn't have anywhere near enough evidence to carry this on so reluctantly he released his grip on Shane Street's clothing, pushing him backwards as he did so.

As he walked back across the road to his car he vowed to himself that he would get to the bottom of the evil that seemed everywhere on this street.

He got into the car, started the engine and drove off, watching the youths gathering around Shane Street on the corner of Hammond Street.

As he drove passed Gary muttered under his breath, 'I'm going to fucking have you Street.'

The youngest of the group gathered on the corner, fifteen-year-old Rocky Street, stared hard at the detective as he drove away. Smiling, he began to jingle the old mans war medals that were safely stashed in the pocket of his brown leather bomber jacket.

Later that afternoon, Gary Watts was sitting at his desk in the CID office at Worksop Police Station. He was waiting patiently for a call from the pathologist carrying out the post mortem on Jakub Kowalczyk.

At two thirty-five the telephone on his desk began to ring, he answered it on the third ring, 'Hello Worksop CID, Dc Watts speaking.'

'Hello detective, you're just the man I need to talk to. It's Mr Simpson, the pathologist at Worksop Hospital. I understand from your colleague, Pc Jackson, that you wanted to be informed of the outcome of the post mortem on Jakub Kowalczyk?'

'Yes, that's right Mr Simpson, what did you find?'

'Absolutely nothing that would set alarm bells ringing, if that's what you mean? The old man died from a heart attack, pure and simple. I understand from his notes that he had a long history of coronary disease.'

'Thanks Mr Simpson. There's just one thing I noticed earlier when I looked at the body, I saw some bruising around his mouth?'

'Yes, the bruising to his lips, I would estimate that injury to be at least three days old and nothing to do with the heart attack that killed him.'

'Okay Mr Simpson, I appreciate the call, thank you.'

Gary replaced the telephone receiver feeling very despondent. Ever since his run in with Shane Street on Hammond Street, Gary had felt troubled.

He couldn't put his suspicions down to anything specific, but he now thought Pc Jackson was right.

Something about the death of Jakub Kowalczyk was definitely wrong.

CHAPTER 17

5.00am 21st July 1987
Secret location, North Nottinghamshire

The air was perfectly still.

The only sound to be heard was birdsong emanating from the tall trees that surrounded the large open expanse of meadow. It was already light, but the sun had not yet risen high enough to clear those same trees. The meadow itself was still in deep shadow and held the chill from the previous night. The ground beneath him was still damp and cold.

Tom Naylor was dressed in full camouflage.

The ghillie suit he wore had taken hours of meticulous preparation. It was worth the effort, he knew the carefully constructed camouflaged suit would allow him to melt into the meadowland he would be slowly moving through.

For two long hours the previous day he had analysed the terrain and the various types and colours of foliage before carefully selecting the different hues necessary to adapt the hessian suit.

If he was to be successful he needed to remain virtually invisible against this particular landscape.

The meadow itself was just over a thousand metres long and six hundred metres wide, a vast expanse of tall grass, wild flowers, heather and dark green bracken. It was bordered on three sides by tall, green conifers and smaller deciduous trees and bushes that grew down to the very edge of the meadow. The conifers had been planted by the Forestry Commission many years before and the meadow itself had been created after the conifer plantation that once stood there had been felled. Within the next five years it would be replanted and the process would start again.

Tom knew that at the far end of the meadow there was a single dirt track that gave the only access into the woodland.

It would be on this dirt track that he expected to locate his quarry; the old man would be waiting in a vehicle surrounded by his entourage.

As his thoughts turned to the target, instinctively Tom checked his rifle. The Ruger M77 was a bolt action rifle. It had been fitted with a telescopic sight which transformed the weapon into an extremely capable sniper rifle. The .243 Winchester ammunition used in the weapon was perfect for the sniper, as over penetration was not an issue with that calibre.

Tom had begun his painstakingly slow and careful journey across the meadow just as the sky began to change from the black of night to the purple hues of the approaching dawn. He knew that his target would also be approaching his rendezvous on the dirt track at around the same time.

The old man would be in or around his vehicle, most likely with a pair of powerful binoculars glued to his face, scanning the terrain around him looking for the slightest glimpse of movement, however small or insignificant.

The hours Tom had spent studying the ground he needed to cross had proved invaluable. Knowing the exact location of every little area of dead ground, where he couldn't be seen from the dirt track, was as valuable as gold dust.

Although extremely useful to the sniper, dead ground could also be a death trap. Knowing where to exit dead ground was a skill in itself as it would often lead to an obvious opening where it would be all too easy for the unwary to be observed.

Tom had been stalking his target for well over two and a half hours now and the physical and mental effort was beginning to take its toll. The weight of the ghillie suit now heavily adorned with foliage together with the heavy Ruger rifle was starting to take its toll.

The concentration required was enormous, the fact that just one mistake was all it would take for the mission to be a disaster also had a very debilitating, wearying effect.

The kill range for the mission had been set between one hundred and one hundred and forty metres, so he needed to get in close enough to identify his target, but not too close. Every metre he got closer to his quarry afforded an even greater opportunity for him to be exposed and compromised.

Tom estimated that he was entering the last phase of his stalk and had already traversed well over eight hundred metres of rough, undulating terrain using the dead ground to its maximum potential. He had also taken advantage of the numerous ridges that had been left when the area had been cleared of conifer trees years before. These ridges were all overgrown now and had provided him with excellent concealment.

As he moved slowly forward to his target he identified an area of ground shaped like an upturned saucer. Once he had traversed around this area from right to left, it would leave him in a very dense patch of gorse and bracken.

The patch of bracken would be the perfect place for him to take his kill shot.

If he could get into position and take his shot from there, he would be completely hidden from the old man and his cronies. The men were clearly in view now and Tom could hear their voices being carried by the breeze across the meadow.

They were all laughing and chatting about incidents from the night before. The younger ones in the group were bragging about conquests with women from the local pubs and clubs, the older ones about the amount of alcohol they had consumed.

Finally, for the first time he could see his target.

The old man was the only person not joining in the banter; he remained alert, constantly watching. Looking for the slightest movement, a shadow or an object that was darker or lighter than the surrounding area.

His concentration was total.

The fatigue Tom was feeling, began to allow doubts that he wasn't up to the task to creep in.

Time wasn't an issue, so he made the decision to rest for ten minutes and regroup. This would allow him to get his breath back and recover physically and mentally before moving into his final position ready to take the shot.

It was the smart move.

He settled down to rest, safe in the knowledge that he hadn't been seen. Provided he remained perfectly still and didn't make any stupid errors, he was confident he would remain undetected.

As he recovered physically, he also began to regain the confidence in his own ability. Making the shot, hitting the target, was not an issue. From this range and with the scope fitted to his rifle it really was an easy shot.

This entire operation had all been about the skill of the stalk, the patience and the tenacity to get it right. Tom had already approached this same area from two other directions that morning only to turn back after being dissatisfied with the concealment on offer. He hoped it was this attention to detail that would make this operation a success.

Feeling fully recovered, Tom was about to start the final approach to his chosen firing position when he noticed a movement on the very edge of his peripheral vision. Something had moved on to the top of the upturned saucer shaped area of ground, immediately to his right and approximately eight metres away.

Slowly, millimetre by millimetre, he turned his head towards the movement. A large rabbit was now sitting out in the open nibbling at the short grass on the very top of the mound.

As he looked at the rabbit feeding, Tom saw a much slower movement directly behind it. Focussing on the second movement, he could clearly see the glint of moisture in the small, beady eyes of the sleek, streamlined stoat painstakingly stalking the much larger rabbit.

He realised that he wasn't the only predator within the tall grass of the meadowland trying to make a kill on this beautiful summer's morning.

Tom remained motionless, breathing slowly. He was now totally transfixed by the life and death drama that was about to unfold before his very eyes.

Suddenly, in a blur of reddish brown fur the stoat pounced, sinking its sharp, needle like teeth into the neck of the unsuspecting rabbit. The rabbit let out a high-pitched squeal and began to thrash its legs around wildly in a futile attempt to break the death grip applied by the stoat's jaws.

The thrashing lasted no more than twenty seconds before Tom could see the rabbit's eyes glaze over as it died, it's throat still gripped by the jaws of the smaller, deadlier predator.

With the drama over, Tom suddenly realised there was no other noise to be heard.

The voices he had heard from the track had now become deathly quiet.

He could now see that every man on the track was completely focussed on the exact spot where the rabbit had met its death.

The question facing Tom was a simple one, had the stoat caused his own demise as well as the rabbit's?

It was too late to do anything.

Tom only had one choice, he had to remain perfectly still and have the courage to trust in his camouflage and concealment. Even though every nerve in his body was screaming at him to get up and run for cover, he lay motionless hardly daring to breathe.

He desperately tried to melt into the ground below him and closed his eyes tightly, thinking it was only a matter of time before he was discovered.

After what seemed like an eternity, gradually the voices began to chatter once more and the attention of the men on the track began to waver again.

Tom knew that one pair of eyes would still be focussed intently on that spot, desperately searching for any sign of his presence.

After remaining rooted to the spot for another fifteen minutes, finally he found the courage to move. Almost imperceptibly he began to slowly move sideways, getting ever closer to the high bracken. Once in the bracken the only thing he had to be wary of was the very tops of the tall ferns moving in an unnatural fashion, betraying his presence below their tall stems.

Half an hour of extremely slow progress passed before Tom was at long last in his final firing position. Having reached his goal, he once again took time out to recover and relax.

He settled down onto his rifle, drawing it into his right shoulder until the weapon felt as one with him. Slowly reaching across with his left hand, he removed the two lens covers from the telescopic sight, taking care to replace the front cover with a fragment of dull, gossamer thin muslin. This cloth allowed him to obtain a clear sight picture of the target and prevented any danger of reflected light bouncing off the lens. Any such reflection would instantly compromise his position.

Looking through the scope, he slowly made minute adjustments until he could see the head of his target.

The image was so magnified, Tom felt as though he could just reach forward and touch the man's face. Every line and every wrinkle of the targets rugged and weather-beaten face was clearly defined. He could clearly see the blue smoke rising from the obligatory cigarette hanging from the old man's lips. For a fleeting second Tom wondered if the cigarette was ever smoked or if it just hung from the old man's mouth like some nicotine stained pacifier.

As if in a direct answer to his unspoken question, he watched as the old man drew deeply on the cigarette, pulling the smoke deep into his lungs before exhaling smoke from the other side of his mouth, the cigarette never leaving his lips.

The target's eyes were hidden behind a large set of binoculars that appeared to be permanently attached to his face. He never put them down, constantly scanning the area, constantly searching.

Taking great care, Tom used his right hand to slide the bolt action of the rifle down into the firing position. During the stalk, the action had been forward to prevent any rattle from the moving parts. Only now he was in position to fire did he push the bolt down locking the weapon, a round already in the breach, ready to fire.

He consciously slowed his breathing even further and placed the cross hairs of the scope directly onto the bridge of the old man's nose. This point of aim would ensure the bullet smashed directly through the cortex of the brain at the base of the skull.

The effect would be catastrophic.

An instantaneous kill.

The old man would never hear the shot that ended his life.

Maintaining sight picture, Tom slowly exerted a gradual pressure on the trigger, using just the pad of the index finger on his right hand until the rifle barked into life and he felt the recoil drive into his shoulder. Instantly, he slid the bolt action of the rifle up and back, carefully ejecting the spent cartridge. He then moved the bolt smoothly forward, sliding another bullet from the magazine into the breach.

As he reloaded his weapon, Tom continued to stare through the powerful scope.

There was a fleeting moment when he could see the expression on the old man's face as he allowed the binoculars to drop from his face. The initial expression was one of surprise, which quickly changed into a slow smile.

Tom continued to observe through the scope as the old man placed the binoculars back up to his eyes. He could see the old man begin to shout and could hear his raised voice ranting, 'Didn't any of you fuckwits see that? Where is the twat?'

The old man picked up a radio and started to bark commands', Tom could see the cigarette in his mouth dancing on his lips as he shouted orders into the radio.

After a few minutes, Tom heard footsteps approaching from behind and to his right.

He remained totally motionless, lying in exactly the same firing position ready to take a second shot if he got the opportunity.

The bullet he had fired was a blank.

The target, the old man, was Police Sergeant Ray Wilcox. A veteran of the Royal Marines Mountain and Arctic Warfare Cadre sniper school and now the chief instructor of the Regional Police Firearms Training School.

From his position, Tom could hear the sergeant's voice getting angrier; the thick West Midlands accent becoming even more evident as he shouted, 'Come on, find him! That was very close in, are you lot all blind?'

Tom couldn't help but allow a small smile to play on his lips. He was confident they would never spot him in this dense undergrowth. After all, it had taken him long enough to search for the perfect location.

The footsteps now came to within two metres of Tom's position, he heard a voice, 'I'm at the location you directed me to, there's nothing here sarge.'

Tom recognised the voice. It was Bob Baker, another ex-sniper who was now a member of the training school staff. Baker was doing the spotting role for today's exercise.

Tom then clearly heard the voice of Ray Wilcox on the radio being held by Pc Baker, 'Bob, move two metres to your right. There's a shadow at the side of the gorse bush with the yellow flowers on. That's him isn't it?'

Tom smiled again, getting colder, he thought.

Bob Baker moved as instructed, then replied over the radio, 'No, nothing here either sarge.'

'Okay, tell the sniper to take his second shot', growled a clearly disgruntled Wilcox.

Bob shouted, 'Sniper, take your second shot!'

Instantly, Tom's rifle cracked into life as he fired the second shot.

This time he didn't move a muscle, he lay absolutely still to see if the spotters on the track could establish his firing position by sound alone. He felt no inclination to give them a clue by moving his hand to unload the spent blank round.

Having regained his composure after Tom's second shot was fired from less than two metres away, Bob Baker said, 'Sniper, describe to me exactly what your target is doing right now?'

Tom replied just loud enough for the spotter to hear, 'He's scratching his ugly nose on his ugly face.'

Bob Baker chuckled then spoke into the radio, 'He's got you boss. You're stone dead. Did you spot him?'

After an agonising ten minutes Tom finally heard the old man's voice on Baker's radio, 'Okay Bob, tell him to stand up and identify himself so I can put the range finder on him. That sounded way too fucking close. I'll personally kick his arse if he's within one hundred metres!'

Tom didn't wait for Bob's instruction.

He was only two metres behind him, he stood straight up

holding his rifle over his right arm. His sudden appearance caused Bob Baker to jump back with a start.

Tom again heard the old man's voice over Bob's radio, 'One hundred and fifteen metres! What the fuck's he been messing about at? The smart arse could've taken that shot an hour ago. Who is it Baker?'

'It's Tom Naylor, sarge.'

'Well tell Naylor to get his arse in here for a well-deserved brew. I think I'm going to need more than a Disprin to get over the hole he's just put in my head', he said, chuckling.

Tom knew the old man would already have the binoculars back up to his face searching for the other three snipers that were still out there stalking him, desperate to put another proverbial hole in his head.

One of those snipers was Matt Jarvis, Tom's rifle team partner on C Section.

Wearily, Tom made his way back to the vans parked on the track. He made safe his rifle and secured the weapon in the armoured vehicle that acted as a temporary armoury before making his way over to the transit van being used by the Special Operations Unit.

Inside this van were flasks full of hot water and tubes of instant coffee cups. Needing an instant energy rush, he made himself a coffee with three sugars before reaching into his personal kit bag and retrieving two bananas, greedily devouring one of them on the spot.

Stalking always gave Tom a real appetite.

He removed the ghillie suit and took off the head and shoulders attachment. The dirty combat trousers and jacket he wore below the ghillie suit, now felt damp and cold from sweat.

He pushed up the sleeve of his jacket exposing a white crepe bandage on his forearm. He removed the bandage and vigorously rubbed the fresh scar tissue. It had only been four weeks since he'd been badly slashed with a knife as his Section had ended a siege at Cuckney. Although completely healed, the exertion of the stalk had made the area around the scar tissue throb and ache.

The ache dissipated as he rubbed his forearm.

The olive green and dark brown camouflage cream was still smeared over every exposed area of skin on his head and neck. It gave him the appearance of being some green headed monster from the black lagoon.

He quickly swapped the damp combat jacket for a dry sweat shirt from his kit bag, then grabbed his own binoculars and hung them around his neck.

Carrying the steaming hot cup of coffee and his second banana, he made his way over to Sgt Wilcox.

Wilcox had a fold away camping chair placed on the roof of the armoured vehicle. From this vantage point he could sit in relative comfort with an elevated view over the stalking ground.

Without looking down and with the binoculars still glued to his face he grunted begrudgingly, 'Nice work Naylor, though why you have to get in so frigging close is beyond me. You really must work on your JD's.'

JD's was sniper slang for judging distances, a vital skill for any rifleman especially when shooting over longer distances. Being an accomplished exponent of the sniper's art was not just about the ability to fire a weapon accurately. The sniper needed self-discipline, a keen observational eye, an analytical brain that's able to calculate range and wind speed quickly and then competently judge the effect those two elements would have on the accuracy of a shot.

But by far the single most important attribute for any sniper was an abundance of patience.

Tom didn't respond to the sergeant's comment, but just tucked into his second banana.

Wilcox tutted and said in his black country drawl, 'Jesus H Christ! Look at you putting that frigging banana away! You're like a frigging ape!'

Apart from smoking cigarettes, the old man's next favourite thing was to say the word "frigging".

As a direct result of this quirky habit he was fondly known as Frigger Wilcox to all who knew him well.

Tom grinned, 'Sorry Frigger, but killing you has given me a bit of an appetite.'

'Very funny, I don't think. It must have been a frigging fluke for an ex Para like you to get me Naylor. Can you see any of these other muppets?'

'I wouldn't tell you if I could.'

'No, I didn't think you would.'

The brief conversation ended and having finished his banana and his coffee Tom placed his own binoculars to his eyes and began to lazily scan the vast area in front of him. The binoculars were very powerful so to eliminate the shake caused by the magnification he rested his elbows on the bonnet of the armoured vehicle.

Methodically, he began to scan the vast meadow from left to right. He started at a distance of one hundred metres and slowly worked away from the vehicles.

After fifteen minutes he was at a point around one hundred and thirty five metres from the track when suddenly something registered in his brain. He stopped and slowly worked his way back.

He stopped at an area of thick gorse. There was a patch of lighter grass immediately behind it and a dead log to the left of it.

Tom stared through his binoculars at this one particular area of the meadow and began an even slower sweep.

Something wasn't right, his eyes were constantly drawn to the patch of light-coloured grass. Try as he might he couldn't identify what was out of place.

Suddenly, he realised what was wrong.

It wasn't anything on the lighter coloured grass, but something just in front of it. A small object that was too dark, that looked out of place. There was something about the shape of it that didn't belong in that environment.

He stared hard at the object trying to determine exactly what it was he was seeing. His brain desperately trying to decipher the signals his eyes were sending.

Finally, Tom recognised exactly what the object was, he could see it clearly now and he knew that it definitely shouldn't be there.

This was definitely one of the three remaining snipers.

The sniper was lying perfectly still and to the untrained eye looked like an extension of the gorse bush. Just in front of the light grass, Tom could clearly see half the heel of the sniper's boot. It looked like a very small, very black, crescent moon.

From the roof of the van Wilcox growled, 'You've spotted it too, haven't you Naylor?'

'Spotted what?'

'That dozy twat's boot!'

'I can't see a thing.'

'Oh, I think you can Mr Naylor.'

Wilcox was on his radio now, 'Bob, start making your way in. I've definitely got one this time.'

Baker was guided into the area where the dead log, the gorse bush and the heel of the boot was.

'Right Bob, move forward two metres. Stop. Put your hand down, what are you touching?'

'It's a boot, boss.'

'Is it a frigging police issue boot?'

'Afraid so boss.'

'Well don't keep me in suspense Baker! Whose frigging boot is it?'

'I think it's Matt Jarvis.'

'Well tell him to stand up, he's well and truly pinged.'

On that command, Tom's best mate stood up.

Half of the gorse bush disappeared as he stood up. Only then did Tom realise just how brilliant his partners concealment had been.

Apart from the half heel of his boot that had compromised his position and given him away, his camouflage had been perfect.

Wilcox lowered the binoculars and spoke into the radio, 'Tell him to make his way in for a cuppa Bob, I'll debrief him later.'

Tom watched as his mate slowly trudged towards the vehicles on the track. He knew Matt would be gutted. The location where he'd been spotted was definitely his firing position, another couple of minutes and he would have taken his shot.

All snipers know there's no such thing as bad luck, just bad field craft.

Matt had made the fatal error of not concealing every part of his kit. All it had taken for him to be given away was for one leg of his ghillie suite to drag up a fraction as he crawled into his final firing position.

No doubt Sergeant Wilcox would ram home that message later. He would also take great delight in telling Matt exactly where he'd fucked up. Tom knew his partner would just have to accept it and suck it up, because what the old man was nagging about today could save his life tomorrow.

More importantly, as Tom and Matt were a two-man team, indirectly it could save his life as well.

Matt made his way directly over to the Special Ops van, reluctant to hear what Wilcox had to say. Tom was waiting with a hot coffee.

Matt secured his rifle in the back of the van, took the steaming hot brew and said, 'Thanks mate, I'm well ready for this.'

He took a sip of the hot drink before continuing, 'I can't believe I blew it at that stage Tom. I was all set to shoot the old git. What gave me away?'

Tom replied matter of factly, 'He clocked the heel of your boot sticking out from under your ghillie suit.'

'For fuck's sake! I don't believe that, my head's a shed today.'

'Why? What's the problem?'

'I've got major dramas going on at home Tom. Kate's going ape shit about me being on this fucking course. Apparently, now that I'm on the Unit she never fucking sees me. All we seem to do at the moment is argue, big style. I reckon she's ready to piss me off for good.'

Matt and Kate had been married for just over three years.

A few years older than Matt, Kate Jarvis was a Crown Court barrister who specialised in criminal law. She had recently come to prominence both at her chambers and in the public eye after being the chief prosecutor for the Crown in the trial of Barry Tate.

Barry Tate was a major villain, a gangster, who virtually ran the drugs trade in Nottingham. He would stop at nothing, including murder, in order to hang onto his vicelike grip of the narcotics trade in the city. Although surrounded by violent men who would readily kill on his command, Tate was himself an extremely dangerous and menacing individual who enjoyed the administration of violence. He would very often take it upon himself to badly beat, or worse, anyone who crossed him.

Tate had made one uncharacteristic and very stupid mistake. For a reason known only to himself he had instructed Tony Banks, a relative newcomer in his organisation, to carry out the murder of a rival dealer.

Banks was an overweight middle-aged man with an eye for beautiful women. He was not a good-looking man but carried a certain charisma that some women found attractive. Banks regularly supplied Barry Tate with naïve, compliant young women that he could use as sexual playthings.

Banks had a serious cocaine addiction and had come to the notice of the police a week before the murder of the rival dealer, after a young Italian student had been found dead at his penthouse flat.

The cause of the student's death had been a cocaine overdose. Banks had denied all knowledge of the young woman's drug habit and claimed he had fallen asleep the night before when the woman was fine, only to find her dead the next morning. With insufficient evidence to prove otherwise, no charges were ever brought against Banks.

The murder of the rival dealer had been ordered by Tate just a week later.

Banks had stabbed the man to death in a city centre bar in front of several witnesses. The killing was so sloppy and unprofessional that within three days Banks had been arrested and charged with murder.

Facing the prospect of life imprisonment, Banks had quickly elected to inform the detectives interviewing him about the criminal organisation Barry Tate directed. A deal had been struck and Banks began to give chapter and verse on Tate's involvement as the head of that criminal empire.

Banks believed that by co-operating fully with the police he would get a substantially reduced prison sentence.

It was an extremely dangerous decision for Banks to take but it was one that was readily accepted by the police. After five months of painstaking, dedicated detective work by a squad especially formed to bring him to justice, Barry Tate had been arrested and subsequently charged with offences ranging from murder, drug trafficking and money laundering.

Kate Jarvis had then skilfully presented all the evidence of Tate's criminal enterprise to the jury at Leicester Crown Court.

Subsequently, the jury had taken only four hours to find Barry Tate guilty of all charges.

At the conclusion of the trial His Honour Judge Stockwell described Tate as a dangerous, violent individual with no regard for human life. He sentenced him to life imprisonment with a minimum period of thirty years to be served.

Tom was well aware how worried Matt had been at the time of the trial, as Barry Tate had made numerous veiled threats that he would achieve vengeance both on the grass Tony Banks and on the legal team that had been responsible for him being sent to prison.

Even though he was now in custody and serving life, Tate was still a very dangerous, powerful man; his threats were not to be taken lightly.

Matt was totally dejected and still feeling sorry for himself when Sergeant Wilcox came over.

Standing with his hands on his hips, Wilcox said, 'What the frig was all that about numb nuts? You'd done the hard bit.'

'I know, I know, I fucked up! Anyone can make a mistake, can't they?'

The outburst from Matt was totally out of character.

Tom couldn't understand it, Matt knew he'd cocked up, why not just accept what was coming?

Tom glanced at Wilcox who looked fit to explode at the undisciplined response he'd received from the younger officer.

The experienced sergeant stared hard at Matt and said through gritted teeth, 'Luckily for you Pc Jarvis, I've just received a radio message from your headquarters, apparently they need you and golden bollocks here to get back to HQ urgently. There's a job on and the rest of your Special Ops sniper teams are already deployed on the frigging royal visit in Newark today. Don't think you've heard the last of this, Pc Jarvis, we'll be continuing this conversation another time you cheeky frigging twat!'

Matt never said a word and just glared back.

For a split-second Tom thought the two of them were about to start throwing punches. He'd never seen Matt so agitated. He quickly grabbed him by the arm and pulled him away saying, 'Come on pal, let's get the gear loaded.'

Tom retrieved his weapon from the mobile armoury and the two of them stowed the rest of their gear into the Special Ops van before setting off down the track.

The drive back to headquarters would take three quarters of an hour. Tom had been driving in silence for twenty minutes with Matt brooding and sullen in the passenger seat.

Finally, Tom broke the awkward silence, 'Look mate, whatever's going on, if you want to talk, you know I'm always here to listen.'

Tom could see tears welling in his mate's eyes, then suddenly Matt blurted out, 'I think it's over mate, I reckon she's seeing someone else.'

'No way Matt, not Kate. She's solid as a rock mate. Bloody hell, everyone can see she worships the ground you walk on.'

'If she ever did, she doesn't now mate. Ever since I transferred on to this bloody unit ten months ago things have just gone from bad to worse. We were going along great before, nothing ever came between us. Ever since she finished that bloody trial I see her constantly sneaking looks at that new mobile phone she's got. A couple of times I've walked in on her talking quite animatedly on the mobile, then she suddenly stops the call as soon as I walk in. When I asked her who it was, all I get is the "just someone from work" line. She hasn't been the same since the date for Barry Tate's appeal was fixed. She spends hours at work preparing for the appeal, or so she says, I'm sure she's seeing some wanker barrister from her chambers.'

Tom was totally shocked. He couldn't believe what he was hearing. Matt's wife was a fantastic woman, not only stunningly beautiful but extremely intelligent. He found it hard to imagine her ever being unfaithful to Matt, she really did adore the guy.

Tom said, 'Look mate, you both probably need to do some talking and clear the air. I'm sure there's a perfectly innocent explanation for all this.'

'You could well be right Tom. I think we do need to talk, but now I've got another massive problem. I'd already booked a table at Mario's in town for this evening so we could sit down and have a long quiet talk, but now it looks like I'm not even going to be able to make that. Depending, of course, on what this fucking urgent job turns out to be.'

Trying to sound positive Tom replied, 'Let's wait and see, it's only just gone two o'clock now. We may well be done and dusted before this evening.'

Matt stared out the window and went quiet again.

Tom didn't really believe that the job would be over that quickly. He drove the rest of the way to headquarters in silence.

His head was spinning.

Matt and Kate seemed like the perfect couple. Whenever he and his new girlfriend Bev went out with them in a foursome they were fantastic company.

Although they were from very different backgrounds Bev and Kate had hit it off straight away. They both shared a passion for horses as well as both now having cops for partners.

Tom couldn't recall seeing any sign of what he'd just been told. He wondered if Bev was any the wiser, he knew both women talked to each other often but he wondered how much Kate would confide in Bev, as theirs was very much a fledgling friendship.

It wouldn't hurt to ask Bev if she knew anything.

That conversation would have to wait until after this job, whenever the fuck that maybe.

CHAPTER 18

11.00am 21st July 1987
Wakefield High Security Prison,
West Yorkshire

The showers were all being used, the water was red hot and the room was filled with steam.

Tony Banks was well aware that the large communal shower room contained other bodies, he was also extremely pleased that all those other bodies were male.

On the outside, in his home town of Nottingham, he'd always been considered as a "Jack the Lad", the archetypal "Ladies' Man".

Whichever way the world saw him, secretly Tony Banks was very definitely a gay man. Unfortunately for him, the world of drugs and crime he'd frequented for most of his adult life still revered the womaniser, but vilified homosexuality.

His decision to adopt the persona of the ladies' man had been one that was forced upon him by his circumstances; he would have dearly loved to come clean about his sexuality, but he daren't.

He smiled to himself as he thought about what his previous associates outside of these prison walls would have made of that revelation.

Tony Banks was now a lifer in Wakefield High Security Prison and had been ever since he was found guilty of stabbing to death that ponce, Will Jackson. He felt bitter about being inside as he'd only carried out the stabbing as a personal favour to Barry Tate.

Banks had never been a violent man, but there was something about Barry Tate that he just couldn't resist. When Tate had asked him to kill Jackson over a personal insult he'd readily accepted the task. Having said he would do it there was no way he could back out, that would have spelled the end for him in Tate's organisation.

Banks had snorted five lines of cocaine in the toilet of the club to get himself pumped up, before walking back into the bar and plunging the four-inch blade into Jackson's chest. The razor-sharp filleting knife had slid between Jackson's ribs and pierced his heart. In a drug induced daze, Banks had quickly dropped the blade and staggered out of the bar.

He had tried on many occasions to work out exactly what it was that caused the overwhelming attraction he felt towards Barry Tate. He didn't know if it was the power that Tate obviously possessed within the criminal underworld, the undeniable wealth, the access to a plentiful supply of cocaine or simply the man's well-tanned muscular physique.

Whatever the reason, the fact of the matter was that Banks constantly wanted to be around Barry Tate, it was borderline worship. Much to his own personal distaste, Banks had regularly supplied Tate with beautiful young women that he then drugged and defiled in the basest most disgusting way.

Tate paid handsomely for these young women and the currency was always cocaine.

Whenever Tate was actually abusing the women, Banks always made sure he stayed around to watch. He would find himself getting extremely aroused watching the object of his sexual fantasies force himself onto the drugged and vulnerable women. There had been a number of occasions where Banks found he'd become so aroused watching Tate that he had joined in with the sexual assaults on the drugged women, just to placate his own lust.

As he climaxed though, he would always close his eyes and think of Barry Tate.

However, much he fantasised and lusted over Barry Tate, Banks was also a realist. Very quickly after being arrested for the murder of Will Jackson, he made the decision that he couldn't spend the rest of his life behind bars, he was already the wrong side of forty and he still had a lot of living left to do.

As much as he revelled in the all-male environment, he knew that the prisoners surrounding him were basically scumbags.

Banks felt he deserved better, the ironic fact that he was probably the biggest scumbag in the prison was completely lost on him.

The decision to grass up Barry Tate had been made in a heartbeat.

No sooner had the offer been made by the police than Banks had started talking. The police had promised that his sentence would be reduced considerably to reflect the enormous help he'd been to the criminal justice system by providing the information that convicted Barry Tate.

When sentencing Banks to a mandatory term of life imprisonment, the trial judge had failed to stipulate a minimum time to be served.

The police and the lawyers, especially Kate Jarvis, the chief prosecutor, had been as good as their word. Banks was pleased to be considered a lifer by all the other inmates, but only he knew that once he had served four years he would become eligible for parole and released. He'd been promised a new name and a new identity upon his release. No one would ever need to know of his criminal past.

Banks dreamed of setting himself up in a little flat in Brighton where he could finally express his hitherto hidden sexuality.

All Tony Banks had to do was get through the four years, he knew that surviving his sentence would not be easy.

Barry Tate desperately wanted him to pay for grassing him up and he knew that if he got the chance he would have him killed.

After being found guilty and sentenced to life, Barry Tate had been sent to Parkhurst maximum security prison on the Isle of Wight. Banks reasoned that while ever Tate was in Parkhurst and he was in Wakefield, it was unlikely that Tate's vengeance would be able to reach him.

As the months went by and nothing happened, he had started to believe this was indeed the case and he started to feel less threatened around the other prisoners.

Banks had never been to Wakefield prior to him being imprisoned there and he'd never had any reason or desire to visit the city in the past. What he couldn't get used to was how cold the prison itself was, even in July, supposedly the middle of summer, it was freezing. It seemed that the only place in the entire prison where he ever felt really warm was in the steamy shower room.

Maybe the steamy heat and warmth were the reasons why Banks lingered in the showers, or maybe it was simply because he enjoyed checking out the parade of young naked men, some of whom were also obviously gay.

The fact that the shower rooms in any prison are the least supervised, most dangerous places to be was completely disregarded by Tony Banks.

For probably the fifth time since he entered the showers, Banks got a handful of shower gel and began to lather his genitals. As his hands explored his own manhood he stared intently at the buttocks of a young man two showers along, who looked to be around nineteen years of age and who was busily shampooing his own long dark hair.

As he watched the young prisoner in front of him Banks began to get aroused and was totally oblivious to the fact that a very muscular, dreadlocked West Indian had occupied the shower immediately behind him.

The West Indian prisoner obviously spent hours in the prison gym lifting weights and the muscles in his huge arms rippled as he placed his towel on the hook situated on the opposite wall. Looking quickly around him, he stealthily removed a three-foot length of piano wire that had been secreted in the stitching of the bath towel.

Grabbing a flannel in each hand he wound the wire around the flannels until it was pulled taut and there was only eighteen inches of the lethal looking wire exposed.

Tony Banks was slowly becoming fully aroused, totally engrossed by the young man washing his hair. He could smell the heady lemon fragrance from the man's shampoo. He half closed his eyes, looked up towards the shower head and allowed the hot water to cascade on his face as he fantasised about having sex with the stud two showers along.

Suddenly, he became aware of a presence behind him and opened his eyes. He saw a flash of steel pass before his eyes and immediately felt the wire bite into the podgy flesh of his fat neck.

Instinctively, his hands reached up to his throat as he desperately tried to grasp the wire that was slowly but surely biting into his skin under the pressure exerted by the muscular black man behind him.

As the wire bit deeper into his flesh, blood began to seep from wounds in his neck caused by his own long fingernails as he desperately tried to claw beneath the wire.

Banks couldn't breathe now, he could feel his tongue starting to swell and block his airway as it began to protrude grotesquely from his mouth. His head felt like it was about to explode and he could feel his eyes bulging in their sockets.

His entire head was hurting now and the room started to close in as if a dark curtain was slowly being drawn in around him. Just as he was about to pass out he felt a pop in his neck and saw a fountain of blood spurt from the carotid artery in his throat as it was severed by the wire. The red arc of arterial blood sprayed across the tiled wall opposite.

The last thing Banks saw before he died was the smiling face of the young stud two showers along.

He was already dead when his fat, bloated body slammed into the hard tiles on the shower floor.

The stainless-steel shower head was still pelting the hot water down onto the grotesque, swollen face of Tony Banks.

The blood pumping from the wound in his garrotted neck washed away in a constant crimson stream down the plughole. His glassy, bulging eyes stared sightlessly up at the shower rose and the steel piano wire dangled limply from either side of his slit throat.

The shower room was now totally deserted.

The only noise to be heard was the drumming sound of water as it cascaded down onto the lifeless body of the grass, Tony Banks.

CHAPTER 19

2.30pm 21st July 1987
Nottinghamshire Police Headquarters

It was already two thirty in the afternoon by the time Tom and Matt arrived back at headquarters. They quickly carried all the equipment from the van into the Huts; the secretive buildings that housed the Special Operations Unit, tucked away behind the main headquarters building.

Chief Inspector Jim Chambers was waiting for them as they walked in.

After the debacle of his relationship with Jaycee Stasuik, Tom had only recently found himself back on good terms with his boss. Had the outcome of the siege in Cuckney been any different, he was under no illusion that his time on the Unit would have been over.

As both men placed their rifle carry cases carefully on the table, Jim Chambers said, 'Right you two, you need to get cracking. I want those rifles stripped right down and cleaned, then you need to draw kit and ammunition for an urban sniper scenario. I want you ready by five o'clock for an initial briefing by Detective Inspector Kavanagh. Any questions?'

'No boss.'

The response came from Tom, Matt said nothing and just got to work taking out the Ruger M77 rifles from the carry cases.

He extended the bipod legs of the two rifles and placed them on the work bench in the equipment store, ready to be stripped down and cleaned thoroughly.

Rifles pick up all sorts of grime and dirt during a stalking exercise. Tom had also fired two blank rounds during the stalk. A considerable amount of time and effort would be needed to ensure that both rifles were properly cleaned and oiled ready for use on tonight's operation.

As both men started to strip down and clean their rifles, Tom wondered what the urban sniper scenario would be. Unusually, there was none of the normal conversation or banter between the two of them. Tom glanced across at his partner and wondered if Matt was mentally in the right place to be going out on a live job, where decisions made could literally mean the difference between life and death.

By a quarter to five, both Tom and Matt had cleaned down the rifles, drawn the appropriate kit and ammunition from the store and the armoury and had taken a quick shower to get the grime and camouflage cream from their bodies.

Both men now sat in stony silence sipping a hot coffee in the briefing room, waiting for Detective Inspector Bill Kavanagh to arrive.

Breaking the oppressive silence Tom said, 'Matt, you know I'm your mate and that's the reason I need an honest answer from you. Do you think your head's in the right place to be going out on a live op? If you don't you, should say so now mate.'

Matt was thoughtful for a couple of seconds then said, 'I know what you're saying and I understand why you're saying it. Trust me, if I didn't think I could handle what's going on at home and still do a professional job I would've gone home by now. You've known me long enough to know I won't let you or anyone else down. Having said that, don't expect me to be cracking too many jokes either.'

After saying his piece Matt flashed Tom a wide grin.

Seeing the grin, he knew his mate would be fine on the op.

He asked, 'Have you called Kate yet?'

'Not yet. I'll call her straight after the briefing, that's if this wanker Kavanagh ever fucking gets here!'

Right at that very moment, as if on cue, Jim Chambers walked into the briefing room followed by Detective Inspector Bill Kavanagh.

Bill Kavanagh was very fat, with a large ruddy face and a mop of uncombed straw-coloured hair. He wouldn't have looked out of place sitting on some tractor ploughing a field out in the sticks.

He wore an ill-fitting, scruffy, food stained navy-blue two-piece suit. His appearance was the legacy of chain smoking cigarettes, and too many late-night drinking sessions that were all too often followed by the obligatory full English fried breakfast.

The middle-aged detective was a heart attack waiting to happen.

Jim Chambers waved the two SOU men to sit down then said, 'Right gents, this is Detective Inspector Kavanagh, he's here to give you a preliminary briefing on tonight's job.'

Chambers stepped to one side to allow the detective to start the briefing.

Taking a deep drag on his cigarette, Kavanagh started the briefing. The first words coming out as he exhaled blue smoke, 'Okay gents, I'm not going to take all night, I'll keep this short and sweet. I've already briefed the rest of your section, they're waiting for you at Radford Road nick. We've had reliable information that a murder is going to take place tonight at a flat in Radford. This is the very brief background story behind that information; a man by the name of Winston Small rents a flat at 34, Roman Walk on the Berringer Estate in Radford. Until very recently, Small had a man by the name of Junior Rhodes staying with him at that address. Both men were heavily involved in the supply of cocaine and heroin at pubs and clubs in Nottingham city centre. However, they soon encountered a problem with their activities. They hadn't informed a certain Barry Tate of their fledgling criminal enterprise. Our information is that this oversight resulted in Winston Small getting a visit from Tate's henchmen and being taxed on the spot to the tune of twenty thousand pounds.'

Kavanagh took another deep drag of the cigarette and continued, 'Be under no illusions gentlemen, even though Barry Tate is currently languishing in prison at Her Majesty's pleasure, he still rules the roost when it comes to the supply of drugs in Nottingham. He also has an appeal coming up very soon. At the time of the visit from Tate's gangsters to Winston's flat, Rhodes was visiting his "yardy" mates in London. He's not inclined to believe Small's version of events that the cash is now missing due to the taxing by Tate. He believes that quite simply Winston Small has ripped him off to the tune of twenty grand. Which wouldn't ordinarily be a problem if it wasn't for the fact that Junior Rhodes is a particularly evil shit who's suspected of being responsible for several killings back in Jamaica. One of the main reasons for him being here in England, is to avoid the law back home.'

He took in another lungful of smoke, 'Our informant's adamant that Junior's intent on returning to Nottingham tonight so he can kill and rob Winston Small at his flat in Radford. Rhodes has a key for the flat and plans to just walk in, waste Winston and steal whatever he can get his hands on. It's believed he'll be in possession of a firearm to do the job. On this point, the informant isn't one hundred per cent sure, but he believes the weapon of choice will be a sawn-off shotgun. The informant has made it clear to us that Rhodes intends this murder to be a warning to Tate's henchmen and other drug dealers in the city. Apparently, he's decided to try and fill the void left by Barry Tate and with his obvious connections to the yardy gangs, this is not beyond the realms of possibility. Having just got rid of Tate, the last thing we need is this crew moving in. If we thought Tate and his cronies were violent, it seems they couldn't hold a candle to this mob, so we need to try and nip this in the bud. The informant has suggested that Winston Small is only the first of a number of smaller dealers that Rhodes intends to dispose of.'

Kavanagh reached behind him and stubbed out the remnants of the cigarette, before immediately reaching for the open packet in his jacket pocket. Taking out another cigarette and his lighter, he quickly lit up and continued, 'Earlier today, the Drug Squad executed a Misuse of Drugs Act warrant at 34 Roman Walk. This was done so Winston Small could be detained and taken out of harm's way. Our intention tonight is to put your colleagues into Small's flat and await the arrival of Rhodes. Hopefully, he'll turn up with the weapon and your mates can nick him. We can then get the horrible bastard shipped out of here back to Jamaica where they can deal with him for the murders he's suspected of committing over there.'

Kavanagh paused, he seemed out of breath from the effort of doing all the talking.

Finally, he said, 'Have either of you two got any questions before we travel down to Radford nick?'

Matt asked, 'Has your informant given any indication when Rhodes is likely to arrive in Nottingham to do this job?'

'The only information we've got is that it will be some time after one o'clock tomorrow morning. Rhodes knows Small will be back in the flat by then.'

Tom saw Matt's shoulders sag as the realisation there was no way he'd be having an Italian meal and any meaningful conversation with his wife tonight hit home.

Tom turned to Jim Chambers and asked, 'Why do you need a sniper team on the job boss?'

'There's a derelict factory that overlooks the block of flats. From the factory you'll be able to get a perfect view of the landing to Winston Small's flat on Roman Walk. You'll also be able to get a clear line of sight into the only car park that services those flats. Rhodes will have to park his motor there when he arrives to do the job. The car park has plenty of street lights so I want you and Matt to be the eyes for the team waiting inside the flat. They have the shit end of the stick on this job and are putting themselves in extreme danger waiting for an armed criminal to arrive and enter the flat. I want the team inside to know exactly when this piece of shit is putting the key into the door of the flat. I want them to know what he's carrying, where the weapon is etc. If you two can give them all this information, along with the element of surprise, then there's every chance they'll be able to take this bastard down without firing a shot. That's why I want a sniper team, is that clear?'

'As crystal, boss.'

'There's also a contingency plan that you'll be briefed on when you get to Radford nick and see Sgt Turner. Basically, if any shots are fired inside the flat and Rhodes steps back outside onto the landing, it will be your task to take him down. Now if there are no other questions, I suggest you two get cracking and get down to Radford nick and join the rest of your section.'

Nothing more was said.

Tom and Matt picked up all their kit and walked outside with Bill Kavanagh.

They loaded the equipment into the boot of the unmarked Ford Mondeo and sat in the back. Kavanagh got in the driver's seat and the car was soon speeding down the driveway of police headquarters.

Matt stared out of the window as the car sped through the districts of Arnold and Sherwood, then along Gregory Boulevard and into Radford.

He imagined his wife sitting at home looking at the clock getting more and more annoyed and agitated as it became obvious that once again her useless husband wasn't going to be home on time.

CHAPTER 20

5.00 pm 21st July 1987
Oxton Village, Nottinghamshire

Kate Jarvis was in a desperate mood.

She sat alone in the lounge of the large Georgian house she shared with her husband Matt. Once again, he had failed to get home on time leaving her bereft with worry.

She stared at the Nokia City Man 900 mobile phone on the arm of the leather armchair, willing it to ring. The mobile phone was the latest must have gadget at the law firm of Peregrine and Charteris, where she worked.

At the same time as she purchased her mobile phone she had also purchased one for her husband. Matt's remained in the utility room still in its packaging, he had been reluctant to face the banter and ridicule from his colleagues at work who still saw the new mobile phones as nothing more than a yuppie gadget.

As much as she was willing the phone to ring and to hear from her husband, in equal measure she was also dreading another call from the husky voiced stranger.

The calls from this unknown man had become gradually more graphic in the violence they threatened. They were also becoming more frequent and insistent.

Kate Jarvis was an intelligent woman, a brilliant barrister who was surely destined to become a QC. Her ultimate ambition was to become a judge. As she had steadily risen through the ranks of her chosen career she had always feared that at some point an attempt would be made to intimidate her into taking a course of action she knew would be wrong.

She had always believed that whatever form any threats or intimidation would take, she would be able to deal with it promptly and correctly. After she had met and married Matt this resolve had become even stronger.

As her career progressed, she had been presented with ever higher profile cases and there were rumours that she would soon be elevated to Queens Counsel. The ultimate test of her suitability for that higher role arrived when she had been selected to be the Chief Prosecuting counsel for the Crown in the trial of Barry Tate.

Colleagues at chambers who she knew very well and had respected for a long time, warned her about the dangers of taking on such a high-profile trial. Kate was extremely ambitious and knew this represented a massive opportunity for her to progress to the next level.

She was only too aware that Barry Tate was not your normal run of the mill villain, he was an enormously powerful drugs baron who virtually ran Nottingham city and the surrounding county's supply of narcotics.

It had once been said of Barry Tate, that he took seventy-five pence of each pound made in the supply of every single gram of controlled substance sold in Nottinghamshire.

Tate's was a multi-million-pound business and he lived a lifestyle that matched his ill-gotten wealth. He owned four glittering properties, two in the UK, one in the south of France and one on the Costa Del Sol. He owned a huge private yacht that he kept moored in the marina at Cannes and had a fleet of luxurious cars. Each of his properties had garages containing Bentley's, Ferrari's and Lamborghini's.

He spent most of his time at the penthouse apartment he owned in an area of Nottingham simply called The Park. This property alone was worth well over four million pounds.

Tate ran a gangland empire that employed hundreds of individuals, ranging from his close confidants and enforcers right down to low level street dealers, selling ten-pound bags of dope.

He had risen to these heights from very humble beginnings, being raised on the huge Clifton council estate on the southern edge of Nottingham.

Tate first ventured into drugs supply when he was employed as a bouncer in one of Nottingham's premier night clubs. He'd then established a company that provided door security for every club in the city and subsequently the county. Once he controlled the doors of the pubs and clubs he was free to supply drugs into those establishments. The rise from there had been meteoric. Any opposition to his activities was met with ruthless physical violence. Tate was a sadistic, violent individual who enjoyed the beatings and torture of rival dealers. His reputation was fearsome and he was believed to have been personally involved in at least five murders as well as sanctioning countless others.

He was a driven individual, determined to hold onto his empire. He would readily do whatever it took to maintain the iron grip he had on the drugs trade in Nottinghamshire.

Despite all the warnings and sage advice she had been given from colleagues in the legal profession, Kate Jarvis had readily accepted the challenge of prosecuting this evil individual.

After a two-month trial, she had secured the conviction, before a jury, of Barry Tate on three separate charges of murder, drug supply and money laundering.

The trial judge had sentenced Tate to life imprisonment with a minimum tariff of thirty years.

Even though she'd been expecting some reaction from the defendant as he was sentenced, Kate had been shocked at the graphic nature and level of the menacing threats made by Tate towards the chief witness, police detectives and herself.

After the trial she had tried to reassure her husband Matt, that these kinds of threats were all part of her job.

Matt had expressed serious concerns over the level and specific nature of the threats issued by Tate, he was acutely aware of just how far the gangsters network stretched and realised how easily those threats could be turned into a devastating reality.

The menacing voice on her mobile phone had made it clear to Kate that those threats were indeed now becoming reality. The worry for her was that the threats she had received had not been aimed at her. They were targeted at the person she loved most in the world, her husband Matt.

The first of the calls had been made to her place of work, the receptionist innocently putting the call through to Kate.

The male voice on the phone had informed her coldly that Matt had been involved in an accident at work, that his injuries were severe and that he was not expected to pull through.

Having given her the message, the caller had then hung up immediately. She had sat there numb with shock, unable to move or speak.

After a few seconds, the telephone had rung again, it was the same dispassionate, cold voice, 'How did that make you feel Mrs Jarvis? Your husband isn't dead or dying.'

There was a pause before the voice said simply, 'This time.'

Another pause then the voice continued, 'Listen carefully, if you mention this phone call to anyone, especially your precious husband, he will be dead. Trust me lady, this is not an empty threat. Give me a contact number where I can reach you day or night, give me the number now or your husband will die.'

In a state of shock Kate had given the caller the number to her new mobile phone.

The voice had said icily, 'I'll be in touch, I will demonstrate to you how easy it will be for us to kill your husband if you force us to. Remember, not a word to anybody, Mrs Jarvis.'

Kate remained motionless and had sat at her desk for over an hour, numb with shock. Slowly the shock had turned to anger and at the very last moment that anger dissipated, substituted by a forlorn inevitability.

Whoever had made the call, they were obviously linked to Barry Tate, even languishing in a prison cell he would have the means to reach out and make those threats a brutal reality.

After agonising for over an hour Kate finally made her decision. She would say nothing for now.

She would play the waiting game, see which way the calls developed, she could always tell somebody about the threats at a later date.

That first call now seemed like a lifetime ago.

Since then the calls to her mobile phone had become more and more frequent, describing in detail exactly what Matt was doing at any given moment of the day, describing his routine and giving graphic accounts of the various ways they would be able to kill him and make it look like some tragic accident.

Two or three times Matt had walked into the room as she was attempting to reason with the voice. She had immediately terminated the call and then lied to Matt explaining that it was a problem at work. Although he never questioned her further about the calls, she could intuitively tell that Matt was becoming suspicious and noticed that their relationship was beginning to suffer.

He was becoming cold towards her, shunning any and every outward show of affection she offered. There was a rapidly growing distance between them, where they had previously been so close. Now, when they were alone together they barely spoke.

Throughout the weeks of veiled threats, the only thing the voice had never been explicit about was what they expected her from her in return for her husband's life.

That had all changed two days ago.

Now Kate knew exactly what was expected of her.

The menacing voice had informed her that all she had to do to ensure no harm came to her husband was to gather all the paperwork, files and other documentary evidence to be used by the Crown at Barry Tate's forthcoming appeal against conviction. The appeal was listed to be heard in two weeks' time at the High Court in London.

Kate Jarvis was then instructed to destroy every scrap of documentary evidence before that date, so the Crown could in effect offer no evidence.

She knew that if the Crown offered no evidence the only other thing barring Tate from being released would be the personal testimony of Tony Banks.

As if reading her mind, the voice had said menacingly that the main witness would not be giving evidence at the appeal and that provided Tate was released from the High Court without a hitch no harm would come to her husband.

She had been backed into a corner and felt there was no choice but to do exactly as the voice demanded. She knew it would be the end of her career and most probably the end of her relationship with Matt. At least he would still be alive, he would never need to know why she had done what she did.

The only thing that mattered to her at that moment in time was keeping her husband alive. There was no doubt in her mind that if she chose any other course of action Matt would be killed.

It had taken well over an hour to load all the paperwork, court files and documents into her Range Rover earlier that day. She had assured the clerk at her chambers that it was vital she took everything home to research it thoroughly for the two weeks prior to the appeal so she didn't miss anything. Begrudgingly, the clerk had helped Kate load the boxes of documentary evidence into the boot and the back seat of the big car.

On her way home from work she had withdrawn as much cash as she could. She had resolved to drive over to Tom Naylor's house later that night and talk to his girlfriend Bev.

She had become good friends with the paramedic and she wanted to talk to somebody to try and explain why she was leaving her husband.

Kate knew she would be able to convince Bev that there was nobody else involved and that she just needed a little space from Matt. She hoped that Bev would pass this message on to Matt as at that moment in time she didn't trust herself to be able to deliver the same message to him personally without breaking down and telling him the truth about what was going on.

With an overnight bag packed she walked out of her house and got into the grey Range Rover that was packed full of the evidence for Tate's appeal.

She started the engine and steered the big car off the driveway. As she drove away from the house she pondered exactly how she was going to be able to destroy all the documents. Not only did she need to destroy them, she also needed to ensure that the menacing voice would know they had been destroyed and understand that she had kept her side of the bargain.

Driving along the winding country lanes, Kate was so engrossed in thought, she failed to notice the black Mercedes van with the tinted windows following her at a discreet distance.

CHAPTER 21

7.30pm 21st July 1987
Radford Police Station, Nottingham

The CID car was driven at speed directly into the rear yard of Radford Police Station well out of the view of any passing members of the public. As soon as the vehicle came to a halt Tom and Matt got out and began removing all their kit from the boot.

Following Detective Inspector Kavanagh through the labyrinth of corridors inside the station, they found the remainder of C Section congregated in the canteen.

The canteen had been chosen for the privacy it offered at this time of night. Looking around the room they saw their colleagues studiously checking their kit and chatting quietly about the operation they were about to be deployed on.

Seeing Tom and Matt enter the room Sgt Turner walked over and said quietly, 'Not before time you two. What was the hold up?'

Neither man said a word, but both unconsciously glanced across to the portly Detective Inspector who was now sweating profusely after the brisk walk through the station corridors.

Det Insp Kavanagh looked at Graham Turner and said, 'Okay, now that they're all here, I'll leave you to brief your team.'

With that Kavanagh turned and walked out.

As soon as the detective left the room, Sgt Turner raised his voice and said, 'Gather round so I can tell you exactly what this job is all about.'

The men gathered round so Graham Turner could give a full and concise briefing, explaining fully the intelligence that had brought about tonight's operation.

He then spoke to each member of the team outlining their individual responsibilities. At the conclusion of the briefing every member of the team not only understood their own role, but was also fully aware of every other team member's individual role.

Tom and Matt as the sniper team were to be deployed inside the derelict building that was once Baxter's Textiles factory. The local CID had identified a position on the third floor of the disused building that had a view overlooking the car park and the walkway that led to 34, Roman Walk, the flat that was rented by Winston Small. The observation point for the sniper team was one floor higher than the walkway. This vantage point provided a clear view down to the front door to Small's flat.

The reasoning behind this was simple. If people are scanning an area looking for anything suspicious they very seldom consciously look up.

Graham Turner continued to give deployments to the remainder of the team.

Eddie Keane and Steve Grey would be inside flat 22, Roman Walk. This flat was currently unoccupied and was located at the extreme left of the walkway, and was the nearest property to the stairwell that led from the car park to the walkway.

Turner informed the team that this position would be known as 'Green' for all radio communications.

Jack Rimmer and Colin Morgan would be located inside flat 42, Roman Walk. The residents of this flat had been asked to vacate their flat for the duration and were currently at Radford Police Station. This flat was on the extreme right of the walkway and would be position 'Red' for radio communications.

Graham Turner outlined to the four officers in the two flats that their role was to intercept and detain Junior Rhodes at gunpoint if he either aborted actually going inside flat 34 or in the very unlikely scenario that he had gone inside the flat and somehow got out again without being engaged and taken down by the sniper team.

In a calm flat voice, he informed the team that he would be deployed inside the target premises with Tony Garner, Fran Kubica, Jimmy Hope and Luke Goddard.

Undoubtedly, these five men had the most dangerous role of the operation.

They would wait inside the target premises until Junior Rhodes walked through the front door carrying a firearm, hell bent on murdering Winston Small. Using the element of surprise, they would endeavour to overpower and detain Rhodes before he had the chance to use his weapon.

All five men inside the flat realised that if they didn't achieve this quickly and decisively it could end in disaster with a real possibility of people being injured or worse.

Turner finished the briefing by reinforcing the contingency plans that had already been put into place. Should the target arrive in a vehicle and then abort he would be intercepted away from the flat by four armed traffic patrol officers who would perform a hard stop of the vehicle.

A paramedic team was also on standby in the area should the worst happen.

The last part of the briefing was formal; all the officers deployed were reminded by Sgt Turner of the law in relation to the use of deadly force. This was a legal requirement prior to any operation involving the Police use of firearms.

As soon as the briefing was over and no questions had been raised about the operational plan, the men began to gather their kit ready for deployment.

The men deployed inside the three flats on Roman Walk were all dressed in civilian clothes and carried grip bags that contained their body armour, fluorescent green baseball caps marked POLICE on the front, Heckler and Koch Mp5's the standard issue Smith & Wesson .38 revolver and holster along with ammunition for both weapons.

The men inside the target premises also carried with them two Dragon Lamps. The enormously powerful hand-held torches would be switched on at the precise moment Junior Rhodes walked into the flat. The lamps would instantly turn night into day and would be aimed directly into the eyes of Rhodes dazzling and disorientating him enough to give the team the opportunity to take him down without having to draw their weapons.

Before deploying to the disused factory, Tom and Matt made one last check of their equipment in the large holdalls they carried. Each man had their individual Remington M77 sniper rifle, a .38 revolver, ammunition, binoculars and night vision goggles. Both hoped the latter wouldn't be needed as they had been assured that the lighting of the car park and the walkway itself was excellent.

As the team deployed, Tom and Matt remained in the canteen. They were going to be driven to the disused factory by the local CID in a covert vehicle.

After a long ten minutes the canteen door opened, Tom recognised the detective immediately. He had worked alongside Dc Nick Quinn previously on a number of enquiries in the city.

Nick Quinn reached out and shook Tom's hand saying, 'Hello Tom, I wondered if you'd be involved in this job.'

Tom grinned, 'Yeah, lucky me as always.'

He then pointed to Matt and said, 'Nick, this is my partner Matt Jarvis.'

Again, Nick Quinn reached out and shook Matt's hand, 'How's it going Matt?'

Matt returned the handshake and just nodded.

As both the snipers picked up their kit bags Nick turned to Tom and said, 'I'm not kidding mate, this building's a proper shit hole. It gets used by all sorts of pond life. Druggies get in there to shoot up, pissheads doss in there and totties take their tricks there. In fact, you should feel right at home.'

Tom grinned, 'Yeah, thanks for that mate. Seriously though, will you be able to secure us in there? The last thing we need is to be interrupted by some wino wanting to finish off his litre bottle of White Lightning!'

'No problem Tom, me and my partner are going to be deployed at the rear of the property for the duration of the operation and will intercept any problems coming your way.'

'Cheers Nick, let's get this gear stowed in your motor and get down there.'

Nothing more was said and after loading their gear into the boot, the sniper team was driven to the disused factory.

As the car pulled to a stop on waste ground behind the derelict building, Nick Quinn said, 'Good luck gents. By the way Tom, did you hear what's happened to that piece of shit Tony Banks?'

Tom replied, 'Nah mate, we haven't heard a thing. We've both been away on a course.'

Matt was suddenly very interested and said, 'What's happened to Banks?'

'Well, it seems that he lingered a bit too long in the prison showers and somebody took him out. This is the unusual bit though, he wasn't stabbed or beaten to death like you would expect when there's a murder between cons. He was garrotted with a three-foot length of piano wire!'

With a note of concern in his voice Matt asked, 'Have they got anyone for it?'

'Nah, it's the nick, nobody's saying a dicky bird! Obviously, everybody's looking squarely at Barry Tate after Banks grassed him up but there isn't a scrap of evidence connecting him to the killing. Tate's still locked up in Parkhurst on the Isle of Wight and this happened way up north in Wakefield jail. Everyone knows it's Tate behind it and no doubt he'll have given the order, but as per usual he's kept his hands well and truly clean.'

Matt looked at Tom with a worried expression.

Tom said, 'Don't worry mate, I know what you're thinking. Kate will be fine. It's one thing going after a druggie grass who's banged up with hundreds of hardened criminals who given half a chance would kill him just for being a grass. It's a totally different ball game going after the judiciary. Tate's appeal is coming up shortly and he's not going to risk doing anything as high profile as that. No doubt after the appeal, whichever way it goes, the security arrangements for Kate will be reassessed.'

Matt nodded and looked away.

Tom gripped his shoulder and said, 'Come on mate, let's get the gear and get inside this shithole. The sooner this job's done the sooner we can get home.'

CHAPTER 22

8.30pm 21st July 1987
Nottingham City Centre

'Come on Billy, you can do this.'

Billy Swan muttered the words to himself as he psyched himself up getting ready to raise the bar for a second time.

He was lying on a bench and supporting the bar as it rested on his chest, preparing himself mentally and physically for the enormous effort it would take. At both ends of the chrome benching bar were four blue metal plates each weighing twenty kilograms. The combined weight of plates and bar was close to one hundred and seventy -five kilos.

As usual Billy was training alone, but he was confident in his ability to raise the enormous weight without the precaution of somebody spotting for him.

Closing his eyes, he pushed upwards against the weight with all the strength he could muster. He felt his eyes strain and start to bulge as ever so slowly the bar and the weights began to rise from his chest. As he pushed the bar upwards further away from his chest the strain on his body became ever greater.

He was unconcerned and knew he could handle the huge weight. Bench press had always been his speciality in the gym.

As his arms extended fully he felt the elbow joints start to lock at the top of the push. He immediately began to slowly release the pressure allowing the bar to descend slowly back towards his chest. Just before the bar reached his chest he gritted his teeth, repeated the process and pushed the heavy weights aloft once more.

This time as he allowed the bar to descend he let it settle gently and silently onto the stand.

He despised the posers in the gym who when benching half that weight would allow the bar to smash noisily onto the stand causing everyone in the gym to turn and look.

Having completed the last of his bench press routine Billy slowly sat up on the bench and reached behind him for the towel he carried with him around the gym. He always finished his hour-long weight training session with a heavy set of bench press.

His session finished, he needed to get a quick shower before heading across town to complete the little bit of business he had planned.

A regular at the Hang Ten Gym in the city centre, Billy was well liked and respected by everyone who used the place. He religiously trained with weights four times a week and when he trained he worked his body very hard. He stood an impressive six feet four inches tall and weighed nineteen and a half stone. There wasn't an ounce of fat on his body. Not only did he regularly train with weights, he also ran two or three times a week and swam every fortnight.

To say he was a keep fit fanatic would do him a disservice; everything he did and everything he consumed was geared towards maintaining his health, strength and well-being.

He even kept his hair in short corn rows now as he found

that the dreadlocks he had sported as a youth just got in the way when he trained.

He wiped the bench down with the towel and made his way towards the changing rooms. As he walked to the door he smiled at two women who were chatting to each other as they walked briskly on the treadmills. Both the women giggled as they wrongly assumed he was smiling because he found them attractive. In reality Billy was chuckling to himself at their half-arsed attempt at fitness. He was thinking to himself, if the two of them spent as much effort training as they did gossiping about trash and trivia they would be like Olympic athletes.

Without pausing to answer the women, as they tried to engage him in conversation, Billy walked straight into the changing rooms to shower and get dressed.

Twenty minutes later, he was heading out of the front door of the Hang Ten Gym. He walked briskly to his car and breathed in deeply relishing the feel of the cooler night air. A short drive to Basford to take care of that small bit of business and then Billy could relax for the night.

The business was getting to grips with a late payer.

Goods had been supplied as requested and now the man needed to pay Billy what he was owed. There would be no second chances, he intended to get payment in full tonight or there would be consequences.

The reason Billy Swan had all the time and money to develop his physique and live a life of luxury was because his chosen profession was that of drug dealer.

Billy had been dealing drugs since the age of eighteen. He was now twenty-one years old and although still young, by sheer persistence and brutality he had forced his way almost to the top of a very competitive but lucrative trade.

He also had the smarts required to understand that he needed to pay certain people to continue plying his trade relatively untouched. He had always paid the Barry Tate organisation a fair percentage of everything he made.

However, since Tate had been jailed he hadn't paid a single pound. Without Tate calling the shots he was aware that there was nobody left in the organisation to concern him. Billy was biding his time carefully. He was aware that Tate had an appeal against his conviction coming up, if that failed the time would then be right for him to make his move for the top spot.

It was a far cry from when he had first started out and was striving to establish himself as a major player. In those early days he had been helped out by a white guy he met in prison when he was serving time for an assault.

Shane Street was a lot older than Billy, he was also an extremely violent, sadistic racist thug. Billy tolerated Street because he knew he could help him achieve his ambitions within the drugs trade in Nottingham. He was well connected with Barry Tate and had facilitated Billy's first meeting with Tate.

Just under a year ago Shane Street had contacted Billy and told him he was moving out of the city and returning back to the north of the county to be with the fat fuck he called a wife and his brood of inbred brats.

Billy had been glad to see the back of him. As well as being one less business rival to contend with, Shane Street sickened him with his racist views.

He still did some business with Street but as far as Billy was concerned Shane Street was now strictly small time supplying amphetamine to the muppets up in Worksop.

Still, it was a nice little earner supplying amphet that far north. He would continue to provide Street with as much amphetamine as he could shift.

As he got into his car and started the engine, his thoughts turned back to tonight's business. If the money wasn't there waiting he would need to send out a clear signal that would be heard by both his customers and potential competitors. If he was to be considered as the man ready to replace Barry Tate the message he sent out tonight would have to be as unequivocal as it was brutal.

As he drove towards Basford he played out in his mind how the meeting with Frankie Squires, the late payer, would pan out.

He grinned, he was going to enjoy this.

CHAPTER 23

8.30pm 21st July 1987
Radford, Nottingham

When Tom and Matt finally got inside the derelict factory they both realised that Dc Quinn had actually understated how awful it was. The place was ten times worse than he had described. Carrying their equipment carefully, they scrambled up the crumbling stone staircase to the third floor.

Taking care not to fall through the holes in the floor, they made their way over to the windows that overlooked Roman Court. The windows here were floor to ceiling and made up of numerous panes of glass that measured two feet by two feet. As most of the panes of glass in the windows had been smashed years earlier, rain had constantly soaked the floor of the factory and there was standing water in puddles all over the area nearest the windows.

There was a constant low whine as the wind whipped through the broken panes. The constant wind did nothing to take away the stench of the place. It was a disgusting mixture of damp, decay, human excrement and vomit.

After a quick look around the third floor, they selected an area that at least had a few panes of glass still intact and where the floor was still relatively dry. With no better alternative on offer, this would be their observation post for the operation.

Grabbing the binoculars from his bag, Tom scanned the area below their position and quickly located the target premises. He removed his personal radio from his belt and tuned in to the back to back channel stipulated in the briefing.

Using this channel meant that any communications made would only be heard by officers actually involved on the operation. It also meant that there would be no interference on the radio from local officers.

Tom said quietly, 'Tom to Graham, are you receiving? Over.'

'Yes Tom, loud and clear. Over.'

'We're in position, but it'll be another ten minutes before we are good to give you any commentary. Over.'

'Received that. I want an update from your location every ten minutes, understood? Over.'

'Understood. Over.'

The ten-minute update meant that everyone on the operation got to check their communications. If nothing was happening the signal given would be, "No Change. No Change".

Tom concluded his signals check by changing channel and speaking to Chief Inspector Chambers in the Operation Control Room, 'Sniper Team Charlie, Pc Naylor and Pc Jarvis in position. Over.'

The reply was instantaneous and brief, 'Received. Over.'

Tom knew that the Chief Inspector would stay in the control room until the operation had been completed.

Matt removed his rifle from the carry bag and set it up on its bipod legs to keep it raised off the damp floor. He checked the scope and said, 'The lights look great at the moment but we'll have to reassess it again when it's full darkness. I don't think we're going to need the night vision.'

This was a real bonus as the quality of the optics used was never good and they needed to identify their target positively if and when he arrived at Roman Walk.

While Matt busied himself with the preparation of his rifle, Tom plotted out the target area. He quickly identified the direction vehicles would enter the car park. There was only one way in and one way out of the car park, another bonus. The distance between the factory and the block of flats was just under one hundred yards. A railway line ran between the factory and the block of flats which meant there were no physical obstructions between their position and the flats. No large trees or other buildings to impede their view.

As observation points go this one wasn't bad; apart from the stench and the damp floor they were lying on, it was perfect.

With the time fast approaching eight thirty, Tom and Matt were finally fully operational in the observation point.

Once again Tom tuned his radio onto the back to back channel and said quietly, 'No change, no change.'

He heard a series of clicks as the other members of C Section acknowledged his signal. The operation to arrest Junior Rhodes was underway.

CHAPTER 24

9.30pm 21st July 1987
Newark, Nottinghamshire

Dc Sue Jenkins was getting worried.

She had been passed another message from the control room advising her that an informant had requested to see her tonight at eight thirty.

Sue knew that the informant would be the gypsy Pip McGuire and that although he was sometimes a little late, he was never normally this late. As she glanced down at her watch and saw that it was fast becoming an hour past the arranged time, she wondered to herself if the old man had made a mistake and had been caught out trying to obtain information on the Smith brothers.

It had been a month since she had last had any contact with the old gypsy.

She waited patiently in the CID car parked up behind the ruin of Newark Castle. It was another of Pip's favourite meeting points because of its secluded location.

With another nervous glance down at her watch, Sue realised she would very soon have a decision to make.

She placed the car key in the ignition and was just about to start the engine when she saw the familiar shuffling figure making his way very slowly along the cobble street towards the car.

She leaned over and opened the back door.

An out of breath Pip McGuire climbed in and closed the door.

Sue said, 'For Christ's sake Pip, where have you been? I thought the brothers had sussed you out and given you a good hiding.'

The old gypsy chuckled and said, 'Oh ye of little faith! Those two have got it all on to suss out which shoes to put on which feet in the morning. They aren't the sharpest knives in the drawer, if you understand me Miss. I know I'm late and I can only apologise, I had a little accident with a bottle.'

'You mean you fell into a bottle, I could smell it on you as you walked down the street!'

'I know, I know. It really is the devil's brew, but I'm here now and I've got some very good news for you.'

'Go on Pip, I'm listening.'

'Well, the brothers are indeed planning another little venture out next Thursday, a week today.'

'Come on Pip, you told me that a month ago. Haven't you got any more detail than that?'

'My but aren't you the impatient one! The good news is they'll be using an old Ford Transit van for the trip out.'

'Do you know the reg number?'

'No, I don't, but you won't need it. This particular chariot is bright bloody orange! It's like a fucking Jaffa orange on wheels, so it is!'

He laughed like a drain at his own joke.

'That's great Pip, any idea where they're heading on this planned trip?'

'I'm sorry Miss, that I can't help you with. All I'm hearing is that it's out in the sticks again and is something to do with antiques. Did I do alright though?'

Sue took out five ten-pound notes and handed them across to McGuire.

'If I look a little disappointed Miss, please don't take any offence, but I was hoping for a little more.'

'That's all I can do at the moment Pip, but I promise you if this information comes good and we catch them at it, I'll double that for you.'

'Didn't I always say you were the most beautiful detective I've ever seen Miss! It will come good, you can trust old Pip. I'll be seeing you soon to pick up my cash.'

'Enough of the blarney Pip, I mean it. If it comes good you'll get another fifty. Take care now.'

Pocketing the fifty quid, McGuire got out of the car and said, 'You too detective.'

He quietly closed the car door and began to shuffle away down the street.

As she watched her informant disappear into the darkness, Sue muttered out loud, 'I do hope you're on the money this time old timer.'

CHAPTER 25

10.30pm 21st July 1987
Basford, Nottingham

It had taken Billy Swan twenty minutes to drive from the city centre to Basford for the pre-arranged meeting with the debtor.

He'd deliberately chosen a car park near the centre of a run-down industrial estate that was closed for the night. He knew there were no CCTV cameras covering these dilapidated, scruffy units. The industrial estate was a desolate place at night, far from any prying eyes. He would be able to conduct his business there without any unexpected interruptions.

The debtor he was meeting was Frankie Squires.

Squires was a forty something night club owner who allowed his door staff to supply amphetamines and other Class A drugs to his customers as a side-line. The seedy night club on Summer Leys Lane in the Meadows area was on its arse and would have closed a long time ago without the illegal drugs sales. The profit he made from selling drugs was the only thing keeping him in business.

Squires was in debt to Billy Swan for six thousand pounds and had been promising payment for over a month. The debt problem had arisen after one of the bouncers he employed had disappeared with the drug profits, leaving Squires with no way to pay his supplier for the drugs he'd already been supplied with.

Billy Swan was aware of the bouncer's disappearance but as he had outlined to Squires during a previous conversation that wasn't his problem. He'd given Squires a couple of weeks to come up with the money owed.

As far as Swan was concerned, Squires was now starting to take the piss.

Whether Squires paid in full or not, that would end tonight.

Swan could not afford for his other customers and rivals to believe he had any weakness. He needed to send out a clear message to his customers that he was not a man who would tolerate late payment. With the Barry Tate situation how it was, the message would need to go out to any rival dealers as well.

As a result, the fate of Squires was already sealed. Even if he turned up with cash to clear the debt in full, an example would be made of him tonight.

As Billy drove into the car park he saw that Squires was already there, slouching against the side of his tacky old Porsche sports car.

Everything about Frankie Squires disgusted Billy.

The club owner was a physical wreck, his long, dyed black greasy hair was unwashed and pulled back in a pony tail. He was unshaven and had a week's growth of stubble. His cream coloured suit was grubby and stained and his pot belly strained against the tight-fitting trousers.

Swan drove a single circuit around the car park to ensure Squires hadn't brought any enforcers with him.

Satisfied that Squires was alone, Billy parked up two spaces away from the Porsche, switched the engine off and got out.

Squires remained leaning against the Porsche with his arms folded as Billy got out.

In his reedy, effeminate voice Squires said, 'Alright Billy, how's things?'

'Fuck all that how's things bollocks Frankie, have you got my six grand or what?'

'I've almost got it for you Billy. As you know I've had a bit of a cash flow problem, but that's all been taken care of now. You know I'm good for the money.'

Billy shook his head and growled menacingly, 'I'm warning you man, don't fuck with me. I want that six grand tonight!'

With a lazy movement Squires pushed himself away from the Porsche and stepped towards Billy with both arms outstretched and his hands open in a gesture of appeasement, 'Look Billy, I've got five grand cash in my pocket right now. I can let you have the other grand by the end of next week.'

Billy turned away, he was sick and tired of this horrible little shit taking the piss.

He turned to face Squires, sighed heavily and said in a low voice, 'Okay Squires, give me the five-grand man.'

As Squires reached inside his jacket pocket for the brown envelope, he allowed the faintest smirk to pass fleetingly across his rat like features.

Billy noticed the change of expression as he was handed the cash by Squires.

He opened the envelope and quickly counted the grubby notes. There was exactly five thousand pounds, still a grand light.

Swan walked over to his car and placed the five thousand cash in the glove compartment.

Just as Squires was about to get into his Porsche, Billy shouted across to him, 'Not so fast Squires. Step over here a second my man. You and I need to talk about the interest rate on the remaining grand.'

Squires closed the door and with a wide grin on his face he walked across to Swan, both hands thrust deep inside his trouser pockets. He looked at Swan, smiled and said, 'Anything Billy, you're doing me a massive favour. You just name your price, whatever you want.'

Without saying a word and without changing his facial expression, Billy Swan stepped forward and smashed a huge, clenched fist straight into the grinning mouth of Squires. The force of the blow knocked the club owner two yards backwards.

Squires went down backwards, with both hands in his trouser pockets he could do nothing to prevent the back of his skull hitting the tarmac of the car park hard.

He made no attempt to get back up, he lay flat on his back, unconscious and twitching.

Swan stepped forward and began to repeatedly kick the head and face of the unconscious figure for a full five minutes. Each of the kicks got progressively harder until eventually the face of Frankie Squires was a bloody, unrecognisable pulp.

As he turned to walk back to his car, Swan snarled under his breath, 'You can keep the fucking grand, you worthless piece of shit.'

Swan opened the boot of the Jaguar XJ40 and removed an old cloth. He quickly wiped the blood from the top of his training shoes before throwing the rag back into the boot.

With the tops of his trainers wiped clean of Squire's blood, Swan closed the boot, got into the car and drove off, leaving Squires dead in the car park.

The club owner had been dead from the moment his head had smashed into the tarmac after that first concussive punch.

CHAPTER 26

12.45am 22nd July 1987
Radford, Nottingham

Every ten minutes the same message had been broadcast over the radio, 'No change, no change.' The time was now fast approaching a quarter to one in the morning and absolutely nothing had happened. No vehicles had come into the car park and nobody had ventured onto the footway of Roman Walk.

From past experience of operations similar to this one, Tom knew that if anything was going to happen it would be within the next hour.

Always assuming that the information provided to the detectives by their informant had been correct.

Another ten minutes ticked slowly by. Tom stretched his aching body and sparked up his radio again, 'No change, no change.'

The rest of the team acknowledged this latest signal one by one. Twenty seconds later and the radios were silent once again.

Tom glanced to his left and watched as his partner once again checked that everything was correct with his Remington rifle. Matt was fastidious in his preparation on every job, that was why what happened at the stalking exercise the previous day had been so out of character.

If the shit hit the fan on this job it would be Matt that pulled the trigger. He was the shooter and Tom the spotter for this operation. If anything, Matt was the more consistent shot of the two. Tom, with his military background had the experience but Matt had the skills, even if those skills were as yet untested on a live operation.

Tom knew his partner would have no hesitation pulling the trigger and administering a fatal shot if the circumstances dictated that course of action.

He kept his own rifle loaded and ready to fire at his side, just in case there was a malfunction with Matt's weapon and he was unable to respond to any threat if and when it presented.

Tom again applied himself fully to watching the entrance to the car park that serviced Roman Walk. Hardly a word had passed between the two men all night, they were completely engrossed in their respective tasks. Matt may have had things on his mind but he remained the consummate professional.

Suddenly, the hairs on the back of Tom's neck stood up as he saw a dark coloured Ford Sierra saloon being driven very slowly into the car park of the flats. The vehicle had no lights on and was barely moving.

Tom immediately spoke over the radio, 'All units. Stand by, stand by.'

A series of clicks chattered into Tom's covert ear piece as the rest of the team acknowledged his signal.

Tom muttered under his breath to Matt, 'Looks like we might be in business here mate.'

'Not before time', came the matter of fact reply.

Both men strained to identify the driver of the vehicle as it was driven slowly into the car park and came to a stop.

Tom through his binoculars and Matt through the high-powered scope of his rifle.

Tom spoke evenly on the radio, 'The vehicle has stopped. It's now parked and facing the exit of the car park. There's no movement within the vehicle. I can only see one occupant. Vehicle's a dark blue Ford Sierra saloon; registered number is D440TAU. Stand by for further.'

Tom knew that someone would now be quickly checking the registered number on the Police National Computer to establish exactly who the vehicle was registered to.

Although from his position Tom had a good view of the front of the vehicle, it was parked in deep shadow, meaning he couldn't see the face of its single occupant.

Lying on the floor by his side was the latest surveillance photograph of Junior Rhodes. Tom had been glancing at the photo all night and knew he would instantly recognise Rhodes if he could get a glimpse of his face. The image of the target's face, the two gold teeth at the front, the wispy goatee beard and long dreadlocks was burned into his brain.

Suddenly, the driver's door of the Sierra opened a fraction. It opened just enough for the interior light to illuminate the driver's face. Instantly the driver realised his mistake and quickly closed it again. Seconds later and with the interior light now disengaged the door was opened again.

It was too late.

Tom had already identified that the driver of the Sierra was indeed Junior Rhodes.

'All units be advised, I have a positive identification. The driver of the Ford Sierra is the subject Junior Rhodes. I say again the subject Rhodes is now on plot. Stand by.'

Again, there were the instant clicks of acknowledgment from the rest of the Section.

Tom spoke to Matt quietly, 'Did you clock him through your scope Matt?'

'Oh yes, that's definitely our man', Matt replied with a half-smile on his face.

Down below in the car park, Junior Rhodes slowly got out of the vehicle. Tom could see by his body language that the tall, slim Rasta was totally wound up. He was like a spring that's been depressed and is just waiting to bounce free again. He was constantly scanning from left to right, assessing the situation, checking everything, every sight, every sound.

Tom subconsciously held his breath, he knew that if the least little thing looked out of place to Rhodes or he heard the slightest noise that sounded wrong he would bolt.

Having checked every direction Rhodes then turned and faced the block of flats, staring long and hard at the windows of Winston Small's flat located in the centre of the block.

'This is definitely going down Matt', Tom whispered.

'Yep, it certainly is', replied a fully concentrating Matt as he slowly moved the rifle back into his shoulder, placing the cross hairs of the scope onto the front door of the target premises.

Tom now began the running commentary on every movement that Junior Rhodes made. His whispered communications through his throat mike would make him the eyes of the entire team as they lay in wait for this would-be assassin.

In an even, hushed voice that was barely a whisper Tom said, 'All units I have radio priority. I want complete radio silence until I say otherwise, understood?'

Acknowledgement of the request came again by a series of clicks.

'All units be advised, subject is now out of the vehicle. He's been clocking points and has done a thorough visual on the target premises. Subject's now walking to the rear of the Sierra with keys in hand. Subject's opened the boot. Stand by.'

Having opened the boot of the vehicle Rhodes then spent another two or three minutes standing stock still staring out over the raised boot at the surrounding area before finally moving again.

'Subject's now leaning into the boot of the vehicle. I've no view. Stand by, stand by.'

Rhodes then removed the spare wheel and placed it by the side of the vehicle.

'All units, subject's removed the spare wheel from the boot and has placed a small package wrapped in sackcloth on the roof of the car. Spare wheel now being returned to the boot. Subject's also removed a three-quarter length black leather coat from the boot. The boot's now been closed. Subject's put on the coat and has removed blue plastic gloves from the right-hand pocket and has put them on. He's now removing the sacking from the package on the car roof. Stand by.'

Tom knew instantly what that package was.

The package contained a deadly sawn-off shotgun with silver metallic tape on the sawn down stock. The weapon was a double-barrelled, side by side shotgun. The barrels had been sawn off about two inches in front of the fore grip. The total length of the weapon now measured no more than sixteen inches.

It was a lethal weapon adapted for no other purpose than to kill and maim at very close quarters.

'All units be advised, subject's in possession of a sawn-off shotgun. The weapon is double barrelled and a side by side configuration. Subject has now broken the weapon and placed two cartridges into it. Weapon has been closed and is now loaded. The cartridges were removed from the right-hand coat pocket. The coat isn't fastened and the subject is holding the weapon in his left hand through the left-hand coat pocket. Subject's holding what appears to be a set of keys in his right hand. Stand by.'

Once again Rhodes stood stock still just staring up at the windows of Winston Small's flat.

Finally, he turned and began to walk slowly away from the Sierra and towards the stairwell of Roman Walk.

Tom remained icy calm and said, 'All units, subject now on the move. Walking slowly towards Green entrance. At the stairwell now, subject is walking up the stairs. He's picked up the pace and now looks like a man on a mission. Subject is on the landing and is approaching the target premises. I'll give you a countdown to the target premises. Five, four, three, two, one. Subject's now at the door, key is into the lock. Subject still holding loaded weapon in his left hand through his coat pocket. Door opening NOW!'

The door to the flat opened and Junior Rhodes stepped inside, pushing the door closed behind him.

Suddenly, night turned to day inside the flat as the Dragon lamps were switched on.

Tom heard shouts from within the flat, 'Armed Police! Get your hands out of your pockets! Do it now!'

This was followed by further shouted commands, 'On your knees! Face me! Look at me! Keep your hands where I can see them! Lie down, keep looking at me!'

Tom recognised the assertive voice of Sgt Graham Turner barking out the commands to Rhodes. From the commands being issued Tom also knew that Rhodes was being controlled and that the operation was almost over without a shot being fired.

Tom looked at Matt who was still fully focussed on the front door of the target premises. He was peering down the scope looking for the first sign of any drama, with just the slightest pressure already exerted on the trigger of his rifle.

Suddenly, Tom's ear piece crackled into life, 'All units from Sgt Turner, subject secured. Weapon and ammunition recovered. Let's get some transport in here.'

Chief Inspector Chambers responded to the message on the radio, 'All units. As soon as the CID have lodged your prisoner and obtained your statements, debrief at Headquarters. Well done all. Over.'

Tom and Matt immediately stood up and began to gather their equipment together. Both men did a final check of the area to ensure no kit had been inadvertently left behind on the factory floor.

Tom changed the channel of his radio back to that being used by the local officers and said, 'Pc Naylor to Dc Quinn over.'

'Go ahead Tom, over.'

'We're done here Nick; can you arrange for transport to get us out of our location?'

There was a chuckle then Nick said, 'Will do Tom. You sure I can't tempt you to stay in there for the hotel's full English?'

'I think we'll pass, thanks anyway.'

Within ten minutes Tom and Matt had been extricated from the disused factory and were on their way back to Radford Police Station to give their statements to the waiting CID officers.

As he drove away from the factory Nick Quinn said, 'Good job with the commentary Tom. I was listening into your channel to see what happened. Hopefully your statements won't take too long, I bet you're both knackered.'

'Roger that, I need to get home', said Matt.

After all the statements had been provided to the CID, the two vans containing the men of C Section left Radford Police Station and headed back to Headquarters.

Jim Chambers was waiting for them at Headquarters and was met with a small cheer when he stood the team down and announced that the debrief would keep until later that morning when the men returned to work.

Chambers was no fool, he could see that the men were exhausted after what had been a long and very tense operation.

After the weapons had been returned to the armoury and their kit stowed away, Tom turned to Matt and said, 'Have you spoken to Kate yet?'

'I've been trying her mobile ever since we got back to Radford nick, nothing. I've tried the house phone and that's going straight to answer phone as well. I need to get home and find out exactly what's happening.'

'Okay mate, I'm sure everything's fine, there'll be a perfectly feasible explanation. I bet she's gone to bed early and is out like a light. It's very late now, or should I say it's very early.'

'I don't doubt that she's probably gone to bed early, the question is who with?', said Matt bitterly before letting out a resigned sigh.

'I'll see you later Tom.'

CHAPTER 27

1.00am 22nd July 1987
Linby Village, Nottinghamshire

Kate Jarvis had spent most of the night at the small cottage owned by Tom Naylor. When it became clear that Matt wasn't going to be home anytime soon she had driven to the cottage for a talk with Tom's girlfriend, Bev Wilson.

The last call she had received from the mysterious, threatening voice that was plaguing her life, had instructed her to leave home with all the documentary evidence for Tate's appeal in her Range Rover and drive to a small hotel just outside Lincoln. The voice told her she would be contacted the next morning with further instructions.

Kate had done as instructed, but as she began to drive away from her house in Oxton, she suddenly felt the need to talk to a friend. At that time of night, the only person she could think of to confide in was Bev.

Although from very different backgrounds, the two women had become close after initially meeting through their respective partners.

Bev immediately realised something was drastically wrong as soon as a tearful Kate had turned up on the doorstep just after nine o'clock that night. She had opened a bottle of wine and listened sympathetically as Kate explained that she was leaving Matt and that it was the hardest decision she'd ever had to make.

Desperately, Bev had tried to change her friends mind, giving any number of ways that she could try to rekindle her relationship and save her marriage. It had made no difference. Whatever tack Bev tried, Kate was adamant and towards the end of the night she reluctantly agreed to pass on a message to Matt on her friend's behalf, acknowledging that it would have been virtually impossible for Kate to give such a message herself.

The two women embraced and Kate, her voice cracking with emotion, said, 'Bev, you're such a good friend to me and I'm so sorry to put you in this position, but if I don't leave now I never will. If Matt knew the truth of the situation, believe me he would understand that what I'm doing is the best thing for both of us.'

Bev was puzzled by this comment but didn't press her friend, instead she said quietly, 'Don't worry sweetheart, I'll make it clear to Matt that you still love him and that all you need is a little space.'

'Thanks, I knew I could rely on you to help me.'

Placing the half full glass of red wine on the table, Kate stood up and walked out of the front door, leaving a stunned Bev trailing in her wake. Bev stopped at the front door of the cottage and called after her friend, 'Kate, I don't really know what's going on here, but I think there's far more to this than what you're telling me. You're my friend and you know you can tell me anything and it will remain in the strictest confidence. I won't breathe a word to a soul, least of all Tom. What is it? What's wrong?'

Kate turned on the cottage path and faced Bev. She said nothing straight away as she could feel the tears starting to well up in her eyes, then she suddenly blurted out, 'I'm sorry Bev, I've got to go.'

'Ok sweetheart, but please take care. If you need anything just call me, please. Promise me that much. Stay in touch, I'm here if you need me, okay?'

Kate nodded, then got into her Range Rover. She sat motionless in the car with tears streaming down her face.

After a couple of minutes, she had regained her composure. She wiped her eyes and started the powerful V8 engine. Very slowly she drove the Range Rover away from the cottage down the unlit country lane.

The driver of a black Mercedes van parked fifty yards down the lane also started his vehicle's engine and slowly began to follow the Range Rover. The driver never turned the van's lights on and the vehicle moved along the lane in darkness.

Kate Jarvis was totally unaware of the black van's presence.

As the lane became narrower, bordered on each side by a high hedgerow, the Mercedes began to close on the Range Rover.

Two miles further down the narrow lane and Kate slowed her vehicle to a stop at a T junction. The Mercedes van was deliberately driven into the rear of the Range Rover. It wasn't a significant collision but it was enough for Kate to be shocked and dazed by the impact.

As she shook her head and rubbed the nape of her neck both the front doors of the Range Rover were suddenly ripped open by two men dressed totally in black and wearing black ski masks.

The first thing Kate registered was that the man who had opened the passenger door was holding what looked like a black handgun in his right hand which was pointed at her chest.

Before she could speak she saw a small dart trailing a wire had been fired from the gun. The dart slammed into her chest just above her breasts. Instantly she felt her entire body go into spasm, writhing uncontrollably in a massive convulsion as hundreds of volts passed through her.

The Taser had done its work; she immediately lapsed into unconsciousness.

Moving quickly, the two men dragged her from the Range Rover and placed her unceremoniously into the back of the Mercedes. One of the men bound her ankles and wrists, tied a blindfold tightly round her eyes and finally placed a gag in her mouth. The other man returned to the Range Rover carrying two full petrol cans.

Quickly and efficiently, he poured petrol from the cans all over the interior of the vehicle, paying particular attention to the boxes of documentary evidence.

Once the cans were empty, he stepped back and nonchalantly tossed a lit match into the open passenger door. He hastily stepped back further as the vehicle erupted into a huge ball of flame.

In that instant, every scrap of documentary evidence and original exhibits ready for the High Court appeal of Barry Tate was consumed by the intense fireball.

Both men got into the front of the Mercedes and it was driven away at speed down the dark country lanes. In the back of the van, Kate slowly began to come to her senses. She soon realised that she was now bound, gagged and blindfolded. She was lying on her side on a mattress on the floor of the van. As the vehicle was driven at speed through the winding lanes, the motion caused her to roll from one side of the mattress to the other. On sharp bends she would end up hurtling into the side walls of the van.

Her whole body ached from head to foot and her head was pounding as if she had the migraine from hell.

Her only thought was for her husband. She tried to speak his name but the word was stifled in her throat because of the cloying gag that had been thrust deep into her mouth.

She began to sob, feeling the warm tears trickling down her cheeks and wondered if she would ever see her husband again.

CHAPTER 28

3.30am 22nd July 1987
Linby Village, Nottinghamshire

Finally, Tom Naylor drove his car onto the small driveway of his cottage after what had been an extremely long and eventful day. It was now almost three thirty in the morning and Tom was exhausted.

The adrenalin surge he'd experienced as the operation to arrest Junior Rhodes had come to a successful conclusion had long since worn off and his body was starting to feel like it had been awake almost twenty-four hours.

He switched the ignition off and was surprised to see the lights in the kitchen of the cottage were still on. He knew his girlfriend didn't start her shift as a paramedic until later that morning.

There wasn't any reason for the lights to be on.

As he got out of the car the front door of the cottage burst open and Bev emerged from inside to greet him. She flung her arms around his neck and hugged him closely. It was obvious she was upset and Tom could see that she had been crying.

Holding both her shoulders he looked her in the face and said urgently, 'What is it sweetheart, what's wrong?'

With more tears not far away she blurted out, 'It's Kate, she's left Matt.'

Tom ushered a now distraught Bev back inside the cottage, walked in the kitchen and put the kettle on. He made them both a coffee and listened as she told him about the events of the previous night, repeating word for word what Kate had told her earlier.

Having composed herself Bev said quietly, 'It doesn't make any sense. It's blatantly obvious that she's still madly in love with the bloke.'

She looked thoughtful for a moment then said, 'There was something she said before she left that sounded weird. Something about Matt knowing the truth. If he did, then he would understand. I just don't get it, they always look so great together.'

'I know they do, he only confided in me today that they were having problems. I didn't think for one minute they were this bad. He's going to be arriving home shortly to an empty house. He'll be devastated. Do you think I should drive over there and make sure he's okay?'

'You look shattered. I don't think you should be driving anywhere. Just drink your coffee and get off to bed. He won't thank you for turning up like some half-arsed John Wayne character. If he wants to talk to anyone I'm sure you'll be the first person he calls.'

He knew that Bev was talking sense. If the boot had been on the other foot he wouldn't have wanted to talk to anyone. He would just want a stiff whiskey and some time alone to try and make sense of it all.

Just as Tom drained the last of the coffee from his mug, the telephone started to ring.

Tom answered the phone and said wearily, 'Tom Naylor.'
It was Matt.

'Mate, I've just got home. Something's happened, I need to see you right now.'

Tom was shocked, there was something in the tone of his friend's voice that he'd never heard before.

Matt sounded frightened.

Instantly, any thoughts of fatigue vanished and without pausing to think Tom said, 'Okay, stay where you are mate. I'm on my way.'

He turned to Bev who was standing next to him with a very worried look on her face.

'That was Matt. I don't know what the hell's going on at his house, but something's badly wrong. He sounded terrified and that's something I've never heard before. I'm going over there.'

'Okay sweetheart, but please take your time. You won't be able to do anyone any good if you wrap your car round a tree. Drive carefully, remember you've already been awake for nearly twenty-four hours. In fact, stuff my shift, I'll drive you over there.'

There had been something in Matt's voice that had also unnerved Tom and he said quickly, 'I'll go myself, I don't know what's happening over there yet. I'll be careful and take my time. Don't worry. Go back to bed and try and get some sleep before you start your shift.'

She knew it was pointless to argue and watched from the doorway as Tom jumped back in his car and reversed back out onto the lane to make the short drive over to Oxton village.

CHAPTER 29

4.00am 22nd July 1987
Oxton Village, Nottinghamshire

Twenty minutes later and Tom drove his car through the open wrought iron gates and onto the large driveway of Matt's house in Oxton. He got out of his car and was shocked to see that although the large Georgian style house was in complete darkness, the front door was open.

Matt's car was on the driveway but there was no sign of Kate's Range Rover.

Something didn't feel right and Tom felt a familiar surge of adrenalin course through his body.

Suddenly, his senses were once again fully alert and stealthily he made his way towards the open front door trying his best to lessen the sound his boots made on the gravel driveway.

Using the back of his hand he pushed the front door wide open and crouched low ready to launch himself into an attack if confronted.

The door swung gently open and nothing happened.

It was a dark night with no moon, dawn was still an hour away from breaking and the windowless hallway of the house remained black and in deep shadow. He crept inside, staying low. He peered hard into the shadows and waited for his eyes to become accustomed to the low light.

After a few seconds he could make out a hunched figure squatting on the floor at the far end of the hallway.

Suddenly he heard his friend's voice; it was little more than a husky whisper, 'They've got Kate.'

Tom walked over and helped Matt to his feet.

'What are you talking about? Nobody's got Kate, she's been over at ours all night chatting to Bev. She's fine.'

Matt spoke in a voice devoid of all emotion, 'She's not fine. I've just had a phone call from a bloke who told me they've kidnapped her. He described to me in great detail how they'd watched her leave your place and how they followed her and took her. They said they'd be back in touch later today with instructions I have to follow if I want to get her back alive.'

For the first time his voice cracked with emotion, 'I was left in no doubt that if I even thought about contacting the Police they'd kill her. I just don't know what to do mate.'

Then suddenly the emotion in his voice was replaced by a steely coldness,

'Tom if they hurt her, I'll hunt these bastards down and sure as night follows day, I'll take the last breath from their bodies.'

Tom took his friend into the lounge and sat him down, 'Come on mate, we need to think this through properly so we can decide what we're going to do.'

'No Tom! What we're going to do is exactly fuck all! I need to wait and see what it is they want from me.'

'No mate, that's not the way, we need to get people involved. You can't deal with something like this on your own.'

'Listen to me, I respect you like a brother but if you go behind my back on this and tell anyone what's happening until I know what I'm dealing with and Kate comes to any harm, be in no doubt I'll do you as well.'

Tom was shocked, he knew that at that very moment Matt meant every word he was saying.

Suddenly, the tense atmosphere in the house was interrupted by flashing blue lights illuminating the lounge. The blue lights were turned off and the house was plunged into darkness again. Matt stood up, looked out of the window and saw a Traffic patrol car on the driveway.

He turned to Tom and hissed, 'Not a word.'

Matt turned the hall lights on, wiped his face and walked to the front door.

Having regained his composure, he stepped out onto the driveway and confronted the first of the Traffic officers, 'Is everything okay, mate?'

The uniformed cop said, 'Are you Mr Matt Jarvis?'

Matt nodded.

Tom had walked out of the house behind Matt, recognising the older of the two Traffic officers he said, 'Is that Dave Andrews? What brings you out here, Dave?'

'Hello Tom, I need to speak to Mr Jarvis here.'

'Matt's job as well Dave, he works on Special Ops with me.'

Pc Andrews turned to face Matt and said, 'Sorry Matt, I didn't realise. I'm afraid there's been an accident over at Calverton. We've found a burned-out Range Rover. The rear registration plate was about the only thing not destroyed by fire. I think it's only survived because it was hanging off the vehicle after a rear end shunt. The vehicle's registered to Kate Jarvis of this address, is that your wife, Matt?'

Matt seemed to wobble slightly, Tom stepped next to him to make sure he didn't go down.

Matt looked at the officer and said quietly, 'Was anyone found inside the vehicle?'

Pc Andrews replied, 'Nobody was in it, but it's a total write off. Was your wife driving the vehicle tonight?'

Matt straightened and Tom could see that his friend was once again analysing things, 'No. My wife's staying at her mother's house tonight, I drove her over there yesterday. I was just about to call the Police and report her Range Rover stolen. I've been on a job with Tom at Radford all night and when I got back a short time ago I saw that her car was missing from the driveway and the gates were open. It must have been nicked last night when we were both out.'

Pc Dave Andrews had been on the traffic department for ten years and had over fifteen years' service. In that time, he had probably heard every line going. He knew immediately that he was being fed a crock of shit.

Andrews looked across at Tom who nodded slowly as though confirming Matt's version of events.

There was a brief pause as Pc Andrews considered carefully what to say next, 'Look Matt, if you want to report your wife's vehicle as stolen I'll take the essential details now and call you tomorrow for the rest. The burned-out wreck is being lifted to Johnsons Scrap Yard as we speak. There was nothing left of any value inside the vehicle. I understand that you're on the job, so I know you'll get back to me if anything changes. Okay?'

'Okay thanks for that, I'll talk to you tomorrow. Now if you don't mind, me and Tom are absolutely knackered, we're going to have a quick drink before Tom sets off for home.'

'No problem.'

Dave Andrews then looked at Tom and said, 'Just the one Tom, don't want you over the limit do we?'

Tom looked at the Traffic man knowingly and said quickly, 'Okay Dave, just the one', before adding pointedly, 'and Dave, thanks for that.'

Pc Andrews nodded and the two Traffic officers got back in their patrol car and reversed off the driveway.

As soon as the Traffic car had gone, Tom rounded on his friend, 'What the fuck are you doing? You can't lie to them.'

'Tom, I'll do whatever it takes. Thanks for coming over, but do me a favour now and go home. I'm fine and you look out on your feet. You're just going to have to let me sort this out in my own way. I'll call you later this morning.'

'Okay, I'll go home, just promise me you won't make any rash decisions without at least talking to me first. I'm your mate and whatever these fuckers want, I know that between us we can sort it out and get Kate back to you in one piece.'

'I promise I'll call you first thing. As soon as I've heard from them again. Okay?'

Tom got back into his car and drove away, wondering what news tomorrow's phone call would bring.

CHAPTER 30

8.30am 22nd July 1987
Linby Village, Nottinghamshire

The knocking on the front door of the cottage was becoming louder and ever more insistent. Slowly turning over in bed Tom looked wearily at the radio alarm clock on the bedside cabinet. He groaned when he saw that the time was just after half past eight in the morning.

He hadn't got into bed until just before four thirty that morning and now just four hours later it seemed that someone was determined to drag him out of his much-needed sleep.

His girlfriend had left for work much earlier without disturbing him.

Dragging himself out of bed he yelled, 'Alright, alright I'm coming. Hold your horses!'

Barely awake he staggered down the narrow flight of stone stairs to the front door. He reached for the key from the table in the hallway and opened the door.

As soon as the door opened a breathless Matt pushed past him and strode into the kitchen.

He turned to face Tom and leaned against the sink with his hands held up in an apologetic gesture, 'First of all Tom, let me apologise for anything I said that was out of order. I didn't really know what I was saying, understandably I was a little stressed.'

In an instant all of the dramatic events of earlier that morning came flooding back to Tom.

He reached for the kettle, filled it from the cold tap, flicked the switch to boil it and asked, 'Have you had any more messages?'

'Yes, they called me at eight o'clock this morning.'

Tom put coffee, milk and sugar into two mugs, poured the boiling water in and said, 'Well, what's happening? Why have they kidnapped Kate?'

Taking the mug filled with hot coffee from Tom he said, 'It's that bastard Barry Tate who's behind it all. They've told me this is what I've got to do if I want to see my wife again. They want me to make it common knowledge later today that Kate's walked out on me. I've got to make it clear that the reason she's gone, is because I pressured her into presenting false evidence in Barry Tate's original trial. I've also got to inform the media that my wife has destroyed all the documentary evidence, exhibits and paperwork that she brought home from Chambers last week and that her reason for doing this was because she didn't want to perjure herself further.'

'I don't understand, how's all that going to help Barry Tate?'

'Tom, it's simple. Once I've spread the reason why she's left me, it will then be leaked to the press. Apparently, all the documentary evidence was in her Range Rover when it was burned out by the kidnappers. The main prosecution witness, Tony Banks, is dead. Do you remember that Dc telling us last night that Banks had been murdered in Wakefield Prison? Kate will be held captive so she can't appear at the Royal Courts of Justice in London to represent the Crown at Tate's appeal next week. All of these things taken together will be more than enough ammunition for his defence barristers to call the original trial a mistrial and claim that his original conviction is unsound. The Crown will be left with no option but to offer no evidence and that evil bastard Barry Tate will walk free.'

'Bloody hell, somebody's gone to an awful lot of trouble to set this up. It does all make perfect sense. Have they said anything about what they intend to do with Kate if and when Tate is released?'

'They've told me that if I do exactly what I've been asked, then as soon as Barry Tate walks away from the High Court as a free man, they'll immediately release her unharmed. They stressed to me that if anything goes wrong and Tate isn't released from custody, they won't hesitate to kill her.'

'Do you believe that? Do you honestly think she will be released?'

'I've got to believe it Tom, what choice do I have? I'm backed into a corner here, I've no option but to do exactly as they say. I've got to try and get my wife away from their clutches. If everything goes to plan and I do get her back at some stage further down the line I'll deal with Barry fucking Tate personally. I'll track him down and kill him myself.'

Tom looked squarely at his friend, 'You know I've got your back on this and we'll deal with it however you want, but no more talk about killing Tate. Once we've got Kate safely back we'll go after Tate properly. You do realise that as soon as you mention one word of this story you'll be suspended and there'll be no contact from me or anyone else on the Force? Are you sure you don't want to go to Jim Chambers and tell him the truth about what's happening?'

'I can't risk it Tom. I've got to do what they've told me to do and see what happens. If anything does happen to Kate, I can't make you any promises about Tate. There's only a couple of weeks before Tate's appeal is due to be heard at the High Court. I'd better get cracking, I've got to set up this whole bullshit story, so the press can get wind of it.'

Matt made his way to the door of the cottage.

Tom said, 'Just a second. Before you do anything, let me have the number of that new mobile phone Kate bought for you. That way if for any reason I need to get a message to you I can. If you need anything, anything at all mate, call me and I'll be there for you. If you can't get hold of me, call Bev at Mansfield Ambulance Station and leave me a message.'

'Thanks Tom, I'll call you with the mobile number before I do anything else. I know you think I'm nuts, but I've got to try and get her back.'

Matt thrust his hands deep into his jacket pockets and stalked down the driveway to his car. He turned, held up a hand, got in the car and sped off down the lane.

Later that day as Tom was getting ready to make his way into Headquarters for the debrief of the previous night's operation, he was listening to the radio in the kitchen. The twelve o'clock news came on and the lead story was one of police corruption at the original trial of Nottingham businessman, Barry Tate. The reporter went on to say that a serving Police Officer, a member of the Special Operations Unit no less, had been suspended from duty pending a full investigation. The reporter then gave an opinion on whether this revelation would have any bearing on Mr Tate's forthcoming appeal at the High Court in London next week.

Tom muttered, 'Christ mate, you didn't waste any time.'

He picked up the phone and dialled the number Matt had given him for his new mobile phone.

It went straight to answerphone.

Tom didn't leave a message, instead he phoned Mansfield Ambulance Station only to be told by a somewhat puzzled Bev that Matt hadn't called and he hadn't left any messages.

She had demanded to know exactly what the hell was going on. Tom ignored her remonstrations and told her he would talk to her properly later when they were both at home. He knew he could bluff it out when he got home, he had no intention of talking to anybody about what was happening, least of all Bev.

Tom had an uneasy feeling about the whole thing. He'd seen the look on Matt's face when he left the cottage earlier, he just hoped that his friend wasn't about to do something that would ruin the rest of his life.

CHAPTER 31

3.00pm 28th July 1987
Newark Police Station, Nottinghamshire

The strange convoy of scruffy, rusting vehicles made its way slowly into the rear yard of Newark Police Station well away from the prying eyes of the general public. The small column consisted of two battered old saloon cars, an unwashed light blue Land Rover Defender and a rusting cream coloured Comma van.

Each vehicle contained two men from C Section.

It had been almost a week since Matt Jarvis had been suspended from duty and this operation at Newark had come as a welcome relief to Tom, who was tired of having to bat off the well meaning but unwanted enquiries made by his colleagues.

When the request for assistance had come in from Newark CID to see if the Special Operations Unit had the capability to carry out a vehicle surveillance, the answer from Jim Chambers had been a resounding yes. The newly formed Tactical Surveillance Unit were already committed and the request was urgent as an offence was being planned for that evening.

Tom had been overjoyed. At least this operation will give them all something else to think about, he thought.

As the men got out of the various vehicles, they squinted against the strong late afternoon sunshine.

Steve Grey got out of the Land Rover, stretched and said, 'Where's the briefing, Sarge?'

Sgt Turner responded to the question by addressing all the men in the courtyard, 'Briefing's upstairs in the CID office. We're meeting Dc Sue Jenkins, she's got all the background for tonight's job.'

The eight men made their way through the back door of the police station, up a flight of stone steps and into the spacious CID office.

Waiting for them was Dc Jenkins and Chief Inspector Chambers.

A slightly apprehensive Sue Jenkins said, 'Come in gents, take a seat. Help yourself to a tea or coffee if you want one.'

Sue hated carrying out briefings and looking at this wild bunch of characters sitting down in front of her, this one was certainly going to be interesting.

As she waited for a couple of the men to get a hot drink and sit down, she cast her eyes around the room. Looking at the men from the Special Operations Unit in front of her now, she would never in a million years have guessed their occupation.

Before leaving headquarters, the men had been told they would be required to carry out a covert surveillance on a vehicle. They were instructed to draw two pool cars from the Transport Manager and to take the Land Rover and Comma van as support. They had also been told to take covert communication sets and to dress appropriately for surveillance.

As she glanced around the room at the various T Shirts, ripped and scruffy jeans, baseball caps and training shoes being worn by the men she thought to herself that they had certainly succeeded in following the last part of the instructions.

As the last of the men sat down, Sgt Turner smiled at Sue and said, 'Ready when you are detective, we're all ears.'

Sue took a deep breath and began the briefing, 'Over a period of seven weeks there have been four burglaries at remote country houses in this area, that we believe are all linked and being carried out by the same team of offenders. The MO on all the burglaries is identical. Entry has been gained in exactly the same manner on each occasion and it's only ever cash that's stolen. Valuable jewellery and antiques worth a lot of money haven't been touched.'

Having now got the men's undivided attention, she took another deep breath and continued, 'The signature of these offences has been the totally disproportionate amount of violence used against elderly occupants. To be brutally frank, it's a miracle that none of the victims were killed; all have been left with serious, life altering injuries. There's very little left at the scenes forensically, the offenders always wear gloves and on the few occasions they've been seen by the victims they were wearing masks.'

She continued, 'A week ago, we got a little breakthrough in the case. An informant has given the names of two individuals who may be responsible for these offences. Well, the informant actually gave me just the one name. He thinks the people responsible for these offences are twin brothers named Smith from the gypsy camp on Tanley Road, just outside of town.'

There were audible groans from some of the men and a voice at the back said loudly, 'Smith! On the Tanley site, well that should narrow it down a bit!'

Sgt Turner snapped, 'Shut it, settle down and listen!'

Untroubled by the brief interruption Sue continued, 'The informant also told me that the brothers are planning another burglary tonight and that they'll be using an orange coloured Ford Transit van as transport. I've done all the research I can do on Tanley Road and the only people who come close to fitting the description given to me by the informant are twin brothers called Jimmy and Nathan Smith.'

Sue paused and began passing round mug shot style photographs of the two brothers.

She continued, 'These photographs were taken when the brothers were last arrested, following a brawl outside one of the town centre pubs about a year ago. Both of them are extremely violent, whenever they've been arrested in the past, it's been like a war zone trying to bring them in. They've both got numerous convictions for assaulting the police, the earliest being when they were just twelve years old. Quite simply, they're a nightmare. The only other associate I can find for the brothers on the Tanley Road site is a young lad called Danny Lee. It would appear that Lee's a bit of a soft lad, but for some reason the brothers have taken a shine to him. There's nothing on our systems for Danny Lee, at the moment he has no previous convictions.'

Sgt Turner asked, 'Do we have any idea why these two have suddenly started committing this series of burglaries?'

'From what my informant says it would appear that the motivation for the burglaries is to fund the brothers raging drug addictions. Are there any other questions?'

Tom said, 'Exactly how reliable is this informant of yours? Do you think it's good information?'

'All I can say about my informant is that he's been

extremely reliable in the past, but as we all know, there are no cast iron guarantees when it comes to informants.'

'Fair enough', agreed Tom.

The room was quiet.

Jim Chambers now spoke up, 'Thanks Sue, I'll take it from here, but if I say anything that's wrong feel free to jump in at any point.'

Sgt Turner stepped forward to join his Chief Inspector at the front of the small gathering. Sue Jenkins sat down next to Tom in the seat vacated by Sergeant Turner.

Chief Inspector Chambers said, 'Right lads, fortunately for us there's only one way for vehicles to get in and out of the Tanley Road gypsy site. So, bearing that in mind, this is the plan. You'll plot up at the end of the lane, observe the orange Transit van as it leaves the site and then put a loose surveillance on it until the brothers decide to stop and carry out the burglary. You'll then deploy on foot and take them out as they emerge from the attacked premises with their spoils. However, if the attacked property looks as though it's occupied, just nick them as they break in to the property. We can't afford to let some poor sod get a good hiding or worse just so our case against them is stronger. Is that understood? Are there any questions?'

The men remained silent, it was a very straightforward plan.

Sgt Turner then split the men into pairs and allocated vehicles and call signs to be used during the surveillance. The plan would have to remain somewhat fluid as the intended target premises were as yet unknown.

As the men were getting ready to leave the CID office, Sue Jenkins shouted above the noise, 'I'll be travelling about a mile behind your surveillance with Dc Thomas. We'll be available to interview the brothers should we be lucky enough to get a result.'

Steve Grey grinned at her and said, 'This is C Section, detective, luck doesn't come into it.'

As one, the other men groaned at Steve's terrible attempt at humour, then made their way back to the cars in the back yard ready to commence the operation.

CHAPTER 32

9.00pm 28th July 1987
Tanley Road Gypsy Camp, Newark,
Nottinghamshire

'Oh, nice of you to join us at last, daft lad!'

The voice belonged to Nathan Smith and the barbed, hostile comment was aimed towards Danny Lee as he walked towards Nathan and his brother Jimmy.

Jimmy grinned at Danny and said, 'Leave the kid alone Nat.'

Jimmy put his arm around the youngster's shoulder and said, 'Don't look so worried Danny, we've got a nice easy job tonight. No rough stuff required this time, just a little bit of heavy lifting.'

Danny breathed a sigh of relief and grinned a nervous smile. The reason for his late arrival was due to the fact that he'd very nearly not shown up at all. It was only his fear of the brothers that finally made his mind up to join them. The young teenager had been totally sickened by the brutal and needless attack on the old man at the last burglary. There had been violence on all the other jobs but this was a different level, at one point he genuinely believed that Nathan was going to kill the old man.

Danny had had no problem with committing offences, he would have gladly stolen from the Pope if it meant he could buy more amphetamine, but he didn't see why they had to nearly kill some poor old sod that was pissing himself with fear anyway. Ever since the brothers had introduced him to amphetamines, Danny couldn't get enough of the feeling of euphoria the drug gave him. Lifting him, albeit fleetingly, from his dull, downtrodden, humdrum existence.

Danny had made his mind up, after tonight's job he would slowly try and distance himself from the Smith brothers. He felt confident enough to do jobs on his own now, after all he was the one who always got into the houses. He would still be able to make enough money to buy his fix.

For now, though, he was committed to tonight's job so he listened carefully to what Jimmy was saying, 'Right lads' tonight we're taking a little road trip.'

Nathan said impatiently, 'Where to?'

'If you'd just shut your mouth for a minute, I'll tell you!'

Nathan huffed and Jimmy continued, 'There's a farmhouse out near Sleaford that's got a really old chest inside, like really old from when Oliver Cromwell was a lad. At least that's what Fat Baz reckons anyway. He tried to buy the bloody thing from the farmer for his antique shop in town, but the farmer was having none of it and basically told Baz to fuck off out of the farmhouse. Anyway, Fat Baz really wants this bloody thing, says it's worth a small fortune. He's found out from somebody that this farmer has had to go into hospital for an operation and the farmhouse is unoccupied at the moment. His neighbour only checks on the property once a day, and that's always in the morning. So, the plan is we're going to drive over to Sleaford in the Transit tonight and pick up the chest. Sweet as a nut with no drama.'

Nathan asked, 'What Transit?'

'I've borrowed Mickey Delaney's.'

'What? That fucking bright orange thing that's being held together by the rust and filler?'

'That's the one, what's your problem?'

'Fuck me Jimmy, I'll be surprised if that wreck gets us down the lane never mind over to Sleaford and back!'

'Don't worry, Mickey says it's a good little runner. It will get us there, anyway, we need a van to move the chest.'

Nathan was unimpressed, 'And what the fuck are we supposed to with a fucking antique chest?'

Getting sick of his sniping Jimmy slapped Nathan hard across the side of his head, 'Are you being deliberately thick to wind me up? Just leave the thinking to me numb nuts. I've already agreed a price with Fat Baz. He's going to give me six grand for the chest. How does two grand each sound boys?'

Nathan was now grinning from ear to ear, 'Fuck me bruv, why didn't you say? What are we waiting for, let's go!'

CHAPTER 33

9.30pm 28th July 1987
Tanley Road Gypsy Camp, Newark,
Nottinghamshire

The sky was turning that strange purple colour that you only ever see at the end of a really hot summer's day.

The twilight was slowly starting to fade and night was gradually creeping across the sky when Graham Turner finally broke radio silence, 'All units be aware, I have a visual on an orange Ford Transit making its way along Tanley Road towards our location. Let's get ready gentlemen, this is looking good for our target vehicle. As soon as I know which exit they're taking off the roundabout I'll call it. Be in position to move off and stand by for my message.'

The three teams of two acknowledged the message and started the engines of their respective vehicles ready to follow the Transit.

The Transit drove quickly past the old Comma van parked at the end of Tanley Road that contained Graham Turner and Steve Grey.

As the vehicle passed him, Graham could see the Transit contained three occupants spread across the front seat.

As soon as the Transit passed his location he grabbed his radio and said, 'This is definitely our target vehicle. Registration number is Golf Four Nine Two Hotel Bravo

Tango. It's three up with Jimmy Smith driving. Approaching the roundabout now. Stand by.'

Tom Naylor and Jack Rimmer were in one of the battered saloon cars and were waiting on the forecourt of the garage located just off the first exit of the roundabout. This exit covered the A.46 road and was the most probable exit for the target vehicle as it led straight out into Lincolnshire. Their call sign was Charlie Two.

The rest of the surveillance team comprised of Tony Garner and Luke Goddard who were in the other saloon car, with the call sign Charlie three. Wayne Hope and Eddie Keane driving the Land Rover Defender, call sign Charlie four and finally Sgt Turner and Steve Grey in the Comma van, call sign Charlie one.

Sgt Turner observed the Transit as it approached the roundabout and said, 'There's a nearside indication, looks like the target vehicle's heading for the first exit onto the A46. Charlie two stand by.'

As the Transit turned onto the A46, Jack Rimmer allowed one other vehicle to follow it before driving off the garage forecourt and slotting in behind.

Tom picked up the radio and said, 'Charlie two has the eyeball, we're following the target vehicle onto the A46 direction towards Lincoln. We've got one car for cover. Steady at fifty miles an hour. Convoy check please.'

The rest of the surveillance team quickly slotted in behind Tom's vehicle and contacted Tom by radio, relaying their positions in the convoy.

At the first roundabout, the Transit took the second exit towards Sleaford and Tom allowed Charlie four to move forward and take the eyeball. Eddie Keane was driving and maintained a discreet distance behind the Transit whilst Wayne Hope provided a running commentary over the radio, letting the rest of the team know the target vehicle's direction, speed and current location.

It became obvious to the team at an early stage that the suspects in the target vehicle were not surveillance conscious and were oblivious to the fact that they were being followed. Nevertheless, as a precaution, the men from C Section employed best practice and continually changed their positions in the convoy so that a different vehicle would appear in the rear-view mirror should anyone in the target vehicle start to check behind them.

The vehicle surveillance was uneventful.

A constant stream of communication among the team using the back to back facility on the radio allowed everyone involved to know exactly what was happening at all times. Provided the convoy stayed quite tight the radios would provide comms; if they got scattered, they would have a problem.

Dc Jenkins, following the surveillance team, stayed in close enough proximity to hear the radio traffic.

The target vehicle was driven further and further into the Lincolnshire countryside, heading towards the quiet market town of Sleaford. As the roads became more and more deserted, the team had to drop back further and further. Even more care was needed when darkness fell and the headlights of the surveillance team's vehicles were at risk of being spotted by the suspects.

Almost ten miles from Sleaford, the target vehicle was driven through the pretty village of Fulbeck on the main A17 road. As it left the small village, Wayne Hope spoke over the radio, 'From Charlie four to all units. I have brake lights on the target vehicle. Target has made a right turn off the main and is now travelling down what looks like a farm track. Stand by.'

Eddie Keane drove slowly past the track, there was a sign at the entrance to the lane.

Wayne Hope said, 'All units, target vehicle is now driving towards White Post Farm. I will drive by, park up and meet you by the entrance. Over.'

Having parked the Land Rover by the side of the road some fifty yards from the entrance, Wayne Hope and Eddie Keane jogged back to the entrance to White Post Farm. Already waiting for them, were the six other members of the surveillance team. They'd abandoned their vehicles on the lane about twenty yards away on the other side of the farm entrance.

From their location, the men peered through the darkness down the small valley towards White Post Farm some two hundred yards away. All the buildings were in total darkness, except for the large stone farmhouse now illuminated by the headlights of the target vehicle that had parked up directly outside.

Suddenly, the lights on the target vehicle were extinguished, plunging the whole area back into darkness. Still no lights came on in either the farmhouse or any of the outbuildings.

Graham Turner addressed the team in a voice that was barely a whisper, 'This is looking good. The farmhouse must be unoccupied. These fuckers must know there's no one at home, no way would they have risked driving straight down to the house if they didn't already know it was going to be empty. Right, let's make our way down to the target vehicle. I don't need to tell you that stealth and the element of surprise are both going to be vital if we're to get the upper hand on these nasty fuckers. We get down there, we get into position, then wait for them to emerge from the farmhouse. As they're making their way back to the vehicle with whatever loot they're carrying, we strike. Put your covert ear pieces onto the lowest setting and wait for me to call the strike. Any questions?'

The silence was deafening.

Graham Turner spoke quietly into his radio, 'Sgt Turner to Dc Jenkins, over.'

'Go ahead, over.'

'We're at the White Post Farm just through the village of Fulbeck. We're deploying on foot. Stand by and await my next signal, over.'

'Received that, over.'

Having updated Sue Jenkins, Graham said, 'Right lads, let's go.'

The team knew exactly what was now expected of them and they stealthily set off in Indian file down to the farmhouse in the valley below.

Within five minutes, the men from C Section were outside the farmhouse and had surrounded the target vehicle. Their eyes had very quickly become accustomed to the poor light and they were now hidden in various positions around the farmyard lying in wait.

Still in the same pairs as they were in the vehicles, they waited patiently for the suspects to emerge from the dark farmhouse. Every so often they would see the flash of a torch beam and hear muffled talking and laughter from within the old building.

Tom and Jack were crouched behind a large wooden planter made from old railway sleepers, just to the right of the front door of the farmhouse. The smell of creosote from the sleepers was strong but the planter afforded good concealment. From their location they could see that the front door had been kicked off its hinges, it was splintered and hanging half on and half off the door frame.

Tom could clearly hear the intruders approaching the smashed door from within. He could hear sounds of exertion, grunts and groans. The three men were clearly straining with something large and heavy.

Finally, he heard voices, 'Nathan, get rid of the door, its hanging in the way, shift it!'

A burly figure stepped forward and kicked at the remaining door hinge with heavy boots, after the second kick the door relinquished its flimsy hold and fell from the frame.

The figure immediately stepped back inside the farmhouse and the sounds of exertion began again.

He could hear angry voices now, 'For fuck's sake Jimmy, you didn't say anything about this fucking thing weighing a ton!'

'That's because I didn't know, numb nuts, now stop your bloody whining, get on that end and start pushing while I drag the bloody thing.'

Tom suddenly saw three figures emerge from the darkness of the farmhouse and out into the yard at the front of the house. Two of the figures were sturdy thick set individuals, the third man slighter and much shorter.

One of the larger figures threw something towards the smaller man and said under his breath, 'Danny! Here's the keys, get the back doors open, pronto!'

The small man stepped away from the front door of the farmhouse and opened the two back doors of the Transit van.

As soon as the doors to the vehicle were opened, all three men returned inside the farmhouse. Seconds later they emerged struggling under the weight of a very large, obviously heavy ornate wooden chest.

The heavy-set man nearest to where Tom and Jack were waiting, lowered the chest to the ground at the back of the Transit doors, stood up straight and complained loudly, 'Jimmy, I'm telling you bruv, there's no way we're going to be able to lift this fucking thing into the van!'

'Will you stop bitching? We'll manage it between the three of us. Just think about that two grand Nat!'

The men from C Section, hiding in the shadows, looked on as the three men began to struggle to raise the huge chest, desperately trying to lift it into the rear of their Transit van.

They waited patiently for the order from Graham Turner.

Finally, the three men managed to get one end of the chest into the van.

As the suspension on the Transit's rear wheels sank under the weight of the chest, Graham Turner whispered into his radio, 'All units. Strike, strike, strike!'

Tom and Jack instantly leapt from behind the planter, both shouting 'Police! Stand still!'

Tom grabbed Nathan Smith and Jack vaulted the chest that had now been dropped to the floor and grabbed Jimmy Smith. They were instantly joined by other members of C Section.

Nathan and Jimmy Smith reacted in the only way knew how. Instantly, both men began to fight, violently resisting arrest and struggling to break free.

Tom maintained his grip on Nathan's left arm, but the burly gypsy swung a balled up right fist and punched Tom in the face. The heavy blow landed just above Tom's left eye, splitting his eyebrow. Tom immediately felt the warm blood start to trickle down his cheek. His reaction was instant. He lashed out with both fists at Nathan, landing three heavy punches to his face. Still Smith fought like a wild man, lashing out with both arms and kicking with both feet. One of these wild kicks landed in the groin of Wayne Hope, who grunted loudly before falling to the ground in a heap.

Steve Grey and Graham Turner then jumped into the fight to help Tom.

After a further exchange of blows, the three men were finally able to drag the big gypsy down to the floor. Tom then managed to secure Nathan's wrists with handcuffs.

Even though he was now cuffed, Nathan Smith continued to struggle violently until Steve Grey brought all his considerable weight to bear on him, pinning him to the floor and forcing him face down in the dirt.

Tom and Graham then turned to help Jack and the others who were desperately struggling to restrain Jimmy Smith.

The strong, powerful gypsy was fighting like a man possessed.

He'd already head-butted Jack and landed several heavy punches to his face and body. Jack had gamely hung on and now with assistance from other officers, Jimmy Smith was finally forced down on the ground by sheer weight of numbers and brought under control.

Jack's handcuffs snapped shut around the wrists of Jimmy Smith and for a brief moment the farmyard returned to a relative quiet.

The only sounds were groans coming from the bruised and bloody men.

The silence only lasted a few seconds before the brothers began to hurl abuse at the arresting officers as they used plasticuffs to further secure the feet and legs of the two gypsies.

Graham Tuner switched on a Dragon light portable torch and suddenly the farmyard was bathed in bright white light.

As Tom sucked in air, trying to get some oxygen back into his body after the physical exertion of the violent arrests, he looked over the two snarling, writhing Smith brothers strapped up on the floor, and across the yard to where Tony Garner was standing well back from where all hell had broken loose moments earlier.

Tony was holding onto the right arm of the smallest of the three burglars. Danny Lee was standing perfectly still and sobbing quietly.

Tom couldn't help but grin at the comic scene in front of him, the tall, black, muscular cop holding the small skinny youth by the arm.

He shouted across to Tony, 'You sure you can manage mate?'

As Tom dabbed at his cut eyebrow, Tony replied in a thick accent that gave away his Jamaican roots, 'No problem Tom. How come you blokes are always grabbing hold of the biggest guys? Giving it all that macho shit'.

His laugh boomed out across the farmyard.

Graham Turner stepped forward and said, 'Alright Tony, knock it off. Let's see what we've got here.'

The sight that met the sergeant was not a pretty one.

He could see that four of his team had visible injuries. Tom and Jack had cuts and bruising to their faces and both

Wayne Hope and Eddie Keane had been on the receiving end of vicious kicks and were now hobbling badly.

He looked down at the two handcuffed prisoners and could see that they too had numerous facial injuries and significant bruising. The fight to detain the two brothers had been brief, but it had been intense, bloody and vicious.

Graham addressed his officers, 'Does anybody require proper medical attention or can we get this lot packed off to Sleaford nick?'

There was silence until finally Tony Garner said in a whimpering voice, 'I'm not a hundred per cent certain Sarge, but I reckon I've severely damaged a fingernail over here.'

Again, the booming laugh broke the silence.

'Always the bloody comedian, eh Tony?'

The rest of the men began to chuckle, enjoying the moment of light relief after the tension and violence of the arrests.

Eventually, Graham Turner smiled too.

Regaining his authoritative air quickly he said, 'Right, let's get these two fuckers in the van with me and Steve. Tom, Jack, get some cuffs on that kid and take him to Sleaford in the car with you. The rest of you, divide yourselves up so we've got a driver for each vehicle. Anyone spare, can ride shotgun with me and Steve transporting these two dickheads to Sleaford nick.'

Graham then spoke on his personal radio and informed Dc Jenkins of the arrests. He told her that his intention was to convey them all to Sleaford for booking in. He asked her to radio ahead to Sleaford and let them know they were on their way with three arrested for burglary and for them to arrange uniform staff to travel out to White Post Farm to secure the front door and arrange removal of the gypsies Transit van.

Having handcuffed the youngster, Tom and Jack walked with him back up the farm track to their car.

Jack was driving, so Tom sat Danny Lee in the back of the car and got in beside him.

As Jack started the car and slowly drove away from White Post Farm, Tom said quietly, 'What's your name kid?'

'Danny Lee.'

'How old are you, Danny?'

'Sixteen.'

'What are you three playing at? Do you get off on hurting old people or what?'

'I've never hurt anybody. It's those two that do all that shit. You saw what they're like just then, they're both mental. I just go along on the jobs for the money.'

'Well son, whether you've hurt anybody or not, you're in it up to your neck. Best thing you can do is tell the detectives everything you know about the jobs you've been on and hope they agree to look after you. I'm not joking Danny, this is some serious shit you've got yourself involved in.'

Tom knew that whatever was said between him and the young burglar on the car journey back to the police station could never be used in evidence. He was talking to him hoping to gain some crucial snippet of information that would assist the detectives investigating these cases.

As the car sped through the country lanes heading towards Sleaford, Tom looked at the youngster and said, 'I don't get it Danny, what's the point of it all? I mean, we all like a bit of extra cash, but you three have been at it a hundred miles an hour. Why are you so desperate for cash?'

'I just need it, that's all. If I don't pay for my stuff I'll be in deep shit.'

Tom seized on the slip, 'What stuff Danny? Are you on the gear?'

Danny Lee let out a barely audible whimper and slowly nodded.

'Yeah, I'm on the gear. Those two got me on it and now I owe a chunk of money to some really bad fuckers. They'll kill me if I don't pay what I owe them on time. I'm shit scared of them.'

Tom looked at him with genuine concern on his face and said, 'There's another way Danny. Tell me who you owe this money to. I'll make sure they can't come after you. They'll never know the information came from you, I'll make sure of that. Do you trust me, Danny?'

The youngster nodded slowly, tears dripping down onto the handcuffs on his wrists.

Tom decided to push it, 'Just tell me who they are Danny. I can sort this all out for you and make it go away.'

The floodgates opened and the teenager started to cry.

Between sobs he said, 'It's the crew over at Phet Row in Worksop. I don't know any of their names. There's about seven of them all together. The main man's an evil fat bastard who's already done time for murder.'

Tom pressed on and spoke quietly, 'It's okay Danny. If you don't know their names that's fine. I won't press you for something you don't know, but where's this place you called Phet Row?'

'Phet Row's the nickname we have for Hammond Street on the Renton council estate in Worksop. It's a proper shithole.'

'Alright Danny, this is just between you and me. I'll sort this out, I promise it won't come back on you, got it?'

Danny nodded, sobbing quietly.

'We're nearly there now, Danny. Dry your eyes and remember what I told you earlier. When you're talking to the detectives later, tell them everything you know. You need to try and get ahead of this situation. You're only a youngster, it's clear to me that you're doing everything those two tell you to do, so use that to your advantage, but be straight with the detectives. This is your best option, alright?'

Danny Lee slowly nodded, raised his handcuffed wrists and wiped his eyes on the sleeves of his jumper.

Jack parked the car in the rear yard at Sleaford Police Station and took Danny Lee into the cell block while Tom sought out Dc Sue Jenkins.

He found the detective in the fingerprint room of the cells.

Taking her out of earshot of everybody he said, 'I've got an interesting piece of information for you, Sue. On the way here, Danny Lee told me that this Phet Row place you keep hearing about is actually the nickname druggies have given Hammond Street on the Renton council estate at Worksop. He's also told me that the main dealer there is someone who's already served time for murder. None of this information was obtained under the guidelines for the Police and Criminal Evidence Act so it's only ever going to be good for intelligence purposes.'

Sue Jenkins smiled, 'Thanks for that. Tom, isn't it?'

'Yeah, Tom Naylor. I thought it might help you push this enquiry on quicker.'

'Every little helps Tom, thanks. I'll talk to Sergeant Turner and Chief Inspector Chambers properly later but would you pass on my thanks to the rest of your team? I heard some of them, including you by the look of it, got some knocks from those two animals.'

'I'll pass on your thanks Sue, and good luck interviewing the Smith brothers. I can't see them two being very forthcoming. I think you'll have better luck with young Danny Lee; he'll talk to you, he's way out of his depth.'

CHAPTER 34

11.50am 29th July 1987
Royal Courts of Justice, The Strand,
City of London

It was another beautifully clear day in central London. Even through the permanent haze that is common to all large cities, the sky looked bright blue. There wasn't a cloud in the sky and the sun already felt hot as the time approached midday.

The man stood with his back towards the massive ornate archway that formed the entrance of the historical building that was the Royal Courts of Justice. He blended in easily with the crowds of other people there, the tourists, journalists, legal workers and ordinary Londoners going about their everyday business.

He looked to his left and saw the clamour of press photographers and news reporters all jostling to get in prime position, ready for the press release that was about to be given. They were all waiting for the culmination of a story that had gripped the nation. Today had marked victory in the High Court for a young mother whose infant son had been killed in a Newcastle hospital due to the negligence of some underpaid, overworked junior doctor.

The North East Health Trust had fought the case all the way but today the verdict had gone in favour of the distraught mother and the Trust found negligent. The damages award to the mother had been a staggering seven-figure sum.

The man watching the scrum of newspaper and television reporters jostling for position didn't give a shit about the dead toddler, the young mother or how much she'd been awarded.

All he needed to know was the exact spot where the press would make her stand when she made her eagerly awaited statement to the clamouring media circus.

It had been a tragic story and this would be the dramatic conclusion. The nation demanded every detail of the sorry tale.

The tearful mother was led through the ornate archway by her barrister, who guided her down towards the clamouring media. Prompted by him, she stood on a step just above the scrum of photographers and reporters all baying questions at her.

The mother was overwhelmed by it all and stood mute, dabbing a handkerchief to her eyes as her barrister stepped forward and espoused the righteousness of the decision and that more Health Trusts should be accountable for the actions of their staff. The vicarious liability in this case had obviously been the Trust's and the judgement had been just and would serve as a warning to other Health Trusts across the nation who set impossible rotas for their junior staff.

When he finally finished making his self-glorifying speech, he handed brusquely over to the emotional young woman.

The man watching, listened disinterestedly as she delivered a well-rehearsed, but heart wrenching message to the media; that no amount of money could ever compensate her for the loss of her beloved Brendan.

Finally, the press had obtained all the pictures and copy they needed to file or broadcast the story and they started to dwindle away. The mother was whisked back inside the court building by her pompous barrister who, before leaving, thanked the now empty steps where the press had been, clearly enjoying the sound of his own voice way too much.

Once the crowd had cleared, the man walked across and stood on the exact spot the young mother had been on throughout the press release.

Without making his actions obvious, he slowly began to look around him, taking in the surroundings from this very important position. His eyes were searching for a special place. He looked to his left and away in the distance he could see the spire of The Guild Church of St Dunstan in the West.

To the side of the church at the junction of The Strand and Fetter Lane, he finally found what he'd been searching for.

At that junction stood an unfinished multi storey car park.

The car park was obviously still under construction and had been completed up to about six levels, but work was still needed to complete the project. Strangely, he could see no signs of life on site at the moment. Nobody appeared to be working on the site. For some reason, probably economic, it appeared as though all construction work on site had been temporarily halted.

From where he stood, the multi-story car park appeared to be the perfect location for his task.

The man smiled to himself. It would give him the vantage point he needed at a very low risk of being discovered.

He squatted onto his haunches and pretended to tie his

shoe laces; as he did so he slipped a hand into his trouser pocket and retrieved a miniature spray can that contained a bright yellow paint.

Surreptitiously, he made a single mark on the pavement no bigger than a fifty pence piece. The small yellow dot marked the exact spot where the distraught mother had stood earlier when she made her statement to the press.

In exactly seven days' time the notorious gangster Barry Tate would have his appeal against conviction heard in this very building.

Feeling satisfied with his planning, the man stood up and casually walked away.

He'd taken great care not to expose his facial features to any of the numerous CCTV cameras dotted around the Royal Courts of Justice. It had been a difficult and time-consuming task to locate all the cameras. As a further precaution, he'd worn a navy-blue New York Yankees baseball cap and sunglasses to disguise his features from any potential witnesses, who may later recall a man standing in this particular location.

It had been such a busy morning that he doubted whether anyone would remember seeing him.

Crowds of people were a massive benefit to him, there was nothing better than hiding in plain sight.

He walked away from the High Court knowing that he still had a lot of preparation work to do and only seven days left to complete it.

CHAPTER 35

10.00pm 29th July 1987
Junction of The Strand and Fetter Lane,
City of London

As night finally closed out the last twilight and the shadows deepened, the streets of the capital became progressively more and more deserted.

The man who had spent all day around the Royal Courts of Justice now lingered in the shadows, observing the unfinished multi storey car park at the junction of The Strand and Fetter Lane.

He had watched the car park from various locations for most of the afternoon and had seen no sign of any workmen on the site. Typical of redundant building sites, the area was now surrounded by Harris security fencing adorned with the usual signs, warning parents that the unfinished site was dangerous and to keep their children away from the site as they posed a risk of serious injury or death.

Now totally satisfied that nobody was inside the building site, he slowly made his way over to the Harris fencing. After taking one more careful look in each direction, he removed a small pair of bolt croppers from inside his black Reefer coat. Stooping down he neatly cut the two links that joined two lengths of the fence together. Cutting it in this way meant that to the casual observer the fence still looked intact.

The man quickly lifted one of the panels from its securing base, opened it just far enough for him to squeeze through then just as quickly replaced the panel back into its base.

He stepped into the shadows and paused, waiting to see if anyone had observed his actions.

Satisfied that he remained undetected, he began to make his way up inside the car park to the highest completed level on the sixth floor. Everything above the ceiling at that level remained unfinished and exposed to the elements.

Once on the sixth floor he walked to the edge of the building and looked towards the Royal Courts of Justice. He took out a small but very powerful set of binoculars from his jacket pocket, raised them to his eyes, looked along The Strand and began scanning the area immediately outside the court buildings.

He focussed the binoculars on the ornate archway that made up the grand entrance. The area was very well lit. Like a lot of landmark buildings in the capital, it was illuminated by very bright white street lighting.

It was like daylight down there.

Using the powerful binoculars, the man scanned the area, hungrily seeking the tell-tale sign he'd left earlier in the day.

After a few minutes of methodical searching he found the small bright yellow dot on the pavement.

Having found his mark, he began to scan the shadows and recesses of the unfinished car park looking for the perfect position to observe the small yellow dot.

To his right, about ten meters from where he was standing, there was an area of the outside wall that had only been finished with two courses of bricks from the floor.

It looked like a purpose-built firing point.

He smiled at his good fortune, it was a perfect solid base.

He walked over to the edge of the building, got down into the prone position and once again raised the binoculars to his face. Having located the yellow dot once it took him no time at all to relocate it.

The man removed another object from his jacket pocket. Handling the small hand-held laser range finder carefully, he splashed the yellow dot with the laser beam. The delicate, but extremely accurate, instrument revealed the distance to the yellow dot was exactly four hundred and seventeen meters.

As an accomplished sniper, the man knew that the shot he intended to make was easily achievable from that range.

He stood up and once again scanned the sixth floor of the car park. This time his searching eyes fell upon a broken silver conduit just above the firing point.

Six days from now, he would return to the car park and stash the Dragunov SVD sniper rifle and three 7.62 rounds of ammunition within that silver conduit. Both the weapon and the ammunition would be sealed in an airtight bag to protect them from the elements.

Four nights ago, the man had driven to a remote farmhouse just outside of Basildon in Essex where he had met two shady characters from the East End of London. After doing basic checks, the two men had sold him the weapon and ammunition. It was a risk but the man knew that for the right amount of money he would be able to obtain the necessary weapon with no questions asked.

With this kind of illegal transaction money definitely talked and for the man money was no object.

Having checked the rifle he had been pleased to see that the weapon carried no identifying features whatsoever. All the serial numbers had been meticulously removed and the weapon had been thoroughly cleaned down, leaving no trace of any fingerprints.

Now with all the preparatory work virtually done the man allowed himself a self-satisfied smile.

Only one more week to go before Barry Tate had his appeal hearing at the High Court. Barring any last-minute problems, Tate would be released and the man would be waiting patiently.

CHAPTER 36

8.45am 31st July 1987
Nottinghamshire Police Headquarters

Tom Naylor was sitting alone in the briefing room. He'd been contacted by the control room and told to be at headquarters for nine o'clock. When he arrived and saw no one else about he began to feel a little intrigued as to why he was the only person who had been called in.

Three days had passed since the violent arrest of the three burglars at the farmhouse just outside Sleaford in Lincolnshire.

Subconsciously, he reached up to his face, his fingers gingerly touching the area of bruising around his left eye. The skin was starting to turn from a vivid dark purple colour to a softer yellow. The cut hadn't required stitches but his face was still sore.

He was aware there had been complaints from the Sleaford Duty Inspector on the night. Apparently, he'd been unhappy about the amount of force used during the arrests, the subsequent injuries sustained by the prisoners and the fact he hadn't been informed personally of any ongoing operation by a foreign force in his area.

At the time he heard about the Inspector's petty complaints, Tom had laughed along with the other members of C Section, believing that such things were not his problem.

Now as he waited in the briefing room with a mug of coffee he was beginning to get a little concerned that maybe it was going to be his problem after all.

As he sipped his coffee he pondered some more, surely there couldn't be a problem over the amount of force used? Several of his colleagues had received quite bad injuries. The resistance shown by the Smith brothers had been extremely violent and the force used to make the arrests had been both appropriate and necessary.

Thinking back to that night, once again his fingers brushed the bruised area around his left eye.

The Smith brothers were intent on getting away and had fought like wild men to try and achieve that. No, whatever Chambers wanted to see him about it wouldn't be that, the force used to make the arrests hadn't been over the top.

Having discounted the arrests as causing him a problem, Tom now wondered if there was an issue with how he'd obtained information from young Danny Lee in the back of the car on the way to Sleaford nick. Tom had told the detective how he obtained the information and had stressed to her that it couldn't be used for anything but intelligence.

The clock on the wall was slowly moving around to nine o'clock. He finally gave up speculating, he would find out what the problem was soon enough.

A few minutes passed and the door to the briefing room opened.

Sgt Turner walked in with a stranger in a suit.

Tom nodded to Sgt Turner but said nothing.

He thought the suit would either be a visiting detective from the CID, a gaffer from Division or the worst possible scenario, some bubblehead from the Complaints and Discipline Department.

As if reading his mind, Graham Turner paused at the door, turned back and said to Tom, 'Morning Tom. This is Dc Gary Watts from Worksop CID.'

The sergeant then left the briefing room.

'Hello Gary, good to meet you, help yourself to a brew if you want one.'

The detective said, 'Likewise, I've not long had a cuppa but thanks anyway.'

With a slightly puzzled expression on his face the detective said, 'I've been asked to drive here for a meeting with Chief Inspector Chambers at nine o'clock today. Are you here for the same meeting? Any idea what it might be about?'

As the detective sat down Tom said, 'I've been asked to be here at nine too Gary, but what it's all about I haven't got a clue. I'm as much in the dark as you are.'

A few more minutes ticked by in silence, then Jim Chambers stuck his head around the door of the briefing room and said, 'Good morning gents, thanks for arriving so promptly, come through into my office.'

The two men followed Jim Chambers into his office.

Tom was surprised to see Graham Turner and Dc Sue Jenkins already sitting down in the office.

Jim Chambers introduced everyone then said, 'Right, let's get down to business, shall we? Over to you Sue.'

Sue Jenkins smiled and addressed Gary Watts, 'Gary, I appreciate you're not aware of the operation we ran last week and you must be wondering why you're here. Suffice to say that the Special Operations Unit carried out an operation at my request to follow and arrest three particularly violent individuals who we suspected of being responsible for a series of burglaries around the Newark area. One of these individuals, thanks mainly to Tom here, gave us information about a large-scale drugs supply network operating on the Renton council estate, which I believe is in your area.'

Gary immediately sat forward in his chair, 'Are you talking about Hammond Street?'

Sue nodded and continued, 'We're aware that currently there are at least seven dealers, all working out of that location. They're led by a man named....'

Gary interrupted Sue in mid-sentence, 'Shane Street.'

Sue continued, 'Exactly right Gary. It appears that Shane Street is running things, ably assisted by his four sons, Rocky, Tyson, Manny and Sonny along with a couple of other associates. What can you tell us about their operation, Gary?'

Gary Watts shifted uncomfortably in his seat feeling like he'd been well and truly put on the spot, 'Unfortunately, not much. I've had an inclination that there's been drug dealing of some kind or another going on up there, but it's extremely difficult to get any information, let alone evidence. You've got to understand the layout of the Renton estate to know the problems we face.'

Jim Chambers smiled and said, 'Gary, don't be defensive. Stop worrying, nobody's here to point fingers or to try and score points. I know exactly the kind of problems you face every day on that particular estate. A cop can't leave the nick up there without everyone knowing they've left the station and are on their way up to the estate. I really do understand all that and the problems you face. What I want from you this morning is very simple, I need to know everything you can tell me about this Shane Street character, the geography of Hammond Street and anything else that's happened up there recently that you're not happy about. Just take your time and tell me what you know.'

Gary Watts did just that.

He took his time and informed the meeting everything he knew about the Street family. Their propensity to violence to achieve their aims. The fact that as a teenager, Shane Street had been convicted for the manslaughter of another drug dealer in Nottingham and that he'd served seven and a half years of a twelve-year sentence and was now out on a life licence. He asked the others to follow him back into the briefing room where he used the large map of Worksop that was on the wall to describe and point out different geographical features on the Renton estate and in particular the area around Hammond Street.

Finally, he spoke about the recent sudden death of a retired Polish coalminer that he still believed was suspicious but had no evidence to prove this was the case. In particular he referred to the comment made by Shane Street to him on the morning the old man's body had been discovered.

Tom sat quietly sipping his coffee, taking in all the information.

Nobody had said anything directly to him yet. He had an idea where the meeting was heading and he felt quite excited by the prospect if he was proved right.

When the two detectives had finished their briefing, Jim Chambers turned to the two SOU men and said, 'Well what do you think? Do you think we'll be able to set something up over there and put this shower of shit behind bars, where they belong?'

Tom smiled, he loved his Chief Inspector's succinct way of summarising things.

He looked at Graham as if silently asking permission to speak first. Graham nodded for him to go ahead.

Tom said quietly, 'I've listened to everything you've had to say about the area Gary, but I think I'd prefer to do a close recce myself before I can say one way or the other if it's feasible to set up observations on these characters. In the next couple of days, I'd like to go in there on foot and have a good snoop around. In particular, I want to see for myself if there's any way we can set up a covert rural observation post on the pit tip Gary mentioned. From the way he describes it, that corner of Hammond Street, where the dealers congregate, is immediately below the pit tip. If it's possible to get in there we may get a good enough view to be able to log what's going on. As they're dealing throughout the day we may also get photographs identifying both the dealers and the punters. I think if we can gather enough evidence, we should be able to shut their operation down once and for all.'

Gary looked concerned and said, 'It won't be easy getting in there to have, as you say, a snoop around Tom. The dealers literally control everything that moves in that area. If they even suspect you're a cop you'll be in for a good hiding. You'd be a right mess by the time we could get any back up to you.'

Tom nodded, 'I appreciate what you're saying Gary and I'm not being blasé towards the risk, but I've never been up there before in my life, so the chances of anyone recognising me are slim to nil. Anyway, I'm prepared to take my chances. I thought I'd borrow a dog and go for a walk around the pit tip. If they object to my presence I'll have a cover story ready. I'll play it all meek and mild, be very apologetic and do whatever they say. I've got to get in there to know if the observation post is feasible or not. It's got to be worth having a go.'

Jim Chambers nodded in agreement, 'You're right Tom, get that recce organised as soon as you can please. Let's see for ourselves exactly what it's like up there. Let's reconvene back here in two days' time. We'll know where we stand by then and we'll be able to weigh up our options better.'

CHAPTER 37

11.30am 1st August 1987
Hammond Street, Renton Estate, Worksop

For Shane Street, business was good, life was good.

He rocked back on his camp chair and placed his hands behind his head, interlacing his fingers. He drew in a deep breath and exhaled slowly. It was just approaching eleven thirty, the sun was already high in the sky. It was going to be another scorching day. He was dressed for the weather wearing beige cargo shorts, a tatty light blue T-shirt that strained against his massive gut and flip flops. He wouldn't have looked out of place on the beach front at Skegness.

At the side of his chair he had a cool bag full of Stella Artois and a packet of Benson and Hedges Gold in his shorts pocket. Untwining his fingers, he reached down the side of the chair and felt for the blue metal cash box hidden beneath the Sun newspaper. Taking the tin from under the paper he placed it on his lap, opened the lid and looked at the pile of ten and twenty-pound notes that had been stuffed inside.

He quickly counted the cash.

Just short of five hundred quid, not bad for a mornings work.

If you could even call this work, he thought to himself.

He chuckled aloud at his own thought.

Yes, life was definitely good.

He looked around until he saw one of his sons standing nearby, 'Tyson! Get your fat lazy arse over here!'

Tyson was the oldest of the four brothers and was now approaching nineteen years of age. He was tall, naturally broad and very strong. He was at that age where he liked to challenge his father whenever he got the opportunity.

He strode over to his father with a scowl on his face and said, 'There's only one fat fucker round here, Dad and I'm looking at him.'

Shane didn't rise to the bait and simply said, 'We'll have a bit less of your cheek lad! Grab this cash and take it inside the house. I don't know how many times I've got to tell you, never keep too much cash out here. The filth doesn't need a warrant to search us out here. If we just keep the odd twenty quid in the tin and the law turn us over, we just say it's money for beer and fags. Understand?'

Tyson twisted his face, scowling even more at the rebuke, took the cash and wandered off back to the house, muttering and cursing under his breath.

As he reached the garden gate of the house he yelled back at Shane, 'I do know, I'm not thick!'

Tyson disappeared into the house and Shane settled down in his chair and once more surveyed his little empire.

He saw his youngest boy, Sonny, emerge from the house.

The twelve-year-old was still totally scared of his father. He was a spotty, skinny youth who would have been bullied mercilessly had it not been for the reputation of the Street family.

Shane bellowed at the boy, 'Sonny, grab some of that cash from Ty, nip to the cob shop and fetch me a full breakfast cob, I'm fucking starving!'

Sonny didn't moan or argue, he just turned on his heel and went back inside to find his brother. He emerged a couple of seconds later and sprinted off up the road to fetch his father's breakfast.

As Shane watched Sonny sprint off on his errand, he saw a man walking a dog towards the corner.

He didn't recognise either the man or the dog and was instantly suspicious and on his guard.

As the man walked closer, Shane began to scrutinise him. Although he was quite tall he looked a right skinny fucker. He was scruffily dressed with unkempt hair and a couple of days growth on his face. He was mid-twenties, maybe thirty at a push and was walking a little terrier of some description.

As the stranger drew level he nodded at Street and said, 'You look comfy mate, at least you've got the weather for it.'

Shane Street didn't reply straight away, he just stared hard into the eyes of the stranger.

Finally, he said, 'I'm just catching some rays mate. You must've just moved onto the estate, yeah? Only I don't recall seeing you around here before.'

'Nah mate, I don't live round here, my old auntie does. She lives on the other side of the estate but she's laid up at the moment so I said I'd nip over and walk the rat for her.'

Street looked at the stranger and said menacingly, 'Well don't let me keep you. That dog looks like it's getting ready for a shit and if it shits on my corner I'll have to rub your fucking nose in it, if you get my drift?'

'Alright mate I'm going. I didn't mean any offence, I'll take the dog out of your way.'

Shane opened a can of Stella, took a deep pull on the gassy beer and looked away as if dismissing the newcomer.

Once again, he stared down the road. Where was Sonny with that fucking breakfast cob?

Tom Naylor didn't look back as he strode up onto the pit tip with the small dog on the lead. As soon as he'd walked out of the sight of Shane Street and his cronies Tom began his recce in earnest. After ten minutes of searching he found a promising location.

Approximately one hundred and fifty yards from the corner where Shane was now sitting conducting operations, was a large clump of blackberry bushes. Tom tied the little dog to a tree out of sight and made his way over to the rear of the bramble patch, at the point furthest away from where Shane Street now sat.

Starting at the rear of the thick brambles Tom began to crawl towards the front where he stopped about a foot from the other side. From this position, inside the brambles he had an elevated and unobstructed view of the corner of Hammond Street. He was far enough away not to be heard easily and close enough to take excellent photographs and with the aid of binoculars log all car numbers.

The thorny brambles would help to deter inquisitive dogs, so he knew he'd be reasonably safe from a compromise by dog walkers.

As covert rural observation posts went this one was pretty good.

Tom didn't want to risk antagonising Shane Street any further, so he sought out a different way down from the pit tip. He needed to find an alternative route in and out in any case. Although it was his intention that once he was in the observation post he would stay there for three or four days.

He felt satisfied that he now had all the information he needed ready for the meeting with the two detectives and Jim Chambers. Before that meeting he would need to speak with Graham Turner and ask the sergeant who he wanted to accompany him into the observation post.

Preferably it would be someone with good photography skills. It would normally have been his sniper team partner, but Matt Jarvis was still suspended.

The decision would have to made by Graham.

Tom untied the little dog he'd borrowed from Jim Chambers and started to walk down the pit tip.

As he walked a smile spread over his face and he said under his breath, 'Alright Shane Street, let's get you potted. You big fat fuck!'

CHAPTER 38

1.00pm 1st August 1987
Hammond Street, Renton Estate, Worksop

The telephone was ringing constantly.

Standing in the hallway of his house, Shane Street growled menacingly under his breath, 'Come on you shithead, pick up the fucking phone.'

He'd been trying to contact Billy Swan for hours.

Street didn't understand it. What was Swan playing at?

This was the number he always answered, this was the business number.

This situation would never have happened when Barry Tate was running the show. Drugs were always readily available with a phone call made to the right person. He pondered whether it was time for him to return to the city and pick up the reins dropped by Tate. He had the connections and with his fearsome reputation he could quite easily control the other dealers.

He stopped his daydreaming and dialled the number again.

Street was desperate for more amphetamines; his stash of the drug was dangerously close to being sold out. It was the one situation a drug dealer never wanted to be in. He knew that if he couldn't supply his punters they would very soon go elsewhere.

The only person he knew who could supply him with the amount of amphetamine he was regularly shifting was Billy Swan. When the situation had started to become critical Street had put out tentative feelers to dealers across the border in South Yorkshire to see if it was viable to get re supplied from there but the price those Yorkshire nonces wanted was astronomical.

They could go fuck themselves.

For the time being it would have to be Swan.

The situation was now critical, he would just have to keep calling.

CHAPTER 39

1.00pm 1st August 1987
Nottingham Central Police Station

Detective Sergeant Davy Provost of the Major Crime Investigation Unit was like a dog with a bone.

He sighed and said, 'Come on Billy, run it by me once more. Where were you at nine o'clock on the 21st of July?'

'No comment.'

'It's only just over a week ago, surely you can remember what you were doing?'

'No comment.'

'Did you go to the gym that night?'

'No comment.'

'Would anyone have you seen you there?'

'No comment.'

'What time did you go to meet Frankie Squires?'

'No comment.'

Undeterred by the constant answer of no comment the detective persevered, 'Look Billy, we know you've been supplying Squires with gear for his bouncers to sell on. We've got six or seven doormen who've told us as much.'

'No comment.'

The solicitor sitting at the side of Billy Swan interjected and with a smarmy grin said, 'Excuse me, detective. Could you clarify for me, was that six or seven witnesses? It's just that I don't recall seeing any witness statements on your disclosure.'

Ignoring the solicitor Davy Provost pressed on, 'Then Squires writes an entry in his diary for the 21st of July, "Meeting, BS, Basford" I'm not much on coincidences Billy. The initials B.S. That's got to be you, hasn't it?'

'No comment.'

'What was that meeting about, Billy?'

'No comment.'

'Did Squires owe you money?'

'No comment.'

'Is that what this is all about?'

'No comment.'

'Is that why Squires was found the morning after that meeting with his brains kicked around a car park in Basford?'

'No comment.'

'Did he owe you too much money?'

'No comment.'

'Was he starting to take the piss, Billy?'

Swan leaned back, stretched and yawned then said, 'No comment.'

The interview had gone on in this vein for the best part of an hour.

Billy Swan had voluntarily attended Central Police Station after learning that the police were looking to speak to him about the death of Frankie Squires. He had turned up with his accomplished solicitor, Vernon Jones.

He had been detained at the front counter of the police station and had immediately taken up his right to free and independent legal advice.

Billy and his solicitor knew the game well enough to know that the Major Crime Unit were on a fishing expedition, they both knew that the police had no real evidence. His solicitor had confirmed as much when he had his consultation after Detective Sergeant Provost had given him full disclosure on the evidence they had, or rather didn't have before the interview had even started.

Vernon Jones had impressed on Swan to simply answer no comment to every question he was asked and he would soon be released.

Billy Swan loved the rules under the new Police and Criminal Evidence Act.

At their private consultation immediately before the interview, Jones had spelled it out to Billy, 'Just say no comment to everything Billy, they've got fuck all.'

Billy had done just that.

Even when asked to confirm his personal details he had grinned and said, no comment. As the interview went on Swan had decided to try and find as many different ways he could say no comment as possible but even he had soon got bored of that game.

How ever many questions the waffling detective asked, he knew that if he just kept answering no comment, he would soon be released.

Eventually, Davy Provost sighed, sat back in his chair and asked, 'Is it your intention to answer no comment to every question I ask you Billy?'

Swan grinned and said with an almost triumphant air, 'No comment.'

'Okay, that's enough I'm terminating this interview.'

Hallelujah! thought Billy. Finally, I can get the fuck out of here and get some business done.

Three quarters of an hour later and Billy was standing on the front steps of Central Police Station with Vernon Jones.

The solicitor shook hands with Swan and said, 'If they come for you again Billy just call me, I'm always available.'

'The amount of cash I'm paying you Vernon, you bloody well need to be available,' said Billy as he turned and strode away from the smarmy little solicitor.

He flagged down a passing taxi and made the short journey across town to his apartment.

As he walked through the front door he could hear his mobile phone ringing. The phone was hidden inside a book on the large bookshelf in the living room of the apartment.

It was the business phone.

He grabbed the copy of The Chemists Almanac from the bookshelf, took the mobile from inside and answered it immediately, 'Who's this?'

'It's me, Shane Street, thank fuck. Where've you been? I've been ringing this number for most of the day.'

'Hello Shane, the pigs have had their grubby little trotters on me all day man.'

'What's their beef with you Billy?'

'Some lame, bogus shit about a dead club owner. They've got fuck all on me as per usual. So, anyway, what can I do for you my man?'

'I'm in dire straits, my stash is way down and right now I need gear and lots of it to keep my punters happy. I'm on my arse up here. I've got punters coming out of my ears and hardly any product left. If I cut the gear I've got left any more, my punters are going to know it's a pile of shit and fuck off elsewhere. When can you sort me out a delivery?'

'Fuck that Shane! No way am I driving up to that shithole you call home again. If you want gear that bad you can come down here to the big city and fetch it.'

'You've got to be fucking joking, not a chance Billy Boy, not when you've just had the cops crawling all over you. They'll be watching you like a hawk. No, it'll be much easier for you to come here. That way you'll have plenty of time to shake off any surveillance they put on you. You know its safe once you get up here on the estate. The police can't get anywhere near us.'

Swan detested Shane Street calling him Billy Boy. He was a fat, racist condescending twat, but business was business and deep-down Swan knew that Shane was right and that it would be safer all round for him to drive to Worksop to make the delivery.

'Okay Shane, but the earliest I can get up there is next week. How much do you need?'

'A fucking week! Alright Billy, that'll have to do. I'll take all the amphet you've got. Is the price the same as before?'

'It's the same. Been a pleasure doing business with you my old mate', he lied.

As he terminated the call, Billy had a flash of inspiration.

He would make Street wait for ten days not seven. By that time, he would be well and truly on his arse. He would then be able to increase the price for the product and Street would be left with no choice, he would have to pay the higher price or be well and truly fucked.

Swan allowed himself a smile, his day had just taken a massive turn for the better. He muttered to himself, 'Business is business after all, Shane Boy.'

He could already feel himself filling the shoes of Barry Tate.

CHAPTER 40

10.00am 2nd August 1987
Nottinghamshire Police Headquarters

Tom was in good spirits as he arrived in the car park at headquarters. He was looking forward to starting the operation at Worksop. It had been a while since he'd undertaken any covert rural observations. They were always very challenging but exciting at the same time as they always carried a high element of risk.

As he walked from the car park to the huts he saw Jack Rimmer approaching the door from the other side of the car park.

Tom waited and said, 'Morning mate, how's the bruises?'

'All good now Tom, are you here for this briefing?'

'If you mean the Worksop job, then yes. Looks like you're going to be my wingman on this job as well.'

'Looks like it. I got a phone call from the sarge last night to see if I was available for an observations job where photography would be an important part. You know me Tom, I love taking snaps, I'm the next David Bailey me.'

'That's great news Jack, it should be an interesting job. Let's hope it's not as lumpy as the last time we were paired up together.'

Both men laughed and as they walked in the huts Jack said, 'Those Smith brothers were something else, weren't they? Like a pair of wild animals.'

'You're not wrong mate, the bruising around my eye is only just bloody going.'

Waiting in the briefing room already were Jim Chambers, the two detectives Gary Watts and Sue Chambers and another man sitting on a chair in the corner of the room who Tom didn't recognise.

The stranger was tall, skinny and looked to be in his early twenties. He had a pale, spotty complexion and dark black, greasy hair that was just touching his shoulders. Both of his ears had multiple piercings and both skinny arms were covered in full sleeve tattoos. He was wearing a moth eaten khaki coloured vest, unwashed, black Adidas tracksuit bottoms and a pair of scruffy dark blue Converse trainers.

Jim Chambers noted the inquisitive looks on the faces of Tom and Jack and immediately said, 'Tom, Jack, let me introduce you to Dc Phil Webster from the Test Purchase Unit of the South Yorkshire Drug Squad.'

The look of surprise on both the men's faces must have been obvious because Phil Webster immediately stood up and extended his right hand. Shaking hands with the Special Ops men he said, 'Don't worry about it guys, I always get the same reaction whenever I do a job for a foreign force.'

They quickly shook hands and sat down.

Jim Chambers addressed the briefing, 'It occurred to me after the meeting last week that if Tom's recce was a success then what this operation would really need was a Test Purchase Officer. If we can get photographic evidence of Street and his cronies dealing to members of the public and a TPO they'll be well and truly stuffed.'

Tom responded, 'It's a good idea boss, but I don't know how Phil's going to get into them. It's like a closed shop up there on Hammond Street. They're really aggressive and suspicious of any strangers arriving on their patch. I can't see them dealing to a complete stranger, however unlike a cop he looks. Shane Street had a right go at me just for walking my dog on his corner. There's no way those boys would sell drugs to a stranger.'

Phil Webster answered Tom directly, 'When my gaffer told me about the possibility of this job, I went over to Worksop and carried out my own recce on Hammond Street. I agree with every word you're saying Tom, but I think there's a way. It will take a little time but it can be done. I did a job recently over in Manchester that was a very similar scenario to this. To get around the problem I employed a little bit of Greek Mythology and it worked a treat. I made a few visits in a Transit van that had a side door and let the dealers know that I'd be regularly passing through making deliveries in the area. I told them that I was in the market for some gear while I was in the area and various places I had delivered to had suggested that this was the place to score. I knew they wouldn't sell to me straight away, but on my third visit I actually made a small purchase. Patience is the key. After I'd made that initial purchase, I let them know that I'd be very interested in getting a large order for my mates back home. While I was talking to the dealers I let slip that I deliver training shoes for a living. No shit, just top of the range Nike's and Adidas. I told them that on the day I came back for my bulk order I'd make sure that the van would be full of knock off trainers for them to buy at bargain knock down prices. In my experience these boys can't resist getting their hands on the latest trainers. Anyway, when the day finally arrived for me to pick up my bulk order and for them to buy the latest trainers, the back of my van was filled with hairy arsed coppers. When I opened the van doors the dealers got the shock of their lives. It worked an absolute treat over in Manchester. What do you think Tom? You've seen them close up, do you think these boys would buy into that?'

Having listened carefully, Tom thought for a second then said, 'A lot of the dealers up there are quite young, apart from Shane Street obviously, so I don't see why they wouldn't go for it. I was wondering how we were going to be able to arrest the dealers with any gear on them, when the time came. If it worked that well in Manchester I think it's got to be worth ago here. Yeah, I think it sounds like a plan.'

Phil Webster looked at Jack Rimmer who grinned and said, 'Look mate, if it worked for the ancient Greeks in Troy, who let's face it were a whole lot smarter than modern day drug dealing low life scum in Worksop, it's got to be worth a go I reckon.'

Jim Chambers nodded in agreement and said, 'Right then. Tom and Jack, I want you in the observation post at first light tomorrow morning. Is there easy access to get in and out Tom?'

'Yes boss, no problem. There's a way to get off the pit tip that brings you out the opposite side to Hammond Street. The trail leads onto a quiet country lane where we could be met by a covert vehicle.'

'Right, if that's the case I only want you on plot from dawn til dusk. There's absolutely no point being out there all night if you don't have to be. These jobs are exhausting enough as it is. You might as well get extracted at the end of the day and rest up properly. I know there's always a risk of compromise on insertion and extraction but I think it's deserted enough up there to get away with it. Do you agree Tom?'

'I think we'll be alright if we pick our times carefully. It's pretty deserted and desolate up on that old pit tip. I don't think anybody will be up there when its pitch black at night. If things go our way we should be able to get this wrapped up within a fortnight.'

Chambers then turned to the two detectives and said, 'Thanks for coming down today, I'll keep you both posted on any developments and I'll be in touch with your Detective Inspectors to make sure we've got enough interview teams ready for any future strike day. Do either of you have any questions?'

Both detectives remained silent.

The Chief Inspector then took an altogether more serious tone and said sternly, 'Obviously, I don't have to tell you that this operation is not to be spoken about outside of this room, okay?'

The detectives acknowledged the instruction and left the briefing room.

After they had left the room, Chambers turned to Phil Webster and said equally as seriously, 'I've heard really good things about your undercover work Dc Webster, but I don't want you putting yourself unduly at risk with this crew. They're an evil bunch of bastards that aren't beyond causing you some real damage if they get wind of what you're about. Do you understand me?'

'I understand sir, but none of these jobs are without risk, it goes with the territory. Most drug dealers have a propensity for extreme violence, it's how they keep a grip on what is, after all, a very lucrative business. I know the dangers and I never take unnecessary risks. The last thing I want is to get my good looks ruined.'

He grinned and winked at Tom and Jack.

Jim Chambers grunted and walked out, he didn't really appreciate the attempt at humour or the light-hearted manner of the maverick TPO.

Tom and Jack grinned back at the undercover detective acknowledging his cool courage.

Phil Webster shook hands with the two men, grinned and said, 'No doubt you'll be taking my picture soon, make sure you get my best side. Take care gents.'

Tom said, 'You take care too mate.'

Phil Webster left the briefing room and Tom said, 'Right Jack, we'd better start organising our kit. We've got an early start tomorrow morning.

CHAPTER 41

4.30am 3rd August 1987
Disused pit tip, Hammond Street, Worksop

The first deep orange hues of the new dawn were starting to show on the distant horizon above the rooftops of the Renton estate, as Tom and Jack crawled carefully through the bramble patch high up on the disused pit tip overlooking Hammond Street.

It had just turned four thirty in the morning and the birds were beginning the chorus that heralded in the new day. There was a pervading sooty smell from the tip itself. Although overgrown, the artificial hill was still basically coal slag from the now redundant Renton Colliery.

As is usual for the period just before dawn, when the sun is creeping towards the horizon, the temperature appeared to have dropped a few degrees. Tom hunkered down into the spiny undergrowth trying to shield himself from the cold wind that was sweeping over the old tip.

The two men took up positions side by side in the thick brambles, leaving two feet of vegetation in front of them undisturbed. From their vantage point they had an unobstructed view down the slope towards the corner of Hammond Street. The distance from their position to the corner was no more than one hundred and fifty yards.

Moving slowly and deliberately the two men unpacked and made ready the equipment they would need from their small camouflaged rucksacks. They were dressed in full DPM combat gear, including the head and shoulders from a ghillie suit. The exposed skin on their hands and face was covered in black and olive-green camouflage cream.

From the corner of Hammond Street, the two men would be invisible and they were concealed well enough to avoid detection should anybody venture further up the slope to their location.

Both men carried powerful binoculars and a can of pepper spray to deter any inquisitive dogs. Jack was also in possession of a high-powered Nikon camera, equipped with a zoom lens. The camera also had a date and time facility for any photographs taken. The men had carried in the minimum food and water required as well as plastic bags and an empty plastic container to remove all waste including their own faeces and urine. At the end of each day they would leave no trace that they had ever been there. This was even more important now the decision had been taken to extract from the observation point at the end of each day.

While Jack would be responsible for obtaining any photographic evidence that may present itself, Tom had the responsibility to maintain an operational log, making a written record of everything they witnessed. This was a simple and easy task while the weather remained clement but one that rapidly became a nightmare if the heavens opened. Fortunately, the long-range weather forecast for the next week or so was dry but with thick cloud cover.

Having sorted out their equipment, both men settled down and tried to make the observation post as comfortable as possible, carefully removing any stones and other objects that were directly beneath their prone bodies. It would never be comfortable, but it didn't need to be uncomfortable. They were going to be in that position for a considerable period of time.

Talking between the two men would be kept to a minimum as would the use of the personal radios they both carried for use in the event of an emergency.

Tom checked that Jack was in position and the camera was ready to go then said quietly in to his radio, 'Tom to Steve, over.'

Steve Grey who was at Worksop Police Station monitoring the dedicated channel for the operation quickly replied, 'Go ahead Tom.'

Steve would remain on duty at the police station to monitor any urgent radio messages from the two men on the ground. It would be his responsibility to ensure the safety of the men both on insertion and extraction from the observation post. He would also carry out any urgent PNC checks required by the observations team. It would be a long tiring day for Steve as well, but at least he was in the warmth and comfort of the police station.

Tom continued with his radio message, 'In position now Steve. The time is zero four thirty, commencing Operation Puma.'

'Received that Tom. Operation Puma commencing at zero four thirty. Out.'

Unless something drastic happened that would be the last radio message until the two men were ready for extraction as darkness fell later that day.

They were both in full operational mode now and remained silent, concentrating on the area of ground one hundred and fifty yards below their position.

The sun was high in the sky and the time was almost nine thirty in the morning when the first person of interest appeared on the corner of Hammond Street.

Tom and Jack had already been in position for almost five hours, but both men immediately saw the youth saunter across the road and take up his position sitting on the wide grass verge on the corner. The youth sat with his back towards them looking along the length of Hammond Street. He was very near the position Tom had seen Shane Street sitting when he'd carried out his initial recce.

Ten minutes after the youth appeared, the first vehicle of the day, a garish lime green Ford Escort, was driven along Hammond Street. As the car approached the corner, the youth on the verge stood up and waited for the car to stop opposite him. He then sauntered slowly across the road to the driver's door of the car as the window was lowered.

Jack's camera whirred into life as a fistful of banknotes were thrust towards the youth who instantly exchanged the money for three small deal bags containing a white powder.

Tom was surprised at the openness of the deal. There was no attempt made to conceal the transaction, it was as bold as brass.

After that first car, there was a constant stream of vehicles throughout the day being driven onto Hammond Street. Either the driver or the passenger would hand over cash for deal bags of powder before the vehicles were driven off again.

The dealers would be changed at regular intervals as the day wore on.

Tom immediately recognised the bulky figure of Shane Street when he appeared on the corner just after two o'clock in the afternoon.

Jack took photographs of every deal and every new dealer that appeared as well as the registration numbers of the vehicles being driven by the punters.

Tom also noted how Shane Street sat in his chair directing operations, he never actually went to the cars himself. There was a definite pecking order. The other dealers, including Shane's sons, would obtain the cash and hand over the drugs before returning to Shane and handing over all the money. Initially Shane would place the banknotes into a small blue cash tin that he kept beneath his chair. At regular intervals throughout the day he would instruct one of his sons to take the cash into his house on Hammond Street.

On four occasions throughout the day, the observation team witnessed the eldest son, Tyson, leave the corner and walk up the pit tip towards their location. There was a single gorse bush seventy-five yards in front of their position with a large, flat rock at its base. Tyson moved the rock to one side and removed several clear plastic bags containing white powder.

This was obviously Shane Street's main stash and it was kept well away from the area where they carried out the individual deals.

Tom noted that at any given time during the day, the dealers only ever had in their possession probably half a dozen deal bags of drugs and no more than fifty pound cash in their pockets. This was going to prove a problem, as amounts as small as that could only ever amount to a simple possession charge. On those amounts it would be virtually impossible to prove a charge of possession with intent to supply.

This made the evidence they were gathering even more vital, if they were to get the dealers charged with the more serious offence when they were eventually arrested.

The detectives can worry about that, thought Tom.

He checked his watch; it was now almost four thirty in the afternoon and Phil Webster, the Test Purchase Officer, would be driving onto Hammond Street soon.

Peering through his binoculars it was Tom who spotted the white Mercedes Sprinter van first. He whispered to Jack, 'Get the camera ready mate, Phil's just arrived on the plot.'

'I've got him', whispered Jack.

The TPO drove the van slowly down the road. The Mercedes was one of the high sided ones with the sliding door on the side.

Phil Webster pulled the van over and spoke to one of the younger dealers who had strolled warily over to the driver's door. There was a brief conversation before the young dealer beckoned Shane Street over.

Street walked over and stood about two yards from the driver's door and ordered Phil to get out.

Phil got out of the van and walked confidently towards Street.

Watching from above, Tom felt his muscles tense involuntarily, he realised what a dangerous time this was for the undercover officer.

Phil and Shane were soon engaged in an animated conversation, both men pointing and gesticulating wildly. After a few minutes Phil raised his arms out from his sides and spread his legs. Shane stepped forward and searched him, patting him down thoroughly. Phil had deliberately worn thin clothes so a search would quickly reveal that he was not wearing any sort of covert recording equipment.

When nothing was found, there was a half-hearted gesture of an apology from Shane Street and very soon both men were laughing and joking.

Without even attempting to score on this first occasion, Phil walked back to his van and with a cheery wave he jumped in and drove off.

Jack whispered, 'Christ Tom, that kids' got some bottle.'

'Yeah, not exactly the warmest welcome I've ever seen but it looks like he might be in.'

A steady stream of punters continued up until eight o'clock at night. Then the dealers started to drift off, the last one leaving just before nine o'clock.

The observation team waited for the last dealer to leave and then began their extraction routine, gathering up everything they had brought in with them so the observation post would be left totally sterile.

When he was satisfied the ground was clear, Tom reached for his radio and said, 'Tom to Steve. Over.'

The reply was instantaneous, 'Go ahead Tom. Over.'

'Time is now twenty-one fifteen and we're starting to extract. Our ETA to the rendezvous point is one five minutes. Over.'

'Received Tom, one five minutes. Over.'

Both men carefully crawled backwards out of the observation point taking care not to disrupt the thick vegetation any more than necessary, making one last check of the brambles as they did so.

Wearily they stood up, stretched aching limbs before making their way down the pit tip to meet Steve in the Land Rover at the extraction rendezvous point.

CHAPTER 42

11.30pm 4th August 1987
Linby Village, Nottinghamshire

Tom sat in the living room of his small cottage clutching a coffee. He was almost too tired to drink it. He'd arrived home just after nine thirty that night after another exhausting day in the observation post on the pit tip at Worksop.

He really should have gone straight to bed to get some much-needed sleep, but he was filled with trepidation and an anxiety that was preventing him getting any rest.

Tomorrow was the day of the appeal hearing for Barry Tate at the Royal Courts of Justice in London. Ever since Matt had gone missing following his suspension from work, Tom had been in a foul mood.

Since his suspension there had been no contact from Matt and after their last conversation where his friend had spoken so animatedly about exacting revenge on Barry Tate, Tom was worried sick for his friend.

His foul, angry mood, combined with his fatigue from the observations he was doing on Operation Puma, were starting to take their toll on his fledgling relationship with his girlfriend. He was fully aware that he was behaving badly towards Bev, but she had no idea of the strain he was under.

How could she know?

She was totally unaware of what was going on beneath the surface. As far as she was concerned, Kate had left her husband, these things happen. She didn't really understand her reasons for doing so but that's life, get over it.

What she really didn't understand was why Tom was being such an arse about it and in effect taking his foul mood out on her?

To compound this mounting friction between the two of them, there was no way Tom could ever try and explain to Bev what was really happening, as to do so would be a massive betrayal of his best friend's trust.

Bev was on nights and in the twenty minutes after Tom had arrived home and before she left to start her night shift just before ten o'clock, they had barely spoken a word to each other.

There was no goodbye, no see you in the morning sweetheart. Tom barely registered that Bev had gone out the door.

Ever since his leak to the press about corruption and his subsequent suspension, Matt had completely disappeared.

It was this silence that was making Tom really worried. He knew Matt wouldn't disappear completely off the radar for nothing. In his heart, he feared that his best friend had something planned to get his wife released and then extract some sort of revenge against the gangster Barry Tate.

As well as an overwhelming feeling of concern, Tom also felt angry that his friend hadn't trusted him enough to enlist his help in whatever it was he had planned for Barry Tate.

Tom also found it difficult to understand why Matt hadn't even taken the time to make a phone call, to let him know he was okay.

Robotically, he took another sip of his coffee and stared blankly at the clock on the mantelpiece above the fire. The hands of the clock seemed to drag around its face until it almost looked like they were going backwards.

Tom blinked hard, took another gulp of coffee and decided to go upstairs and at least try and get some rest. He needed sleep, he had to be back at headquarters at four o'clock in the morning for another day at Worksop.

He tipped the remnants of the coffee down the sink, rinsed the cup and placed it on the draining board.

The telephone started to ring.

'Finally, thank fuck for that!'

Tom grabbed the phone and said, 'Where the fuck have you been mate?'

'Tom. It's Chief Inspector Chambers. Who were you expecting? Have you heard from Matt Jarvis lately?'

'No, I haven't boss', was Tom's terse reply.

He was disappointed that it wasn't Matt on the telephone, but he also felt a sense of relief that he hadn't had to lie to his senior officer.

Ignoring the abruptness of Tom's reply, Jim Chambers spoke in a flat, measured tone, 'It's the day of Tate's appeal tomorrow, I just needed to check with you that you hadn't heard from Matt. I figured that if he was going to contact anybody it would be you. I need to speak to him Tom, the Chief Constable is raging about all of this. He scored a lot of brownie points when Tate was finally jailed and he's already demanding a full investigation and criminal charges for Matt and his wife, if as expected Barry Tate walks out of that courtroom a free man.'

'I'm being straight with you boss. I haven't heard a thing from Matt since the day he was suspended, not even a phone call. There's something all wrong about his disappearance. I think there's definitely more to this than meets the eye.'

Jim Chambers was quiet for a few seconds then said, 'Tom. I'm only going to ask you this once. Do you know something about all this carry on? Because if you do, you'd better cough it up right now mister.'

Tom swallowed hard.

After the debacle over the Cuckney siege and his affair with Jaycee Stasuik he had only recently started to feel trusted again by his Chief Inspector. He was desperate to tell him everything he knew, but then he thought of his mate's predicament and the danger facing his wife and said quietly, 'Sorry boss. I wish I did have all the answers, none of this makes any sense to me. You know Matt Jarvis as well as I do. I just can't see him being involved in corruption of any sort, let alone with a scumbag like Tate. Can you?'

There was a long pause before Chambers said, 'Look Tom, I know you're good friends but if you hear anything from him or his wife please tell them to contact me any time, day or night. You got that?'

'Will do boss.'

'Okay Tom, sorry to have disturbed your rest. Get back to sleep, you're on duty again soon.'

Tom put the phone down sighed heavily and said aloud, 'For fuck's sake Matt, please don't do anything stupid.'

He slowly walked upstairs to bed and hoped he'd made the right decision by not telling Chambers everything he knew.

He knew sleep wouldn't come easy.

CHAPTER 43

1.00pm 5th August 1987
Royal Courts of Justice, The Strand,
City of London

The man had been inside the unfinished multi storey car park since first light. It had been just after four thirty that morning when he'd arrived at the car park and slipped stealthily through the Harris fencing. It had been very cold, but at least there was no rain and there was hardly a breath of wind.

He had made his way quietly up to the sixth floor where he then sat patiently in the shadows, waiting.

He glanced at his wrist watch, it was now approaching one o'clock in the afternoon, it was time.

He slowly stood and removed a pair of blue latex gloves from his tracksuit bottoms. Slipping on the gloves, he walked across to the side of the car park that gave him a view along The Strand. He stopped a yard short of the edge and looked down the busy road. In the distance he could see the hustle and bustle outside The Royal Courts of Justice.

He reached above his head and opened up the broken, silver coloured corrugated conduit hanging from the unfinished ceiling. He reached inside and retrieved the rifle and ammunition he had stashed there three days ago.

It was exactly as he had left it.

The rifle was wrapped in a muslin cloth inside a plastic sleeve and the three rounds of 7.62 ammunition were in a zip lock bag, which contained a few grains of rice to ensure there was no moisture in the sealed bag.

He knew that inside the court building at any moment, the three judges would be announcing their verdict on the appeal against conviction of drug kingpin Barry Tate.

Everything in the man's elaborate plan had fallen into place. The evidence that had convicted Tate in the first place had been systematically destroyed the key witness removed from the equation and the chief prosecutor under investigation for corruption. The judges hearing the appeal would have no option but to find the original conviction unsafe and release Tate.

Having removed the Draganov sniper rifle from its packaging, he quickly set the weapon up on its attached bipod. The silencer at the end of the lethal barrel protruded slightly over the course of two bricks at the edge of the building.

The Draganov was definitely not his weapon of choice. He'd never liked the Russian made weapon but at short notice and through some very unsavoury contacts he was happy to have obtained any weapon, even if the price of it was clearly extortionate.

Although not keen on the rifle he'd been pleased to see that it was well maintained, in good working order and most importantly sterile. Any identifying marks had been removed thoroughly.

Three days ago, before he stashed the weapon in the car park he'd tested it in nearby Epping Forest. He'd carried out several test shots to centre the weapon and to test both its accuracy and reliability.

He had been pleasantly surprised on both counts.

The weapon had been perfect and the custom-made silencer attachment didn't affect the accuracy of the weapon in any way. The powerful telescopic sight attached to the weapon was clear, had no cloudy patches and gave a sight picture of genuine clarity.

All things considered, it had been well worth the ten thousand pounds it cost him to obtain it.

Looking along The Strand, he could now see the crowds starting to gather around the area where the impending statement to the media would be delivered.

The days big news story was about to break.

The man allowed himself a grim smile.

None of the gathered media outside the High Court had any idea that this particular news story was about to get far bigger and far more sensational than any of them could have imagined when they had arrived that morning.

As the feeling of anticipation grew and he felt the familiar surge of adrenalin course through his body, the man lay down next to the weapon and started a well-practiced routine that enabled him to embrace the rifle. He always followed the same routine, the weapon eventually feeling like a natural extension of his body.

In just a few minutes time he would be able to reach out and deliver a lethal dose of vengeance to Barry Tate.

As he stared down the powerful scope, he became aware of a change of mood among the gathered crowd. There was a clamour, an air of excitement. He could see expectant looks on the faces of the gathered news reporters. There was a definite sense of renewed urgency amongst the gathered media.

Finally, the man saw his quarry for the first time.

The unmistakeable bulky figure, the shaven head and well-trimmed goatee beard, the distinctive diamond studs in both ear lobes.

He had studied this face until it was an ingrained image on his very psyche.

Wearing a cream coloured Armani suit and a black Paul Smith shirt and tie, Barry Tate strode confidently alongside his beaming barrister to the area directly in front of the waiting media scrum.

When Tate finally stopped to address the nation's media, the man could see the beaming smile on the gangster's face through the powerful scope. The cross hairs of the scope were resting on the middle of his forehead.

The sniper made the minimal adjustment necessary until the cross hairs were lined up perfectly on the bridge of Tate's nose.

Very deliberately and without compromising the position of the weapon he slowly slid the bolt action of the weapon forward until the soft nosed full metal jacket 7.62 round was in the breach. With a downward motion on the bolt the weapon was now cocked and ready to fire.

Down below, some four hundred metres away, Barry Tate raised his arms aloft, both fists clenched in a triumphant pose.

Flash bulbs from cameras repeatedly illuminated his grinning features.

In the unfinished car park, the man slowly exhaled and as he did so he exerted an ever-increasing amount of pressure on the sensitive trigger of the Draganov.

The weapon silently kicked into life and with a sense of satisfaction the man felt the recoil from the rifle reverberate through his shoulder.

From his vantage point he continued to stare down the powerful scope as the bullet slammed into the smiling face of Barry Tate.

The effect was instant and catastrophic.

The gangster's head virtually exploded as the soft nosed round pulverised his skull, smothering his barrister and the onlooking reporters in a shower of blood, brain and bone fragments.

Although instantly decapitated, Tate's body seemed to remain standing for a few brief seconds, before collapsing to the floor like a marionette with its strings suddenly cut.

Seeing the devastation and knowing beyond doubt that Tate was dead, the man allowed another flicker of a smile to cross his features. Below him there was absolute pandemonium as people scattered to try and get away from the dreadful event that had unfolded before their very eyes. There was also an overwhelming sense of panic amongst the crowd as they realised there was still a real threat of further danger.

The man slowly crawled backwards away from the Draganov leaving it in position. He had no reason to keep it any longer, it had completed its deadly task. It was sterile and clean.

He gathered up the packaging the rifle had been stored in, the spent cartridge from the breach and the unused two rounds of ammunition. Crushed them down into a small plastic bag and stuffed the lot into a downpipe on the other side of the car park, away from the rifle.

He then quickly made his way back down to the ground floor of the car park. In the distance he could hear the wailing sirens of the emergency services as they battled their way through heavy traffic to the scene of devastation outside the court.

He waited by the Harris fencing and scanned the street for prying eyes, before surreptitiously slipping through the opening and quickly replacing the fence.

Dressed in a nondescript dark blue tracksuit and running shoes, the man popped his Sony Walkman headphones into his ears and set off jogging slowly along the road and away from the ensuing pandemonium on The Strand.

He looked like just another office worker taking advantage of his lunch hour to get a little exercise before returning to his desk.

As he put distance between himself and the chaos, he grinned and said aloud, 'I wonder if that will be on the six o'clock news!'

He laughed aloud at his own joke, then quickened his pace as he jogged down the deserted street.

CHAPTER 44

6.00pm 5th August 1987
Hammersmith, London

From the moment she had regained consciousness in the back of her abductor's van, Kate Jarvis had been kept bound and blindfolded.

Her captors had treated her with respect and she had been given ample food and water. She was aware that two men were holding her prisoner but they deliberately kept any conversation between them down to a minimum.

She estimated that she had been held captive for two weeks, but she had no real way of knowing. She slept when she was tired and ate when she was offered food. Meal times were irregular and she could have water whenever she needed it, but she had to ask.

The place she was being held captive in smelled of damp and was very cold at night. She slept on a mattress on the floor and was only given a duvet when the temperature got really cold.

The cloying gag, that had been roughly forced into her mouth when she was first taken, was removed when they had arrived at their current location. It had been made very clear to her by her abductors that if she shouted or did anything else to try and raise the alarm, the gag would quickly be put back and would not be removed again.

She had been kept bound, her ties would only be loosened to allow her to eat or to go to the toilet. The most degrading part of her captivity was the fact that either one of the men would continue to watch her at all times, even when she was using the toilet.

She had been compliant at all times, determined not to do anything that would antagonise her captors. The crippling pain of the Taser and the stifling unpleasantness of the gag were both still very fresh in her memory.

On one of the few occasions the men spoke to her, she was ordered to comply with every request they made without question. She was informed that if she did this then no harm would come to her and more importantly, her husband would also be spared.

The men had impressed on her that under no circumstances was she to touch or attempt to remove the blindfold that was tied so tightly around her face. Chillingly, they had told her dispassionately that if at any time she saw either of their faces she would be killed immediately and that Matt would be executed shortly after.

The men had graphically described to her how their colleagues had abducted Matt the day after she had been taken and that he was being held at a different location close by. Again, they stressed to her that provided she and Matt co-operated fully and Barry Tate was released from custody following his appeal then they would both be released unharmed.

With a final veiled threat, the man who appeared to be in charge had told her that the last thing they wanted was the blood of a lawyer and a serving police officer on their hands.

Throughout her time in captivity she had obeyed every

command, however degrading. She had no idea how long she would remain captive as she had no sense of how long she had been there already. In her mind she believed that Tate's appeal must be very soon, but she was unsure.

As usual she had been given toast, jam, a banana and a drink of water when she awoke. Trying to estimate how long ago that had been was difficult. She had no sense of daylight, everything was pitch black because of the tight blindfold. From her room she could hear no sounds from outside that might have given her a clue as to the time of day.

Her best guess was that it must be approaching midday.

If by any chance today was the day of Tate's appeal then the verdict would be coming in soon.

She silently prayed that Barry Tate would be released today.

She was now desperate for the release of the gangster and cold-blooded murderer she had worked so hard to see sent to prison for the rest of his life.

Kate Jarvis had no way of knowing if her captors were being truthful and that she would be released unharmed. At the moment that was all she had to cling to. She didn't even want to think about what would happen if they were lying to her.

Suddenly, she heard an animated voice outside her door. It was one of her captors returning. The man who had been watching her unlocked the door to allow his associate in.

He sounded very upbeat, joyous even. He mumbled something that she didn't quite hear. The reaction of the second man was instantaneous, he also became very excitable. Both men were laughing and she could hear them jumping up and down and congratulating each other.

Suddenly, she felt one of the men kneel onto the mattress next to where she was sitting. She could feel his presence next to her face, she could smell the onion on his breath. He said quietly right next to her ear, 'It's done. We've succeeded. We can all go home very soon. Today you can go home to your family.'

She said nothing. But she could feel herself smiling from ear to ear and began nodding.

She felt the weight lift from the mattress and she blurted out, 'What about my husband?'

Both men laughed out loud, 'What about your husband? We never had your husband.'

There was the sound of more mocking laughter and the man in charge said icily, 'Do you think we're crazy? Why would we kidnap a police officer? Especially one with a rifle!'

Kate was now totally confused, she had no idea what was going on.

If the two men had lied to her about holding Matt captive maybe they had lied about other things too. Suddenly she knew that she wasn't going to be released, she was going to be killed and her body disposed of.

She felt a rush of panic and desperation envelop her and she yelled, 'Why are you doing this to me?'

One of the men gripped her shoulders roughly and said, 'Be quiet! Stop shouting! Today, I will keep my word, you will go home. Your husband's been a huge help to us, he's done everything we asked him to do. He's very well and unharmed. If you can just calm down and hold it together you'll see him again soon, okay?

She nodded then slumped back down onto the mattress.

Time passed slowly by and then suddenly the door

opened noisily. Instinctively she knew that both her captors were now standing at the side of the mattress. The leader said, 'On your feet Mrs Jarvis. It's time for you to go home. Please don't do anything stupid now and try to see who we are. It's still the same rules. If you see either of our faces I will have no option but to kill you and please believe me when I say that is not something I want to have to do, okay?'

She had always felt that the way the men spoke was slightly strange. Generally, their English was flawless, but every so often they would pronounce a word differently. Try as she might, she couldn't determine the accent.

She was helped to her feet and her senses told her that one of the men was now standing directly in front of her. In an effort to reassure her he placed both hands on her shoulders and said, 'Don't worry. I'm not going to hurt you, but this is necessary.'

Kate felt the man put a pair of glasses onto her nose and tuck them behind her ears. He said, 'Don't worry, it's just a pair of large sunglasses to conceal your blindfold as we need to go outside.'

He then chuckled and said, 'Please don't take them off, they actually look very good on you.'

He then placed a large floppy hat on her head to finish the disguise.

One of the men then walked at her side, as if he were guiding a blind person and she could hear the footsteps of the second man immediately behind her.

The man guiding her said, 'Be careful here, there are two steps.'

Finally, after being held indoors for what seemed like an eternity she could suddenly feel the sun's rays on the exposed skin of her cheeks. Generally, the weather was cool and she could feel a slight breeze.

She was instantly aware of a lot of traffic noise.

The volume of traffic was heavy and there was the constant drone of vehicle engines that you only get in large city centres. She could hear a jumble of voices and felt people jostling past them, she kept her head down.

They walked steadily for twenty or so minutes with her captor still guiding her by the arm. She noticed that gradually the traffic noise began to diminish and she began to hear birdsong and the breeze passing through leaves on trees.

Suddenly, she was again filled with a sense of dread.

Why were the men taking her away from the busy crowded street?

Were they moving her away from houses to an area of quiet woodland so they could kill her?

Just as she was plucking up the courage to start struggling and make a bid for freedom, they stopped walking.

The man guiding her said, 'Please don't, Mrs Jarvis. I can feel you're getting tense. Your ordeal will soon be over. I've given you my word that if you co-operate I will not harm you. I do not give my word lightly, so please trust me.'

Calming down a little she nodded nervously.

Her guide again put his hands on her shoulders, turned her through forty-five degrees and said quietly, 'Sit down.'

Instinctively, she reached out behind her and bent her legs as the man forced her to sit down. Her outstretched hands touched what felt like a wooden bench.

Growing in confidence, slowly she sat all the way down.

In the distance she could hear children laughing and squealing. She could also hear ducks and the sound of running water. There was the ever-present sound of leaves moving in the wind.

She felt the bench move as the man who had been her guide sat down next to her. He leaned in close and she could feel his breath on her cheek as he said, 'Mrs Jarvis, thank you for your co-operation. The last thing we wanted was to harm either you or your husband. I have one last instruction for you, do this and you will never hear from us again. Be aware that we are still watching your husband and we can still reach out to him if we have to. It would be such a shame to have to kill him after everything he's done for us.'

With her voice breaking with emotion and the stress of the situation she replied, 'Whatever it is, you know I'll do it. Please don't harm my husband, I'm begging you, I love him so much.'

'Just do as I say and he will not be harmed. Sit perfectly still here for fifteen minutes. Do not attempt to remove your sunglasses or your blindfold. Do not attempt to speak to anybody you hear passing by, if they talk to you, ignore them. Do you understand?'

She nodded vigorously.

'Do you understand? Say it!'

'Yes. I understand!'

'After fifteen minutes you can do what you like, up to then we'll be watching you closely, okay?'

'Okay I understand. Please don't hurt my husband.'

She felt the weight lift from the bench as the man who had been sitting next to her stood up.

Nothing further was said.

Kate strained her ears listening for any sound that would betray the presence of her two captors.

The only sounds she could hear were the continued squeals of delight from children playing away in the distance and a dog barking.

She sat bolt upright and perfectly still with her hands tucked under her thighs. Was this another test? Were the men still there watching her or had they simply vanished?

Nobody approached her and after what she estimated was at least twenty-five minutes she very gingerly moved her right hand up to her face. She let her hand linger around the sunglasses for another few minutes fully expecting to hear a barked order not to touch them.

She stayed like that for another five minutes and when nothing happened, she very slowly and deliberately removed the sunglasses and then the blindfold.

She sat with her eyes screwed tightly shut, still no order to replace the blindfold came.

There was nothing but silence so very slowly, she opened her eyes.

Looking around her, Kate saw that she was in a large park.

She was sitting on a wooden park bench that overlooked a vast lake with a variety of different ducks, geese and other water fowl on it. Away to her left, some two hundred yards away, she could see a playground. The squeals of delight and laughter she had heard were from the children playing on the swings and slides.

Turning to her right she could see a busy road in the distance. She saw two red double decker buses and several black cabs racing along the road and she realised where she was.

This was London.

Suddenly, it started to make sense. Her abductors had brought her to the capital where they could witness first-hand the events unfolding around Barry Tate's appeal. Just thinking about Tate and his thugs sent an involuntary shiver down her spine.

His thugs!

The shiver turned to a moment of blind panic when she realised that she had not checked to see if she was still being watched over. Quickly, she scanned the park looking for two men, thankfully there wasn't a man in sight in any direction.

The only person she could see nearby was a woman walking her two Labrador dogs. The woman was twenty yards away and walking quickly towards her from the direction of the road, the large dogs were both on leads.

Kate slowly got to her feet and began walking towards the young woman.

She approached the woman, made a fuss of the two dogs and said, 'Excuse me, is this Hyde Park?'

The woman laughed, 'No darling, this is Ravenscourt Park in Hammersmith. Hyde Park's miles away.'

The laughter stopped and the woman's face took on a look of concern, 'Are you alright love? Only you look a bit shaken up.'

Kate smiled, 'I'm fine, just a bit lost. You don't have a mobile phone I could borrow for a second, do you?'

'No, sorry. I haven't got one of those new phones yet. Still a bit out of my price range really.'

Kate's face must have registered her disappointment because the young woman quickly said, 'Look, I tell you what, there's an old phone box up on the main road back there. It's only a couple of hundred yards away, if you get to the road and just turn left you'll find it. You can always reverse the charges if you're stuck for cash. That is if the little bastards round here haven't smashed the bloody phone box up again. Really sorry I can't help you more love, but I've got to dash. Bye.'

The woman yanked at the dog leads and in a second was striding off purposefully, heading for the swings and slides of the children's park.

Kate took off the ridiculous floppy hat and threw it on the ground before walking towards the busy road. She felt scared and tearful and was only just starting to realise how much her ordeal had sapped her strength. She cursed herself for not asking the woman with the dogs what time it was, but she guessed it was early evening.

She reached the busy road and looked left, sure enough, away in the distance she could see the red telephone box.

Although the road itself was very busy there were few pedestrians around. The houses on the road were quite large and a little set back from the road, surrounded by high walls or hedges.

After what seemed an age she reached the phone box. She opened the door fully expecting to see the receiver dangling down and wires ripped out. To her delight, the phone looked intact, she lifted the receiver from the cradle and was even more delighted to hear the dialling tone.

Apart from the strong smell of piss, the numerous cards advertising the services of prostitutes and the fact that most of the small panes of glass were either smashed or cracked, at that particular moment in time, Kate thought this was probably the best phone box in the world.

She was unsure about trying to reverse charge a call to

Matt's new mobile as she didn't know if this was possible. As she dialled the number to contact the operator she decided who she would call. If she couldn't get hold of Matt direct she might be able to contact him through his work.

She felt the police would definitely accept a reverse charge call in these circumstances.

'Hello operator, how can I help?'

'Hello, can I make a reverse charge call to this number please?'

Kate quoted the direct line telephone number to the Special Operations Unit at Nottinghamshire Police Headquarters.

The operator said, 'That's a direct line number to a department of the Nottinghamshire Police. Are you sure you want to place this call madam? There are large fines for people who abuse this system.'

Trying to remain calm Kate said tersely, 'I'm fully aware of that and I'm also sure that it's imperative that I place this call. Thank you.'

The line went silent, then she could hear a whirring noise.

Suddenly she was through. 'Special Ops, Sgt Turner speaking.'

'Sgt Turner it's Kate Jarvis, can I speak to my husband Matt please?'

'Just a second Mrs Jarvis.'

The line was silent for a few moments, then another voice came on the line, 'Mrs Jarvis, I'm Chief Inspector Chambers, Matt's boss. I'm afraid he's not here at the moment. Where are you?'

'I'm in London, I'm near a park somewhere in Hammersmith. I've been abducted and held prisoner for a week or so. I've just been released but I don't have any idea where I am other than somewhere in Hammersmith and I've got no money.'

She felt the emotion and stress from her ordeal rising to the surface once again and she added tearfully, 'Please help me, I'm cold and scared.'

Jim Chambers couldn't quite believe what he was hearing, but he remained calm and said, 'Is there a number for the phone box displayed anywhere? It's usually in the middle of the circular dial.'

'Yes, I see it.'

Okay Mrs Jarvis, give me that number and stay exactly where you are. I'll get the Met to send a car for you straight away and take you to the nearest police station, where you'll be safe. In the meantime, I'll try and contact Matt for you. Stay where you are, the police will be with you soon. Do you need an ambulance? Are you injured at all?'

'No, I'm not hurt. I'm just very scared and very tired, please hurry.'

CHAPTER 45

9.30pm 5th August 1987
Nottinghamshire Police Headquarters

Tom sat quietly in the back of the dark Land Rover as it was driven slowly into the car park at Police headquarters.

He'd been deep in thought ever since Steve Grey had extracted him and Jack from the lane at the side of the old Renton Colliery pit tip. Steve could hardly wait to tell them both about the shooting of Barry Tate outside the High Court in London earlier that day.

Deep in the pit of his stomach, Tom had a feeling of dread.

Could it really be possible that Matt had something to do with the cold-blooded murder of this ruthless gangster?

As Tom unloaded his gear from the Land Rover Steve said quietly, 'Don't rush off Tom. Chambers is waiting to see you in private as soon as Jack's left.'

'Okay mate, do you know what he wants?'

'No. I just got a radio message earlier this evening that he wants to see you on your own before you stand down.'

Tom nodded, then made his way over to the huts.

Having stowed his gear in his locker, he heard Jack shout from the briefing room, 'I'm off Tom! See you in the morning.'

'Okay mate, see you later.'

Tom walked along the corridor and knocked on the Chief Inspector's door.

'Come in!'

With some trepidation, Tom opened the door and stepped inside.

Jim Chambers stood, walked round his desk and said, 'Follow me.'

Both men walked back into the briefing room, Jim Chambers put a video tape in the VCR, switched the television on and said, 'You need to see this, Tom.'

The television screen came on and Tom saw that it was a recording of the BBC six o' clock news.

With a grave expression, the newsreader introduced the sensational story about the murder of Barry Tate. The scene then switched from the studio to a reporter standing outside the Royal Courts of Justice in London.

The reporter said a piece to camera, then the pictures switched back to the live news feed from earlier that day. The camera was shaking badly but the pictures were of a chaotic scene outside the High Court. It showed the same stern faced, but visibly shaken, reporter giving a live commentary on the dreadful scenes as they unfolded.

In excitable, panicked tones the reporter said, 'You've come to us early as the notorious gangland figure Barry Tate has been shot as he prepared to give a statement to the press outside the High Court. The fatal shooting followed minutes after his dramatic release from custody. His appeal against conviction had been successful. From what I can see, it would appear that Tate's been gunned down by a professional hitman using a high-powered rifle.'

As pandemonium continued in the background, the reporter went on with his sensational bulletin.

His voice got louder and more frantic as he attempted to speak over the chaos all around him, 'I should have been standing here today reporting on the outcome of Barry Tate's release and the fallout from that decision with regard to both the Police and the Judiciary. The verdict itself is shrouded in mystery after the Crown offered no evidence in the appeal. A situation that before today was almost unheard of. The original conviction and subsequent jailing of Tate now smacks of high level corruption and the legal system has been left reeling. However, events have now overtaken us and we've all been witness to the most horrendous and cold-blooded murder. What I've just witnessed resembled some dreadful scene from a Hollywood movie, not what anyone would expect to see on the steps of the very seat of justice in this country.'

The scene then switched back to the reporter, now speaking in calm, flat tones on the same steps. Using a tone in keeping with the sombre mood he said, 'Rumours and speculation are now rife as to who could be responsible for this dreadful assassination. All I can say with any certainty at this moment in time is that Barry Tate is dead, having been gunned down on the streets of our capital city. I have just received a very brief statement from the City of London Police. It says quite simply "No arrests have been made and enquiries are ongoing".

The reporter then looked dramatically over his shoulder towards the very spot where Tate had fallen and said in a grave voice, 'This has been a, horrific day at the High Court. We will of course keep you informed of any developments, as they happen.'

Without saying a word, Chambers stepped forward and switched off the television.

Tom was stunned.

If Barry Tate was dead, where did that leave Kate Jarvis?

His mind was racing.

Where was Matt? Did he have something to do with the shooting?

Better than anyone, he knew only too well that his friend certainly possessed the skills needed to have taken such a shot.

As thoughts continued to flood his brain, Tom was suddenly aware that Jim Chambers was now talking to him, 'The reason I wanted to see you before you head for home is that earlier this evening I received a telephone call from Kate Jarvis. She was calling from a telephone kiosk in London, somewhere near Hammersmith, I believe. She told me that she'd been the victim of an abduction and had been held for almost two weeks in a house near to where she'd been released by her two abductors. Does any of this make any sense to you mister?'

Tom had to think fast and blurted out, 'No boss, I'm shocked. Is Kate okay?'

'It seems that whoever's been holding her captive has treated her reasonably well. I arranged for the Met to send a vehicle to the phone box and get her picked up and taken to the nearest police station so she was safe. I've now got Graham Turner driving down to London to collect her and bring her back here. I don't want the Metropolitan Police or the City of London Police to start thinking that her abduction has anything to do with what happened outside the High Court today.'

Tom remained silent, trying to process everything he'd been told.

In angry tones Chambers said, 'I'm going to ask you one more time, have you had any contact with Matt Jarvis? Obviously, it's even more imperative that we find him now that his wife has turned up safe and well. I don't really know what's going on here but I don't like it. If there's any way you can contact Jarvis, I suggest you do it right now.'

'Boss, the only contact number I've got for Matt is the number for his mobile phone. He doesn't like the new phone so I don't know if he'll have it with him. I've tried calling it before and he never answers the bloody thing.'

'Call it now Naylor, and keep calling it until he answers it!'

Tom started to dial the mobile number, watched over by an increasingly angry and agitated Jim Chambers.

On the tenth attempt, the call was answered by a very tired sounding Matt, 'Bloody hell Tom! This must be urgent if you won't stop calling the fucking number. What's up?'

'Matt, thank Christ I've finally got hold of you. It's Kate, she's been found safe and well in London. Somewhere near Hammersmith. The Met police have picked her up and she's safe. Where the fuck are you?'

Matt was instantly wide awake, 'Thank God.'

There was a long pause.

Chambers growled at Tom, 'Where the fuck is he?'

Tom said, 'It's great news mate, tell me where you are and we can go and fetch her back from London?'

Tom's heart sank as Matt said, 'I'm already in London. I came down on the train the day after I was suspended. I needed to get away from the house. I've been staying with relatives in Chingford. Never mind me, how's Kate? Have you got any more details? Was she released or did she get away?'

'I don't know the answers to any of that. I'm with the Chief Inspector at the moment. He knows everything there is to know, I'll put him on.'

Jim Chambers grabbed the phone, 'Exactly whereabouts in London are you Jarvis? I've got Graham Turner en route to collect your wife. I'll get him to pick you up as well and bring you both back here.'

Matt gave the address where he was staying and said, 'I'll wait for the sergeant here sir.'

'Make sure you do. We need to get you and your wife back up here after today's events.'

'What do you mean?'

'Haven't you seen the news today?'

'No.'

'Barry Tate was killed earlier today.'

The line suddenly went dead.

Jim Chambers was livid, 'The bastard's hung up!'

He immediately contacted Graham Turner by radio and ordered him to drive to the address in Chingford first and pick up Matt before he drove to West End Central police station to collect Kate Jarvis.

He barked down the radio, 'When you've picked them both up, don't hang about down there. Get back in the motor and straight back here. I want them both here at headquarters for a full de brief. I don't give a fuck what time it is when you've picked them both up, something's not right here. I need to know if Matt Jarvis had anything to do with what happened outside the High Court building today. Have you got that?'

Jim Chambers then turned to Tom and said, 'Get off home Naylor. I'll talk to you in the morning when you get back here for Operation Puma.'

'Okay boss.'

The words Jim Chambers had said about Matt being involved had been niggling away at Tom ever since he'd heard about the murder. Chingford wasn't a million miles away from the Royal Courts of Justice.

What he couldn't understand was why someone had gone to all that effort to get Tate released only for him to be then gunned down in cold blood. Had Matt already known that his wife had escaped or was about to be released before shooting Tate?

Whichever way he thought about it, somehow everything pointed squarely at Matt being involved.

CHAPTER 46

12.30am 6th August 1987
West End Central Police Station, London

The drive from Chingford to West End Central Police Station had been made in silence.

Graham Turner had been relieved to see Matt Jarvis waiting on the doorstep of the palatial house. When he first drove into the long driveway of the beautiful property Graham Turner had thought Matt had given Jim Chambers a false address.

Matt had thrown his brown leather grip bag into the boot of the car before getting in the passenger seat.

Graham said, 'Bloody hell mate, who lives here?'

'The house belongs to one of my uncles.'

'I didn't realise you had royal blood mate.'

'Where's my wife sarge?'

'She's at West End Central, it won't take us long to get there.'

The conversation was over, nothing else was said.

Graham Turner had never seen Matt looking so rough, he was unshaven and wearing a scruffy blue tracksuit.

Turner parked the car outside the police station and both men walked in through the large revolving doors.

The desk sergeant showed them into an interview room where Kate was waiting. There was a tearful reunion, they held each other tightly, both of them sobbing with relief.

The sergeant spoke to Graham, 'Is that her husband?'

'Yes Sarge, he's job too. How is she?'

'When we first picked her up she was at a telephone box near to Ravenscourt Park. She was exhausted. We've had her examined by a Police Surgeon. He says she's fit, well and okay to travel. We've spoken to her gently about her abductors and from what she's telling us it happened at a place called Calverton, which I believe is in Nottinghamshire. So, although she's been held down here, I think it's going to be down to your CID to investigate.'

'That's exactly the thoughts of my Chief Inspector. He wanted me to pass on his gratitude at your swift response to pick her up from the phone box.'

'No problem. She hasn't said anything of note about either her captors or where she was held. Seems like she was blindfolded throughout her ordeal.'

'Right sarge, if there's nothing else we're going to head straight off. These two need to get back home after everything they've been through.'

'Couldn't agree more, safe journey home.'

Graham knew that for every minute longer he stayed in West End Central Police Station there was an increased risk that somebody would make the connection between the Crown Court barrister Kate Jarvis and the gangster Barry Tate. If somebody made that connection then the questioning would begin in earnest trying to ascertain if there was any link between her abduction and his fatal shooting.

Within ten minutes of first walking into West End Central, all three were back in the car and speeding through the capital heading for the M1 North signs.

CHAPTER 47

3.00am 6th August 1987
Nottinghamshire Police Headquarters

As soon as they all arrived back at headquarters, Jim Chambers took Matt into his office and instructed Graham Turner to take Kate into the Briefing Room for a hot drink.

Matt and Kate had both started to protest at the lateness of the hour but Chambers was insistent.

The Chief Inspector questioned Matt for half an hour about his actions since he was suspended and his whereabouts leading up to the time Barry Tate had been murdered.

After listening patiently and repeatedly answering the questions, eventually Matt snapped, 'Why don't you just came straight out with it? You think I had something to do with killing Barry Tate, don't you? I only wish I'd been given the opportunity, because I would've gladly taken it. That scumbag got entirely what he deserved. Why should the authorities lock him up and then expect the rest of society to keep him for the rest of his natural life? Good riddance to bad rubbish I say. If you're so convinced that I murdered Tate, arrest me and interview me properly. I've had enough of this bullshit. Arrest me or I'm taking my wife home right now!'

Chambers snapped back, 'Don't try my patience Pc Jarvis, I might just do that.'

Matt took a deep breath, regained his composure and said quietly, 'Listen boss, before you make that decision, and just so we can get this cleared up here and now, you need to know that the person I've been staying with since I left Nottingham is my uncle. You might know him better as His Honour Judge Sebastian Jarvis QC. I've been in his company for the majority of the time I was awake and yesterday afternoon, at the exact time Tate was shot, I was wearing waders and standing up to my armpits in water. I was with the judge fly fishing for trout in his private lake. Do you want to call him to verify this? I know it's very late and he will most definitely mind about being called at this ungodly hour, but I think it's better for all our sakes if you give him a quick call, don't you?'

Chambers sat back in his chair and took a deep breath.

He was quiet for a full minute, then said, 'Tomorrow will be fine. Your story can be verified tomorrow. Surely you can understand how all this looks? If it had been my wife that had been taken I don't know how I would have reacted.'

'Look boss. I do understand, but I had nothing to do with the murder of Tate. I've been down there with my uncle all the time. He's been doing everything he can to try and take my mind off the situation and stop me going out of my mind with worry. Right now, both me and Kate are exhausted. I just want to take my wife home. This can all be cleared up tomorrow.'

'Okay. Take your wife home. The CID will be over to start enquiries into your wife's abduction tomorrow, when you're both fully rested.'

Chambers walked out of his office followed by Matt.

He opened the briefing room door and said, 'Graham, can you drive them home please?'

'It'll be my pleasure boss.'

As he drove them to Oxton, Graham turned to Matt and said, 'Look mate, I know you're probably sick to death of talking about all this, but what I don't understand is who would go to all the trouble of abducting Kate, forcing you to do what you did, to get Tate released only to then have him killed by what appears to be a professional hitman. None of it makes any sense to me.'

'Nor me sarge. Right at this moment, I don't know and I don't care.'

Matt cradled his wife's head in his lap, she was already fast asleep.

CHAPTER 48

9.00am 12th August 1987
Nottinghamshire Police Headquarters

Operation Puma had been running constantly for ten days.

Chief Inspector Chambers had suspended the observations for one day and called all the participants into headquarters for a debrief. He wanted to assess the evidence gathered so far and to plan for the next phase of the operation.

Tom and Jack had welcomed a day away from the pit tip; they were both mentally and physically exhausted. The long hours they had put in every day and the physical strain of maintaining observations had taken their toll.

They sat quietly in the briefing room waiting for the debrief so they could go home and get some much-needed sleep.

Phil Webster breezed into the briefing room, took one look at them and said, 'Jesus! You two have got eyes like laboratory rats!'

Barely managing to muster a grin Jack replied, 'That may well be true Phil, but you've definitely got the teeth!'

The undercover officer laughed out loud and took a seat next to the two men.

The door opened and Jim Chambers strode purposefully into the room. He sat down in front of the three men and said, 'Right. Tom, Jack, you two both need some rest, so I'll keep this short and to the point. I've left the detectives out of this briefing, I can always liaise with them later if needs be. I want to know from you three exactly where we're at evidentially and what you think our next move should be. Tom, fire away please.'

'We've got some cracking evidence sir. I'm sure Steve's told you already that we've witnessed and photographed countless deals with punters. We know how they operate; their plan of operation and we've photographed them collecting drugs from their main stash on the tip. We've also got photographic evidence of dealers taking bundles of cash, obtained directly from dealing, into Shane Street's house, so we'll need to obtain search warrants for that address and the other dealers' houses on the day of the strike. We've also photographed the three test purchases carried out by Phil.'

'Have you had to deal with any compromise issues while you've been engaged in the observations?'

'No sir, none at all.'

'Any problems getting on and off the pit tip?'

'Nothing at all.'

'Good work.'

He then turned to Phil Webster and said, 'Have the drugs you obtained on the test purchases been tested yet?'

'Yes boss. I did field tests on the days I bought them. Everything I've bought has tested positive for amphetamine. I've exhibited all the drugs purchased and submitted them to the Forensic Lab for proper analysis, but I'm confident it will come back in line with the field tests.'

'That's great. Anything else I need to know from your side of things Phil?'

'After the first two scores went okay, on the third occasion I asked the young lad who came to the van if I could speak with the main man. Shane Street came over and we had a face to face. I wanted to ask him if I could make a larger purchase. I told him that I could easily pass the gear on to several mates up in Yorkshire. He went for this big time; I think he's expecting a nice little earner. He told me he was having a problem with supply at that time and said he was running low on gear himself, but that he expected to be resupplied by his main dealer in the next couple of days. He's going to call my mobile as soon as the new gear's arrived. He's told me I can have as much as I want as soon as his supplier's come through. I've also fed him the line about the knock off training shoes. I made sure I did it in front of all his scroty little cronies. They're all well up for it, so everything's looking good from my side. Like I said, I'll be getting a phone call as soon as he's been resupplied so we'll have plenty of time to set up the Trojan Horse scam for the strike.'

'Excellent work Phil. I don't suppose Street was stupid enough to drop any hints about the identity of his main supplier?'

'The only thing he said was that he was from Nottingham and that he would be bringing the gear to him rather than him having to go to Nottingham to fetch it. I think the only reason he told me that was because he's got an ego as big as a bus and he was trying to impress me, bigging himself up.'

Jim Chambers looked thoughtful and after a lengthy pause he said quietly, almost to himself, 'Do you know what would be really sweet? If we could identify his main supplier as well.'

He then looked directly at Tom and Jack, 'How do you both feel about spending a few more days on the pit tip?'

It was Jack who replied, 'We're both fine boss. I promise you my eyes don't look half as bad from this side.'

Tom grinned and nodded in agreement.

Jim Chambers smiled and said, 'Good lads. Two more days, three at the most. Let's see if we can pot this bigger fish from Nottingham as well.'

The briefing was over and Jim Chambers left the room.

Tom waited a few minutes before knocking on his door.

Chambers bellowed, 'Come in!'

Tom walked in and said, 'Sorry to disturb you boss. I was just wondering if there was any update on Matt?'

Tom's friend and sniper team partner had been back home for almost a week now but was still under suspension, the subject of an investigation into possible corruption.

Jim Chambers sat back in his chair, took off his glasses and steepled his fingers below his chin.

After a long pause he said, 'You're aware that your colleague is still under suspension and that I'm not at liberty to discuss any developments about that with you, aren't you?'

Tom nodded, 'Sorry sir, I was just wondering ....' He let the sentence tail off and turned to leave.

Jim Chambers said, 'However, if I was thinking out loud and just happened to think that the CID have so far found no case to answer for either Matt or his wife and that your colleague may well be back at work very soon, that wouldn't amount to a discussion, would it?'

Tom turned, his fatigue vanishing in an instant.

He grinned broadly and said, 'No sir, it definitely wouldn't!'

'Get off home Tom and get some rest. I want you back on that pit tip at daft o'clock tomorrow morning.'

'Yes sir, thanks.'

CHAPTER 49

9.00am 12th August 1987
Hammond Street, Renton Estate, Worksop

Shane Street was getting angrier by the minute.

As far as he was concerned Billy Swan was now seriously taking the piss. He'd promised to deliver the new batch of amphetamines up to Worksop within a week. Nine days had now passed and there was still no word from Swan and more importantly still no gear.

Street could deal effectively for one more day, two at a push and then he would be cleaned out and his customer base would go elsewhere and that would be him fucked. He knew that once a punter was getting sorted somewhere else, they wouldn't be back. Then he would be left chasing the debtors who he'd laid drugs on to without payment.

It was hassle he could do without.

His life was simple and easy at the moment and that's how he wanted it to continue.

He stomped into the hallway of his house and angrily grabbed the telephone. Thrusting his large sausage fingers into the small holes he dialled the number for Swan again.

The telephone was ringing, but once again there was no immediate answer.

Street screamed at the handset, 'Come on you fucking prick, answer the phone!'

As if in response to his raging the telephone was suddenly answered, 'Yeah, who's this?'

Street immediately recognised the lazy West Indian drawl and said through gritted teeth, 'Swan you're seriously taking the piss now. Where the fuck is my gear?'

The answer came in that same laconic drawl, 'Shane, my man. You've got to obtain a little patience. All good things come to those who wait. It's not easy for me you know, getting all your shit together takes a little time.'

'Don't be giving me all that bollocks! Patience my arse! You promised me you'd have it up here within a week. What's the fucking hold up?'

'You see brother, you need to understand the real concept of business. In our game it's all about supply and demand. Now relax and chill, I'll have the new batch up to your little piece of heaven tomorrow morning. Okay?'

'Not before time Billy, I'm on my arse here.'

'There's just one more thing Shane, the price for the gear has now gone up. I'm going to need an extra five grand when I bring the gear up to you.'

Shane Street gripped the handset so tight he was in danger of crushing it; the veins on his head and neck stood out and his face turned bright red as he was overcome with an incandescent rage.

He wasn't stupid, the delay had all been a fucking set up.

With real menace in his voice, he breathed down the phone, 'Don't fuck with me Billy Boy, we had a deal!'

With equal menace Swan replied, 'Yes, you're right Street, we had a deal, past tense. Now, we don't. The new deal is an extra five grand, take it or leave it!'

'Fuck you, Swan!'

'Who the fuck do you think you're dealing with Street? Without me you're nothing, don't ever forget that you fat fuck! You might be kingpin of that shit tip up there, but to me you're just another fucking sad act punter. It's that simple. Now if you want this gear, you'll pay the extra for it, if you don't then this conversation is over!'

There was a long pause as Shane Street tried to control his rage, it had been a very long time since anyone had spoken to him in that way. If Swan had been stood in front of him right then he would have plunged a knife straight in his chest.

Finally, he calmed down enough to speak, 'Alright Swan. I'll pay the extra five grand this time, but if you ever try and turn me over again you'll fucking regret it. Don't forget, I remember you from when you started out in this game, you were a pussy then and you're a pussy now.'

Swan roared with laughter and said, 'Is that so, I'm a pussy now, am I? Shane, you have to understand, this is only business. I get charged extra, you get charged extra. Shit rolls downhill as they say.'

'Right. Of course it does.'

'The drugs will be with you tomorrow morning, make sure you have the cash ready. All of it.'

'Right.'

'One last thing, Street. If you ever threaten me again, I'll do you once and for all. I don't appreciate your disrespect. You won't be the first I've put under the ground and you definitely won't be my last, you get me? I don't take shit from anybody these days and that includes you. Got it?'

Swan put the phone down.

Shane Street was still seething, he'd never been so angry in his life.

His son Rocky walked past him in the hallway and said, 'Anything wrong Dad?'

Shane smacked his son hard across the back of the head, 'When I want you to know, I'll tell you. Now get the fuck out of my face, you little shit.'

As Rocky stomped off up the stairs he shouted back, 'Fuck off you loser!'

Suddenly, a thought came into Shane's head.

That new punter from Yorkshire was after a big score.

A sly smile crossed his lips and he said under his breath, 'Fuck it. I'll pass the cost of the gear onto him. If he wants it that badly he'll have to pay a bit more for it.'

He started to relax a little as he realised that he wasn't going to be that much out of pocket. What was it Swan had said, "shit rolls downhill".

The smile on his face vanished and he felt the tension across his shoulders return when he thought about Swan.

Sooner or later he would pay that bastard a visit and watch him take his last breath.

CHAPTER 50

10.30am 13th August 1987
Hammond Street, Renton Estate, Worksop

Tom was hoping that today would be the last day that he and Jack had to crawl their way under the brambles on the old Renton Colliery pit tip.

It was a cold blustery day; rain clouds were scudding quickly across the dull grey sky. Every so often the heavens would open and the two men would be drenched.

Since they first crawled into position at four thirty that morning, it had already rained hard on three separate occasions. They were totally drenched, feeling tired and miserable.

The only saving grace was that they no longer needed to maintain the observation logs for evidence. They had more than enough drug deals recorded to convict each and every one of the dealers.

As long as they managed to keep the camera equipment dry and fully functioning they would be able to achieve their objective and record the moment Shane Street's supplier arrived on Hammond Street.

It hadn't rained for over an hour now and slowly, one by one the dealers started to reappear on the street below their position. Tom had been worried that the inclement weather could mean they were not in a position to witness any exchange between Street and his supplier. If it was raining, any interaction between the two would take place indoors out of their view.

Shane Street suddenly appeared on the street and stood on the corner. He placed a brown holdall on the ground at his feet before constantly looking at his watch and glancing along the road.

Tom was staring at his movements through high powered binoculars and said softly, 'What do you reckon mate, do you think he's expecting somebody?'

Jack replied, 'Looks that way to me.'

'Is the camera ready?'

'Yep, it's loaded with a new film, ready to go.'

Down on the corner, Street was pacing up and down constantly looking at his watch.

Tom glanced down at his own watch, it was now fast approaching ten thirty. Just as he put the binoculars back up to his face he saw a black Jaguar turn very slowly onto Hammond Street.

Shane Street stopped pacing and stared at the approaching sports car.

Tom whispered, 'This looks like the main man, get photographs of the registration number. I'll relay it to Steve Grey as soon as it stops.'

'Okay.'

The black car pulled to a stop on the corner of Hammond Street, the driver's door opened and a huge black man with short, corn row dreadlocks got out. He stretched, then slammed the door and walked across the road towards Shane Street.

Tom could hear Jack's camera whirring as he took photographs of the Jaguar and its driver; he whispered into his radio, 'Tom to Steve. I need an urgent PNC check on the following vehicle. Over.'

The reply was instantaneous, 'Go ahead with your reg number. Over.'

'It's a black Jaguar, registered number Bravo Sierra One One. Looks like a personalised plate. Over.'

As he waited for the vehicle check Tom whispered to Jack, 'I don't know what it is, but there's something familiar about the big guy.'

Before Jack could comment Tom heard Steve Grey through his radio earpiece, 'Tom. There's several Police Interest markers for this vehicle on the PNC. They're mainly from the Drugs Squad but the most recent one is from the Major Crime Investigation Unit. The registered keeper's an IC 3 male by the name of Billy Swan. There's a Nottingham address recorded for the keeper. It's all on the log. Over.'

'Thanks Steve. Over.'

Tom grinned, turned to Jack and whispered, 'I knew it. I arrested Billy Swan for a burglary years ago when he was just a daft kid.'

'Was he that big back then?'

'No mate, he was a kid.'

'I reckon he hasn't stopped growing since you nicked him.'

'I know what you mean, what the fuck's he been eating? He's a fucking monster. Look at the size of him. Shane Street's not a small bloke but he makes him look like Tiny Tim.'

'They don't look too friendly Tom, there's not been much of a greeting.'

Down below their position, Street and Swan had remained about two meters apart and were now eyeing each other suspiciously.

Swan broke the awkward silence.

He sucked air through his front teeth and said, 'Look Shane, there's nothing I could do. The price of the product has gone up and like I told you on the phone, shit rolls downhill man. You know that's how it is. Just pass the increase onto your own punters, don't be giving me all this grief and shit.'

'Whatever Billy. I'm not really interested in your fucking whining or your bullshit. Have you got the gear or not?'

'I need to see the money first. You know that bruv.'

You could have cut the tense atmosphere with a knife.

Street picked up the brown holdall and threw it across to Swan.

Taking his time and never taking his eyes off Street, Billy bent down and picked up the holdall.

He slowly unzipped the bag and saw that it was full of bundles of neatly wrapped twenty-pound notes.

Street snapped tersely, 'There's fifty-five grand in there. Do you want to stand there and fucking count it?'

'I'm not going to stand out here on the street and count it like some fool! We both know what'll happen if it's short, don't we?'

Street shrugged in a nonchalant manner.

Swan glared at him and said menacingly, 'Remember what happened to that greasy cock sucker Frankie Squires, when he started messing me about over finance!'

Street growled, 'Frankie Squires was a no mark. A snide fucker who got exactly what he deserved. You need to remember that I'm no Frankie Squires. I won't mess you about Billy, the cash is all there, including your fucking increase. Now where's my gear?'

For the first time since he arrived Swan allowed himself to break into a huge smile. He pointed at the car and said, 'Step this way, my man.'

Both men walked over to the Jaguar and Billy unlocked the boot.

The camera used by the observations team once again whirred into action, taking continuous shots as Swan reached into the boot, retrieved a large black bag and passed it to Street.

Immediately, Street took out the bundles of wrapped white powder and placed them onto the roof of the car. There were twenty bundles in all. As soon as he had counted them he replaced each bundle back into the bag. Before he replaced the last bundle, he made a small slit in the top with a pen knife. He slipped the knife back into his pocket and then dipped the very tip of his little finger into the powder.

Carefully, he rubbed his little finger across his gums above his front teeth.

He then broke into a broad grin and said, 'This is some very good shit, Billy Boy.'

'That's what I'm talking about Shane, you can cut this gear to fuck with whatever you like. You can double its quantity before you sell it on bruv.'

'You're not wrong.'

Billy threw the brown holdall containing the cash into the boot and closed it. He then walked round the side of the car opened the driver's door and sneered, 'Be seeing you Shane, I reckon that will keep your punters happy for a while.'

Shane picked up the black bag containing the drugs and started to walk back towards his house, without looking back at Swan he shouted, 'If you want to keep doing business Billy don't keep me waiting so long next time, and no more snide tricks or we're done.'

Billy got in the car, started the engine, said aloud 'Whatever you say, fat boy!' then switched on the cassette player and drove away, singing along loudly to the latest Peter Tosh release.

Both Swan and Street were totally unaware that their every move had been captured on film.

As the rain began to fall with a steady intensity, Tom hunkered down and said, 'Roll on darkness, so we can get the fuck out of here. I don't know about you Jack, but I'm sick of this Brer Rabbit shit! I don't care if I never see another bramble patch.'

CHAPTER 51

11.30am 13th August 1987
Nottinghamshire Police Headquarters

Chief Inspector Jim Chambers was a very happy man.

When Steve Grey had contacted him with the identity of Shane Street's main supplier and the fact that the transaction between Street and Billy Swan had all been photographed by the observation team, he felt like doing a little dance around his office.

Instead, he picked up his telephone and started making calls.

He dialled the number for the newly formed Tactical Surveillance Unit and requested they commence a twenty-four-hour surveillance on Billy Swan.

He then contacted the Major Crime Investigation Unit and the Drugs Squad and told them both about the evidence they had obtained outlining Swan's drug dealing activities.

He explained that within forty-eight hours he hoped to have all the main dealers in custody, including Swan and he had learned of their interest in him when making the checks on the PNC.

The Chief Inspector of the MCIU had confirmed that they would very much like to be involved in the questioning of Swan following his arrest. They had arranged for Detective Sergeant Davy Provost to liaise with Jim Chambers the next morning to discuss the forthcoming arrest.

Feeling very satisfied, Jim Chambers put the telephone down, let out a deep breath and sat back in his chair.

He smiled and began drumming his fingers on his ample stomach.

He loved it when a plan started to come together.

All he needed now was for Shane Street to contact Dc Webster and tell him he was in a position to supply a major deal to him, now he himself had been resupplied.

CHAPTER 52

9.00am 14th August 1987
Nottinghamshire Police Headquarters

The very next morning, Jim Chambers received the telephone call he'd been waiting on tenterhooks for, ever since he learned that Shane Street had been supplied with a large shipment of amphetamine.

His telephone was ringing as he walked into his office.

He snatched the phone off the hook and said, 'Chief Inspector Chambers.'

'Good morning boss, it's Phil Webster. I got a call late last night from Shane Street. I can buy as much gear as I want as soon as I'm ready. I didn't call you last night as it was nearly midnight when he contacted me.'

'No problem, that's great news, did he say anything else last night?'

'Yeah, the cheeky bastard's hiked the price up, but as we're not going to be actually handing any cash over it doesn't matter.'

'That's interesting though. Did he say why the price had gone up?'

'Not really. When I moaned about the increase and tried to haggle, he just fobbed me off and told me that it's top-notch gear and that I'd be able to cut it to fuck before passing it onto my punters.'

'The piece of shit really doesn't give a toss about the damage he's causing, does he?'

'He's a dealer, that's what they do, boss.'

'You're right Phil, it just makes me mad, that's all. Have you made any arrangements with Street yet?'

'No, not yet. It was late so I told him I'd call him sometime this afternoon to make all the arrangements. That way I'd be able to sort out his money for my gear, plus I'd also be able to ensure my van was full of good quality knock off training shoes for him and his lads to buy. I did sort of hint that I'd try to be on Hammond Street some time tomorrow morning.'

'Excellent. That sounds like a plan to me, great work Phil. I'd better get cracking. I've got some major planning and organising to do before tomorrow morning. We're only going to get one crack at this and I want it to be done right. Call Street this afternoon and tell him you've got everything organised and that you can pick your gear up and drop the trainers off at eleven o'clock tomorrow morning.'

'Right you are boss, eleven o'clock tomorrow morning.'

CHAPTER 53

6.30am 15th August 1987
Linby Village, Nottinghamshire

Tom Naylor stirred slowly, trying to ignore the persistent prodding in his ribs.

Eventually, his girlfriend's sharp fingernails did the trick and Tom woke up.

She complained, 'Tom, for Christ's sake, the phone's ringing!'

He'd been asleep in bed ever since he'd got home and crawled up to his bedroom after the observations job at Worksop had finished.

He hadn't realised just how mentally and physically exhausted he was.

The phone was still ringing off the hook as he sat up in bed and looked at the clock on his bedside cabinet, 'It's only six thirty Bev, who the hell's calling at this time of day?'

Without opening her eyes Bev grumbled, 'Why don't you answer the bloody thing and find out!'

He moodily snatched up the phone and muttered, 'Hello, Tom Naylor.'

Immediately he heard the cheery voice of the Control Room Inspector, 'Ah, finally. Good morning Pc Naylor, are you wide awake and raring to go?'

Tom took the phone away from his ear and looked at it incredulously, then with a look of disgust on his face he said sharply, 'I am now.'

'Marvellous. We need you to grace us with your presence this morning. Be at headquarters for a full briefing at seven thirty. Don't be late.'

The call was terminated immediately, leaving Tom holding the phone and listening to the dialling tone.

He replaced the phone and mumbled, 'Yeah thanks', before half stumbling out of bed towards the en suite shower.

Behind him, Bev turned over in bed and groaned, 'Keep it down Tom, I've got to be at work in a few hours.'

'A few hours? Aren't you the lucky one.'

'Shhhh!'

Twenty minutes later and Tom was showered, dressed and heading out the door of his cottage.

He drove steadily to headquarters knowing that he would arrive in plenty of time for the briefing. As he drove his car into the car park next to the huts he could see officers from A and D Sections also parking their cars.

As soon as he saw the staff from other sections arriving, he knew exactly what was happening.

Phil Webster must have received the all-important phone call from Shane Street.

Tom was buzzing.

He could still remember that overwhelming feeling of evil he'd experienced when he walked down Hammond Street and encountered the malevolent presence of Shane Street for the first time.

Hopefully, today would be the finalisation of Operation Puma. As far as he was concerned it couldn't come quick enough.

CHAPTER 54

6.30am 15th August 1987
Nottinghamshire Police Headquarters

Everyone had gathered in the main briefing room and at exactly seven thirty Jim Chambers walked in followed by two men wearing dark suits.

Tom recognised both men, one was the head of the Drugs Squad and the other the Detective Chief Inspector of Worksop Division.

Last to enter the room was Dc Phil Webster, the undercover officer. He was dressed in his usual scruffy clothes and immediately drew the same looks from the assembled ranks as he had from Tom and Jack when they'd first met him.

As he sat down at the front of the room, Phil raised a hand towards Tom and Jack in acknowledgment. Both men smiled back; they had the utmost respect for Phil and the way he calmly carried out his dangerous work.

Jim Chambers called the room to order and there was immediate silence.

He looked at the gathered men and said, 'Listen in gents. Over the last few weeks Tom and Jack have carried out daily covert observations on a gang of drug dealers operating on the Renton Estate at Worksop. During that period of time they've managed to gather invaluable intelligence on this drug dealing operation. They've amassed enough evidence for us to take the operation forward into its final stage. We're now in position to arrest all the dealers, charge them and hopefully get them sent down out of harms way for a good few years. In conjunction with the observations we've also deployed Dc Webster from the South Yorkshire Force as a Test Purchase Officer.'

Chambers looked along the front row and indicated the young detective before continuing, 'Dc Webster's done such a great job of infiltrating this gang, that he's now arranged to make a major purchase of amphetamines from the main dealer up there at eleven o'clock this morning. The main dealer being a man by the name of Shane Street. Dc Webster has also arranged with Street that at the same time he collects his gear, he'll have a load of stolen training shoes in the back of his delivery van for the dealers to purchase at knock down rates. What he conveniently forgot to mention to Street is that those training shoes will be being worn by a dozen of you lot!'

The room erupted into laughter.

Jim Chambers raised his hands and the room became quiet again.

'Okay, okay. This is the plan. Phil Webster will drive the van onto Hammond Street as usual. He'll stop on the corner as usual, get out and call the dealers across to the sliding side door of the van. Once they're all gathered at the van door with their bundles of cash ready he'll open the side door and C Section will emerge and detain the dealers. It's that simple. As soon as the dealers are arrested, Misuse of Drugs Act warrants will be executed on their home addresses. These addresses have been identified with help from the local CID. As I mentioned earlier, the leader of this motley crew is

Shane Street, four of the other dealers identified are his sons. They all live in the same house on Hammond Street. I'm deploying A Section to execute the warrant on the Streets' home address. I want a thorough job doing on this search. I want the place turning upside down, is that understood?'

Jim Chambers then indicated to the Detective Chief Inspector of Worksop CID to continue the briefing.

He stood up and addressed the men, 'I've arranged for plenty of my staff to be available for the interviews of these offenders following their arrest. All prisoners are to be taken to Worksop Police Station. There are going to be two custody sergeants on duty, so there shouldn't be too much of a back log when you're booking people in. I know it takes a little longer since the Police and Criminal Evidence Act came in, but we should be able to get them processed and ready for interview pretty quickly.

Finally, I just want to say that this lot have been a scourge on my Division for far too long and this operation is long overdue. Good luck, gentlemen.'

Jim Chambers then stood up and said, 'Right, C Section, liaise with Dc Webster about the final preparations for your role. The rest of you start making your way up to Worksop nick.'

CHAPTER 55

11.00am 15th August 1987
Hammond Street, Renton Estate, Worksop

The ten men of C Section were all crouched in the back of Phil Webster's Mercedes Sprinter van. The only man missing from the operation was Matt Jarvis, otherwise it was a full contingent.

As Tom looked around the van he could see some seriously grim and determined looks etched onto the faces of his colleagues. The tension in the van was palpable. There wasn't a sound in the van, nobody said a word. Everyone of the men inside that van knew that the drug dealers they were about to confront would not go down without a fight. The briefing had touched briefly on the type of individuals they would be tackling and their propensity for violence and carrying weapons.

No firearms had been mentioned but they were expecting to be confronted with knives, coshes and God knows what else.

Each man carried an extendable baton and several sets of Plasticuffs inside the belt loops of their uniform trousers.

Provided they managed to remain completely silent until the side door of the van was opened, they would retain that all-important element of surprise.

Hopefully, that would be all the edge they needed.

At the final briefing, Tom and Jack had been given the task of identifying and arresting the leader of the group, Shane Street.

As the van was driven into Hammond Street and slowly made its way towards the corner where the drug dealers congregated, Tom once again thought back to that feeling of menace he'd encountered doing that first recce.

He had seen close up what an evil bastard Shane Street was.

As the moment of no return approached, he got the familiar sensation of a rising tension in the pit of his stomach. His mouth was dry and his palms became sweaty as the adrenalin kicked in.

Phil Webster shouted to the men in the rear of his van, 'Fifty yards away now lads, I'm driving up to them. For fuck's sake, don't make a sound. I need this to be a total surprise when I open the sliding door. As soon as you hear me say, "I've got a load of Nike Air on board!" the door will be opened. So be ready lads and good luck. Hit them hard and hit them fast!'

The van came to a stop and Tom could clearly hear voices at the side of the van. He heard the driver's door open and close and heard Phil engaging easily in the banter.

He really was a cool customer, thought Tom.

He heard Phil laugh and say loudly, 'I hope you've all got plenty of dosh, these trainers are the real deal.'

There was a jumble of voices as the dealers all tried to talk at the same time. Shouting about what sort of trainers they were looking for and how much money they'd got to spend.

Inside the van nobody moved a muscle, everyone's eyes were focussed on the side door. The only noise Tom could make out was the sound of his own heart starting to beat ever so slightly faster.

Tom's muscles tensed as he heard Phil say loudly, 'I've got a load of Nike Air on board!'

The sliding door at the side of the van was yanked wide open by Phil.

If it wasn't such a tense and dangerous situation, the sight that confronted Tom and the rest of C Section as the door was opened would have been comical.

Standing in a wide semi-circle, less than two yards from the side of the van, were the entire crew of drug dealers, including Shane Street and his four sons. Every one of them, clutching a large wad of bank notes of various denominations, ready to grab a bargain.

For a split-second time seemed to stand still.

The look of shock and disbelief was written all over the dealers' faces.

Instantly, C Section jumped from the van, diving into the gathered dealers.

As they began to target the individual dealers they began barking instructions at the top of their voices, 'Police! Stand still!'

After the initial shock the dealers had instantly started to resist. Punches were being thrown and scuffles were breaking out all across Hammond Street.

Tyson Street snarled at Phil Webster, 'Bastard copper!'

He lashed out with a wild punch aimed at the undercover officer. Although the detective tried to take evasive action, the blow still landed heavily just below his left eye, knocking him backwards into the side of the van.

Tyson Street was immediately buried under the combined weight of Steve Grey and Tony Garner. To his credit, Phil Webster flew straight back into the fray and landed a punch of his own square in the mouth of Tyson Street, effectively ending any further resistance.

Having been quick to recover from the initial shock of being confronted by a van load of police officers, Shane Street had used the ensuing melee and chaos to try and escape.

Tom saw him running along Hammond Street on the other side of the van and shouted, 'Jack! Shane Street's trying to leg it that way.'

He pointed along Hammond Street and both he and Jack began to chase down Shane Street.

Jack was in front of Tom and was a faster runner; he soon chased down Street, leaping onto the dealers' wide back and putting him in a headlock, before bringing him crashing to the ground. Arriving seconds after Street had crashed to the floor, Tom added his weight on top of the downed dealer.

Street began to lash out, thrashing about wildly trying to break the grip of the two Special Ops men.

Although he still had a fearsome reputation, the reality was that Shane Street was now an overweight, middle aged and very unfit man. Try as he might, there was no way he was ever going to be able to sustain the effort needed for the fight. He was soon out of breath and gasping for air.

Within a minute he'd stopped struggling altogether and had accepted his fate. Instead, he used what breath he had left to verbally abuse and threaten the two officers.

As Jack tightened the Plasticuffs around Shane Street's wrists he looked him in the eyes and said, 'Yeah, yeah, yeah! Whatever you say, gobshite! You're nicked, Street.'

As they frogmarched Shane Street back to the waiting Police vehicles that had now descended onto Hammond Street, Tom looked around him.

Everywhere he looked he could see his colleagues standing next to handcuffed drug dealers waiting for transportation to the Police Station.

The operation had been a complete success and further teams from the Special Operations Unit were now arriving to execute the warrants on the homes of the dealers.

A scenes of crime team had also arrived on the street to help document any evidence seized from the searches and to photograph and recover the drugs from Street's main stash on the pit tip.

Graham Turner ensured that every prisoner detained by C Section was conveyed to Worksop Police Station, accompanied by the appropriate arresting officer.

As soon as all the prisoners had been booked into custody, Graham gathered the men of C Section together and said, 'Okay listen in everybody. Great work. That couldn't have gone any better. Has anybody got any injuries that I need to know about?'

The men stayed silent so Graham continued, 'In that case, we now have another task to complete. Hammond Street was only the first phase of the operation for us today. The Drugs Squad and the Tactical Surveillance Unit have been running a combined operation following a man by the name of Billy Swan. This is the man who Tom and Jack identified as Shane Street's major supplier of amphetamine. Our next task, is to arrest Swan when he goes to a furniture shop in Carlton later today. Drugs Squad officers have been watching this shop for over a fortnight after getting a tip off about drugs being dealt regularly from that location. During these observations Billy Swan has twice been seen going into the shop carrying a large holdall. He's visited the shop on the same day each week and if he follows the same pattern, he's expected to visit again later today. Knowing that Swan has supplied Shane Street with large amounts of amphetamine, it's not a wild leap to suspect the same thing's happening in Carlton. The plan is for us to be there waiting when Swan arrives at the shop today. He's to be arrested for the supply of drugs to Street; if we find any drugs on him at Carlton that will be an added bonus.'

Jack asked a question, 'How many other people will be in this shop?'

'I can't answer that Jack, we've no way of knowing.'

'Are we just arresting Swan? What about anyone else on the premises?'

'We've already got grounds to arrest Swan, as for anyone else in the shop it will depend entirely on what we find when Swan's detained.'

There were no further questions so Graham said, 'Right lads, get your statements of arrest done as quickly as possible and hand them to whichever detective is going to interview your prisoner. If Billy Swan follows the last fortnight's pattern, he'll be arriving at the shop just after three o'clock this afternoon. I want to be on plot in Carlton no later than two thirty, so get cracking and get these statements done. I want to be leaving Worksop at twelve thirty.'

Jack was doing the statement of arrest for Shane Street so Tom took the opportunity to have a quiet word with Graham Turner, 'Sarge, has anybody spoken to you about Billy Swan?'

'Only what I've just told you lot, why?'

'There's something you need to know about Swan, he's literally a man mountain. He looks like the Incredible Hulk on steroids. It's going to be a tough job taking him down sarge.'

'That's why it's been given over to us to make the arrest Tom. We'll tackle him mob handed and hopefully he'll realise that however strong he is, he won't be getting away.'

'I wouldn't count on that sarge, we're going to have our hands full. Trust me.'

'We'll just have to cross that bridge when we come to it, but thanks for the heads up I'll let everyone know what we're going to be faced with.'

CHAPTER 56

12.20pm 15th August 1987
Hammond Street, Renton Estate, Worksop

The men of A Section had been allocated the task of searching the home address of Shane Street, following the arrests of Shane and his four sons.

The house was a shabby, three bedroomed semi located on the corner of Hammond Street. It had been the centre of the Shane Street drug dealing operation.

Pc Jim Hallam and Pc Dave Groves had been given the task of searching the hall, stairs and landing.

Jim Hallam was painstakingly checking all the jackets hanging on coat pegs on the back of the front door. Standing behind him, watching him closely was Dawn Street, the wife of Shane and mother to the four boys.

Systematically, the young policeman removed each jacket from a coat hook then turned to Dawn and asked her who the coat belonged to, before searching the garment in front of her.

He took a brown leather jacket from one of the coat hooks and asked, 'Who's jacket is this, Mrs Street?'

Barely able to contain her boredom, Dawn Street took a long drag on her roll up cigarette before looking at the jacket and declaring wearily, 'That one belongs to our Rocky. It was his Christmas present last year. It's all paid for, I've got a receipt here somewhere.'

Meticulously, the officer began to search all the pockets in the jacket. As he searched, he noticed that one of the inside pockets contained something heavy. Reaching into the inside pocket he retrieved five-coin shaped objects attached to brightly coloured ribbons.

The officer held the objects in the palm of his hand, showed them to Dawn Street and said, 'These are war medals Mrs Street. Where did Rocky get them from?'

Without a moment's hesitation she said, 'Our Rocky's got this thing about collecting war stuff, medals are his favourite. I bought these ones for him when we were on holiday in Ireland last year.'

As the officer looked closer at the medals he said, 'Where did you take your holiday, Mrs Street?'

'We went over to Cork, Shane's got family over there. There's lots of little antique shops in the city. I got the medals from one of them. Paid a pretty penny for them as well.'

'Do you have a receipt?'

'It'll be in the house somewhere, I'm sure I'll be able to find it if I've got to.'

Jim Hallam held up one of the medals and said, 'It says on the back of this one, "Presented to Jakub Kowalczyk for extreme courage in the face of the enemy". Do you know anyone called Kowalczyk?'

'No. Why would I? I've just told you, I bought those medals in Cork.'

'I don't believe you Mrs Street. Wasn't Mr Kowalczyk your neighbour? The old man who died a few weeks ago? The neighbour who you called an ambulance for after being concerned for his welfare?'

For a moment Dawn Street said nothing, the fleshy part of her neck began to redden and flush and she stared wild eyed at the officer.

Suddenly, she exploded with anger and screamed, 'The stupid little bastard! Why's he kept those fucking things?'

'Mrs Street, these medals belonged to your neighbour, didn't they? You never bought them in Cork or anywhere else, did you?'

Dawn Street fixed the officer with a hateful stare.

Ignoring her malevolent glare Pc Hallam smiled and said quietly, 'Dawn Street, I'm arresting you on suspicion of handling stolen goods.'

As he cautioned her Dawn Street began to shout over the top of him, 'Why are you arresting me? I didn't steal them. What happened to the old man had nothing to do with me. They only went around there to scare the old twat! No one hit him or anything, they just scared him and he had a heart attack. It was just one of those things. It's not their fault if the old man had a dodgy ticker, is it?'

Jim Hallam couldn't quite believe what he was hearing. He said calmly, 'Dawn Street, I'm also arresting you on suspicion of the murder of Jakub Kowalczyk.'

'What are you on about? It's not murder. I've just told you they only wanted to scare him. Nobody murdered him.'

Jim Hallam placed Dawn Street in handcuffs and walked her out of the house to a waiting police vehicle.

Dawn Street ranted a tirade of abuse at the officer, screaming her innocence to anyone who was listening. As he sat her on the back seat of the CID car he said quietly, 'Save your excuses for the CID, love.'

CHAPTER 57

3.00pm 15th August 1987
Carlton Hill, Nottingham

Tom Naylor looked nervously at his watch, the time was steadily ticking round towards three o'clock. He licked his lips as he felt his mouth starting to dry, then rubbed the palms of his hands along his trousers, trying to remove the thin film of sweat that was starting to develop.

He hated this part of any operation; the anticipation was always worse than the actual application. He fully expected to be involved in a violent confrontation with Billy Swan when he and his colleagues attempted to detain him.

He and Jack Rimmer were in the Post Office on Carlton Road directly opposite the small furniture shop the Drugs Squad had identified as being used for drug dealing.

C Section had arrived in the Carlton Hill area forty-five minutes ago and Sgt Turner had immediately deployed Tom and Jack into the Post Office to set up observations on the furniture shop, so they could identify Swan and let the rest of the team know when he arrived.

The remainder of C Section had parked their van on Standhill Road, well away from the furniture shop but close enough to respond quickly when Swan arrived.

Tom and Jack had already witnessed the tell-tale signs of drug dealing at the shop. The regular footfall of pitiful humanity, shiftily approaching the premises. Time after time, they watched as desolate, scruffy individuals with sallow skin and eyes sunken deep within their sockets entered the shop, only to leave again a few minutes later.

They stayed just long enough to sort out their next fix of whatever poison the shopkeeper was peddling.

A couple of times they had seen the shop keeper come to the front door, step outside, then look both ways up and down the street.

The shopkeeper was a tall, thin Asian man with a well-trimmed black beard and long black hair. He was dressed in cream coloured baggy trousers, a dark brown Nehru style jacket and leather sandals.

'He's definitely waiting for somebody', said Tom.

Jack suddenly exclaimed, 'That's weird! The shopkeeper's just put the "CLOSED" sign up on the door.'

'Maybe it's good news? Could be a sign that Swan's not far away.'

Tom reached for his radio and said, 'Tom to Graham. Over.'

'Go ahead Tom. Over.'

'The shopkeeper's just closed the shop. Could be Swan's on his way and is imminent. Stand by. Over.'

'Okay Tom, received that. Over.'

After Graham had briefed the men about the physical stature of Billy Swan and what a task it was going to be to detain the man mountain, the level of nervous anticipation felt by all the members of C Section had grown steadily.

Looking across the road from the Post Office, Tom saw a familiar black Jaguar came to a stop directly outside the furniture shop.

The car contained only one occupant.

Billy Swan.

Tom reached for his radio, 'All units be advised, target has arrived on plot in a black Jaguar registered number Bravo Sierra One One. Target is remaining in the vehicle. Stand by. Over.'

Tom and Jack watched intently from their vantage point, as Swan slowly got out of the vehicle. Very methodically and carefully he looked around him in all directions. Finally satisfied that nobody was watching him, he reached back inside the car and retrieved a brown leather holdall from the passenger seat.

Carrying the brown holdall in his right hand, Swan walked confidently towards the furniture shop.

As he approached the door, it was opened from inside and Swan was greeted by the Asian shopkeeper with a handshake.

Swan towered above the shopkeeper. The pair of them made a ridiculous spectacle, the skinny Asian man standing next to the black colossus.

Both men walked inside the shop and the door was closed behind them.

Tom said, 'Swan's entered the target premises carrying a brown holdall. This looks like it Sarge. Over.'

Graham Turner replied instantly, 'I want you to get over there and get inside the shop. We've got a problem here, but we'll be with you as soon as we can. Just delay them until we get there. Over.'

Tom didn't have time to ask what the problem was. He replied quickly, 'Okay we're on our way. Over.'

As they walked across the road towards the shop Tom said, 'Let's just stumble in and pretend we're pissed.

Hopefully if we can cause a bit of a scene it will delay Swan long enough for the rest of the lads to get here and back us up. I don't fancy our chances tackling Swan on our own.'

Jack replied grimly, 'Me neither! Let's just play it by ear and hope they get here sooner rather than later.'

Tom swung the door to the shop open and virtually fell inside, giggling like an idiot closely followed by Jack. In a slurred voice he said loudly, 'Ish in 'ere mate. That coffee table I've been telling you about, the one my lovely gobby wife keepsh nagging me about. I'm going to buy it today so she'll finally shut the fuck up and give me shome peash!'

Jack looked around the shop and said, 'Wish one ish it?'

'I think thash it over there pal!'

The two men then began to weave their way towards the back of the shop where they could see Swan in conversation with the shopkeeper.

The rest of the shop was deserted.

The Asian shopkeeper tutted when he saw the two drunks stumbling through his shop.

Swan growled through gritted teeth, 'What the fuck's this Hassan? Haven't you closed the fucking shop? Get rid of them man!'

With his arms spread wide the shopkeeper approached the drunks and said, 'Sorry fellers, but the shop's closed. Didn't you see the sign on the door? Why don't you both come back later?'

Tom continued to act the obnoxious drunk and slurred, 'Nah, fuck that. I'm here now Abdul. I jush need a coffee table for my wife Mrs Gobby.'

There was real anger in the shopkeeper's voice now, 'Both of you just fuck off! I've told you already the shop's closed now fuck off or you'll be sorry!'

Jack now joined in, 'Who'd you think you're telling to fuck off? You're ashkin to get your fucking shop trashed, dickhead!'

The raging shopkeeper took a step forward but Tom immediately squared up to him, 'Come on then dickhead, I'll fucking do you!'

As Tom threatened the shopkeeper, Jack tipped over a small table at the side of him.

Billy Swan grabbed the shopkeeper and pulled him backwards out the way.

He looked down at Tom and growled, 'Listen you idiot, if you don't want the biggest hiding of your life, you and your pissed-up cretin of a mate had both better fuck off out of this shop right now!'

As Tom looked up at Swan he thought, where the hell was Graham Turner and the rest of the team?

This was about to get very painful.

Jack was still totally in character, he laughed like a maniac and said, 'And who'sh going to give us thish good hiding fatsho!'

Tom was trying to delay the inevitable confrontation in the hope that at any minute the rest of C Section would come crashing through the door.

What the fuck was keeping them?

He grabbed Jack and pulled him away from Swan, 'Come on mate, lesh go. Ish obvious they don't serve white boys in thish shit hole. Fuck 'em lesh go somewhere elsh.'

Playing for time Jack fell over. As Tom slowly picked him up off the floor he shouted, 'Nah fuck it mate. I'm not going anywhere until I've had an apology from that big dope!'

Suddenly Swan exploded with rage and shouted, 'That's fucking it!'

He lunged forward towards Jack.

Where was Graham Turner?

Where were C Section?

As Swan advanced menacingly towards him, Jack threw a punch that deflected uselessly off one of Swan's huge arms. Swan grabbed Jack by the front of his jacket, lifted him bodily from the floor and hurled him across the shop, where he landed heavily onto a pine dining table set, instantly turning the table and chairs into match wood.

Tom jumped onto Swan's back, desperately trying to get the big man into a headlock. Across the shop, he could see Jack untangling himself from the wreckage of the dining table and chairs.

As Swan swung around trying to get Tom from around his neck, Tom saw the shopkeeper advancing towards him carrying what looked like a broken chair leg.

Where the fuck was Graham Turner?

Tom watched on helplessly as the shopkeeper drew his arm back and rained a heavy blow down onto the middle of his back.

Shouting out in pain, Tom was unable to maintain the grip he had around Swan's neck and dropped to the floor.

Swan growled at Tom, 'You're a fucking dead man!'

He dragged Tom up off the floor by his jacket and drew back an enormous fist.

Tom raised his right arm and managed to deflect the powerful punch. He couldn't stop the full force of the punch and he felt the impact connect just above his right temple. The weight of the blow was still enough to send him hurtling backwards across the shop, smashing more furniture as he came to rest.

Through dazed eyes, Tom saw Jack get up and hurl himself back at Swan, connecting with a flurry of hard punches into the face of the giant. The effect of the punches was minimal and Tom winced as he saw Swan unleash a punch that landed flush on Jack's left cheek.

The force of the blow from the huge hambone fist was enough to send Jack spinning to the floor where he landed in a heap.

Swan stepped forward purposefully intent on continuing the assault on Jack who was now lying on the floor barely conscious.

Tom was manfully trying to get to his feet to try and help his stricken colleague when suddenly the shop door flew open and the rest of C Section piled in.

They immediately confronted Swan and an almighty fracas started as the officers desperately fought to bring Swan under control.

'Thank fuck for that', said Tom, as he picked his way through the smashed furniture to help Jack to his feet.

Tom could see at least five members of C Section all hanging onto Swan, trying to dodge the huge haymaker punches being swung by the big man.

He looked towards the rear of the shop and saw the Asian shopkeeper trying to sneak out through the rear entrance.

'Oh no you fucking don't', snarled Tom.

He launched himself onto the shopkeeper, bringing him down. He quickly subdued the Asian, secured him with Plasticuffs and sat him down on the floor next to where Jack was recovering.

Finally, Billy Swan was brought under control.

His eyes bulged as he struggled wildly, desperately using all of his considerable strength to break free from his ties. Even for a man of his power there was no way out of the three sets of Plasticuffs that now bound his wrists, He still continued to lash out at the officers with his feet, trying to kick them.

Through a bloodied mouth and a couple of broken teeth Graham Turner said, 'Get him outside and into the van!'

Jack was now sitting up and painfully grinned at Tom, 'For fuck's sake Tom, look at it, it's like something out of an old cowboy movie. I've never seen so much smashed up furniture.'

Tony Garner, who was nursing an inch-long gash above his right eye walked over to Tom and Jack. With genuine concern in his voice he said, 'Jesus! Are you two alright? I'll say it again boys, what's the news with you two and all this macho shit?'

A very groggy Jack said, 'Nice of you to join us. What the fuck kept you? Couldn't you see what was happening?'

'A bloody traffic warden wanted to give us a parking ticket and he wouldn't move from the front of the van so we ended up leaving the van there with him and running around to the shop. Honestly mate, we got here as fast as we could. By the time we got here you two were already going three rounds with the love child of Mike Tyson and Godzilla!'

Jack groaned, 'A bloody traffic warden! I've heard it all now. I thought I was about to meet my maker.'

Graham Turner walked over carrying a brown leather holdall and asked Tom, 'Is this the bag you saw Swan bringing in?'

'That's the one sarge.'

He opened the holdall, looked inside and said, 'This should interest the Drugs Squad, there's five big packets of white powder in here and no doubt when we've sifted through the broken furniture in here, we'll find a boat load of cash ready to pay for it. Good work you two, sorry for the delay in backing you up. It couldn't be helped.'

'Tony's just told us about the bloody traffic warden, sarge. I'd like a few words with that muppet.'

'Maybe one day. Right now, I want both of you to get down to the hospital and get checked over straight away. Looking at the amount of furniture you've smashed in here, you could've broken anything. Casualty, now!'

CHAPTER 58

10.30am 28th August 1987
Nottinghamshire Police Headquarters

Chief Inspector Chambers looked up as he heard the sharp rap on his office door.

'Come in!'

Tom Naylor and Jack Rimmer walked into the office and stood in front of Jim Chambers desk.

Tom said, 'You wanted to see us boss?'

'Yes. I wanted to let you know that I'm putting you both forward for a Chief Constables Commendation for your work on Operation Puma. Firstly, for the observations in all weathers and secondly for the part you both played in the arrest of Billy Swan. It was outstanding work gents. What you won't know about yet are all the remarkable developments in the cases surrounding Operation Puma.'

Jim Chambers paused before continuing, 'Newark CID have charged the Smith brothers and Danny Lee with all the aggravated burglary offences in that series and have also charged Nathan and Jimmy Smith with a number of Section 18 wounding offences. They will be going away for a very long time. On top of that I've also had a very interesting update from Worksop CID about the Street family. Following the discovery of several war medals at Shane Street's house, the CID have now positively identified them as being the property of the elderly next-door neighbour who died under suspicious circumstances a few weeks ago. Although there were elements about the old man's death at the time the police were unhappy about, there was no evidence that pointed to foul play. Following the discovery of the medals and some brilliant interviews by the CID up there, it now appears that the old man died as a direct result of Shane Street and two of his sons breaking into the old man's house and literally scaring him to death. The CPS are still weighing up the options, but it's looking like the three of them will be charged either with conspiracy to commit murder or manslaughter.'

Tom let out a low whistle and said, 'Bloody hell boss, what a result!'

Jim Chambers smiled and said, 'I haven't finished yet. Obviously those three and the other dealers have all been charged with numerous drugs offences as well. Shane Street was already on a life licence so he can forget about seeing life outside of prison walls for a very long time, if at all.'

He took another breath and said, 'Finally, I've just had a telephone call from the Chief Inspector in charge of the Major Crime Investigation Unit who has informed me that following the arrest of Swan and the seizure of his Jaguar car, the Drugs Squad organised a full forensic examination of the vehicle primarily looking for evidence of drugs supply. Turns out that as well as evidence of drugs being found in the boot, forensics also found traces of blood in the driver's footwell and on an old rag in the boot. This blood has subsequently now been DNA matched to the murdered club owner Frankie Squires. The MCIU always suspected that Swan had some involvement in Squires' murder at Basford. Now they have the positive DNA match from the blood found in the

Jaguar they have charged Swan with the murder of Frankie Squires.'

Tom and Jack looked stunned.

Jack said quietly, 'All that from one job?'

Jim Chambers grinned, 'All that. Well done gents, now before you get back to your duties I need a quick word with you Tom. Thanks Jack.'

Jack Rimmer said, 'No problem boss', then left the office.

After he had closed the door, Jim Chambers said, 'There's also an update on Matt Jarvis. Following a full investigation by the Major Crime Investigation Unit in conjunction with the Complaints and Discipline Department, they've found no evidence of any wrongdoing on the part of Matt Jarvis. Following a consultation with the Chief, his suspension has been lifted immediately. He will be coming back to work in a fortnight's time. I've contacted him at home and told him to spend some time on leave with his wife to try and make some sense of everything that's happened. They both need a little time to take stock and get their careers back on track.'

'That's great news boss. I never could understand what all that was about.'

'I know what you mean, somebody went to a hell of a lot of trouble just to kill one man.'

'Are Scotland Yard none the wiser who was behind the shooting?'

'No, it's a complete dead end. There are no leads at all. I think it will remain one of those forever unsolved cases. My guess is that it will have something to do with drugs that we know nothing about yet. With Barry Tate dead there's still a massive vacuum in this city for a new organisation to move into. Anyway, that's something for the Drugs Squad and the

Regional Crime Squad to monitor. Either way, I don't think too many people will be mourning the demise of Barry Tate, do you?'

'No boss, I suppose not. Like you say, maybe it's destined to remain a mystery.'

Jim Chambers grinned and said, 'Anyway, that's enough chit chat Pc Naylor, I'm sure you've got work to be getting on with?'

EPILOGUE

November 1987
Acquedolci, Northern Sicily

Roberto Visiglio sat in his favourite high-backed wicker chair on the vast balcony of his palatial residence watching the early morning sun rise slowly into the clear blue sky.

As it rose steadily above the horizon, he became almost mesmerised by the golden rays reflecting off the crystal clear, cobalt blue waters of the Mediterranean Sea.

The only sounds he could hear were the waves lapping gently against this beautiful rocky stretch of Northern Sicily and songbirds greeting another new day.

At one time, not so long ago, he would have regarded this as his favourite place and his favourite view in the whole world.

That had all changed now.

Now he felt that to appreciate such stunning beauty from this very spot would be a betrayal to the sadness he felt deep within his soul.

Almost a year had passed since he had sat in this very chair looking out over the ocean and noticed the blue and white Polizia Di Stato car arriving in the courtyard way below his balcony.

He had been curious at first when he saw Commissario Capo Matteo Ricci get out of the car. He had been driving himself, which was unusual in itself for an officer of that

342

rank, but what really made him take notice was when the policeman walked round to the passenger side of the car and opened the door for the elderly priest Father Alfonsi.

He had known both men for many years but could not understand why they would visit his residence together.

He had received his visitors sitting in this very chair and his blood ran cold as he relived that awful day.

It had been the elderly priest who had broken the most heart-breaking news to him that day.

Commissario Capo Ricci had received news from the Italian Embassy in England that Roberto Visiglio's granddaughter Francesca De Luca had been found dead in Nottingham, where she had been studying medicine, and her body was being repatriated to Italy. The arrangements had been made by the embassy.

The chief of the local police feared Don Visiglio's reputation and had begged the priest from the local church to accompany him to the villa to break the sad news personally.

The police officer had stood in the background wringing his hands as Father Alfonsi gently broke the awful news.

Don Visiglio's body felt racked with pain just remembering that day.

At the time it had felt like history repeating itself.

Francesca's own parents had died fifteen years before when their Maserati sports car had inexplicably left one of the many winding mountain roads on the island. The car had plunged two hundred feet into a rocky ravine, killing them both instantly.

The pain of losing his only daughter Marguerite and his son in law, Franco De Luca, in such a futile way was only eased by the beauty and innocence of his grandchild. The old man had raised her as if she were his own daughter.

Francesca De Luca wanted for nothing and she rewarded her grandfather with an unconditional love that only a grandchild can give.

The old man had watched, filled with pride, as Francesca blossomed into an intelligent, stunningly beautiful young woman.

She had her father's dark eyes and raven black hair and her mother's poise and grace. She was also extremely bright and gifted academically. When the time came for her to choose a University to further her education, she could have chosen anywhere. Harvard, Yale, the Sorbonne.

Francesca had always loved England and her passion was for medicine, so after much deliberation she left Sicily to train to become a surgeon at the world-renowned Nottingham University and the Queens Medical Centre.

To his eternal regret and eventual damnation, it had been he who had greased the wheels to enable his granddaughter to achieve a place at the University in England.

He had been so proud that she wanted to dedicate her life to saving the lives of others, but instead of saving lives she had ended up forfeiting her own precious life.

After receiving the awful news, he had made all the arrangements for his granddaughter to be buried back alongside her mother and father.

Once the funeral had passed he instructed two of his most loyal associates, Mario Battaglia and Salvatore Pincette, to travel to England and discover the circumstances that had led to Francesca's death.

Roberto Visiglio wanted to know everything that had happened. How she had died? Why she had died? Most importantly of all if anyone else had been directly responsible for this abomination.

If this was the case then that person would have to pay the ultimate price.

Tradition demanded it.

Vendetta demanded it.

It was the Sicilian way.

It was most definitely the Sicilian Mafia way.

Mario and Salvatore had served him well. Using a combination of money, threats of violence and violence itself, they had soon discovered that Francesca had died as a result of a cocaine overdose. Their enquiries found that two men were indeed culpable for her death.

By some freakish twist of fate, both of the men responsible were now being held in prison serving long sentences for other matters.

One of the men was a lowly street dealer named Tony Banks.

He had been responsible for getting Francesca hooked on cocaine in the first place. Their painstaking research revealed that Banks was no better than a pimp who used cocaine to entrap beautiful young girls, who he then supplied to his gangster boss for sexual gratification.

It had been Banks who had supplied Francesca with the cocaine that killed her.

The second individual culpable for her death was the man Banks answered to.

A Nottingham gangster called Barry Tate.

Tate was ultimately responsible for the supply of most of the narcotics in the city of Nottingham.

Their enquiries also revealed that Barry Tate had defiled Francesca in the basest of ways after she had been rendered insensible by the cocaine given to her by Banks.

Armed with their findings, Mario and Salvatore had returned to Sicily and informed Don Visiglio of the information they had learned. The Don had asked for the truth, so both men told him exactly what they had discovered about the events leading up to his granddaughter's death and more importantly who was responsible for her death.

The old man had cried as he listened to the men's accounts.

It had then taken him the time of a single heartbeat to sanction the deaths of Tony Banks and Barry Tate.

He ordered the men to return to England straight away and to carry out his wishes at their earliest opportunity. He had declared that Banks and Tate were both men devoid of any honour and should die like the pigs they were.

Upon their return to England, it had taken no time at all to organise the killing of Tony Banks. It had been a simple task of paying the right amount of money to the right people to get the job done.

Even though he was incarcerated in an English jail, he was considered a low risk prisoner and wasn't subject to overwhelming security.

It had not been difficult to arrange and pay for his murder. The only stipulation they had given to the men tasked with the contract was that Banks should die using the age-old method of Sicilian vendetta killings.

They wanted Banks to be killed by the garotte.

Mario had made this stipulation as he knew it would please the Don.

As soon as the two Sicilians had learned of Banks' death, they turned their full attention towards the murder of Barry Tate.

Before the men had left Sicily, Don Visiglio had decreed that as Tate was the person ultimately responsible for his granddaughter's death, his killing must be carried out by one of the Family; either Mario or Salvatore were to undertake the contract.

Unlike Banks, Barry Tate was being held in a maximum-security jail and was considered to be a Category A prisoner. This made it impossible for either of the two Sicilians to get close enough to carry out the task as decreed by their Don.

A different more patient strategy had been needed to get to Tate.

This had been the reason behind the elaborate plan to manipulate the Courts into giving Tate his freedom. Once released and beyond the security prison had given him, it had been a routine task for the accomplished assassin Mario to shoot Tate on the steps of the High Court.

As Don Visiglio stared out across the blue ocean he waited patiently for his two trusted lieutenants to visit the villa.

He knew that Mario and Salvatore had flown into the Catania- Fontanarossa airport the previous evening and would now be on their way to see him.

The Don was impatient for news.

Looking down from the balcony he saw the black Mercedes arrive at the villa gates. He watched as the gates opened slowly and the car was driven along the driveway lined with olive and lemon trees.

The Mercedes came to a stop below the balcony and he heard the car doors open and slam shut again.

He waited patiently in his wicker chair.

After a few minutes Mario and Salvatore walked towards him across the marble floor of the balcony.

Both men were dressed in dark suits, crisp white shirts and black ties as a mark of respect for the still grieving Don. Both wore Aviator style sunglasses to shield their eyes from the glare of the bright morning sun.

The two men came to a stop at the side of the Dons' wicker chair. He continued to stare out to sea never once acknowledging their presence.

Mario put his hand to his mouth and coughed politely.

In a flat, sombre voice he said quietly, 'Don Roberto, it is done. The English pigs are dead.'

Very slowly, the Don reached out an ageing hand in the direction of the men.

Mario took the Don's hand and kissed the back of it very gently, before releasing it and stepping back, allowing Salvatore to do the same action in the same reverent manner.

In a voice filled with emotion Don Visiglio said softly, 'Mario and Salvatore, you have served me well. I'll never forget this act of kindness you have done for me. You're a credit to yourselves, to your own families and to our greater family. I thank you from the bottom of my heart.'

Neither Mario or Salvatore said anything, they both just nodded in acknowledgment of the Don's words before slowly walking away.

As the sound of their footsteps receded off the balcony, Don Visiglio looked down at the floor and breathed out a long heavy sigh.

Now that Francesca's death had been rightfully avenged, maybe he would once again be able to appreciate the natural beauty of the world and enjoy the remaining days of his life.

With both of the English bastard's now dead, maybe he would be able to move on, maybe not.

Only time would tell.

Don Roberto Visiglio, the all-powerful head of the Sicilian mafia, leaned slowly back in his wicker chair and once again stared out over the blue waters of the Mediterranean.

This time the sun's rays were glistening off the tears that were streaming down the old man's face.

Sobbing quietly, he whispered a single word, 'Francesca.'

COMING SOON

The Root of all Evil

Nottinghamshire 1988

A fanatical group of animal rights activists are planning the abduction and murder of the Company Director of UK Pharmaceutical Ltd in revenge for a young woman's death. The activists involved have an unprecedented, ruthless attitude and will use firearms to achieve their aims.

Standing in the way of this plot are armed officers from the Special Operations Unit and an undercover officer from the Metropolitan Police who has infiltrated the group.

Meanwhile, in the North West of the country a gang of armed robbers callously gun down an off-duty officer during a raid on a security van in Liverpool.

The sickening, cold blooded murder is captured on CCTV.

The graphic images of the killing cause Pc Tom Naylor to confront a ghost from his past and lead him into undertaking a dangerous undercover role.

As the plot unfolds and tragedy strikes, Tom is left facing unpleasant truths that make him question his role as a police officer and that throw doubts upon everything he ever believed in.